SWITCHBACK

By S.W. Andersen

Edited by S.W. Andersen
and Cindy Bamford

Cover Design by Cindy Bamford

©2017

swandersenwrites.com

ISBN-13: 978-0-9990616-1-9

ISBN-10: 0-9990616-1-5

Published by S.W. Andersen Books

MORE NOVELS BY S.W. ANDERSEN

Love By Design

Somewhere Between Love and Justice

The Price of Payback

ACKNOWLEDGEMENTS

A huge thank you to all of you who have read my books and supported my writing endeavor. So many of you have been there from the start and it means the world to me. I strive to improve with each passing story and I hope to keep you all entertained for years to come.

I couldn't do this alone. I am so very lucky to have such a wonderful, supportive team to help me create these books. Georgia, Samantha, Laura, Kyle, and Kathy B. Your feedback and willingness to submit to my many opinion surveys help shape the finished products.

To my co-editor and cover designer, Cindy, you always come through, even when I can't seem to verbalize what I really want to achieve. You're amazing in every way and I am so grateful that you're my friend. *Hugs*

And to my wife, Dianna. Without you, I may have missed out on the joys of mountain biking and skiing. More importantly, I would have missed out on an amazing twenty-year journey. Your love and support is unwavering and appreciated more than you will ever know. Here's to another twenty years and then twenty more after that.

My wish for everyone is that you find your passion and ride hard all the way to the finish line.

Much love and thanks to all of you.

CHAPTER ONE

A brief moment of serenity followed by total reckless abandon—that's how Sierra Cody lived her life. Whether she was throwing her body or her heart off a cliff, she was all-in from the start, consequences be damned. Unfortunately, thus far in her life, her heart hadn't fared so well. Professionally, however, she was on fire, living it up as her dream of becoming a professional women's downhill racer had finally come true. Next stop was World Cup, but that wouldn't come easily.

She stared down the mountain, excited for the ride ahead. Mountain biking filled her soul with things she could never explain—wonderful, powerful things that made her smile stretch from one end of the horizon to the other.

It was a shame some people would never experience such joy.

In moments like these, she felt sorry for the masses who never stepped foot outside of their safety zone, never pushed for more, never challenged their abilities. They were the living dead, merely breathing air, taking up space and doing nothing worthwhile with the gift of life they had been given.

That would never be her.

Whether it was music, sport, love, or any other passion, what was the point in taking a breath if you weren't going to go full throttle to the end? Call her crazy, and they have more times than she could count, but this right here...*This* was what being alive was all about.

Straddling her bike inside the starting gate, Sierra basked in the majestic view that the seven thousand foot altitude allowed—the practiced rhythm of her breathing and her trusted friend, a red Scott Gambler downhill bike, were her only company. Their shared mission to conquer the mountain was steadfast and unwavering. Every race, every course, was a new puzzle to be finished as quickly and skillfully as possible. Once the buzzer sounded, there would be no more peace, only a finite number of hair-raising minutes until this ride would end and Sierra would begin to crave her next fix.

The seconds ticked down. Soon, the frenzy would begin again, but until then, a brief, pleasurable silence. Sierra's eyelids drifted shut behind her goggles, hiding the open blue skies that were interrupted by jagged peaks, whose landscapes were dotted with giant green cedars. Mother Nature's beauty faded into the background until there was only the course and every detail of her journey ahead visualized to perfection.

The steep slope out of the gate led into the high banking of the first turn. Then a wicked rock garden awaited approximately thirty seconds down. She would have to dial back her speed through there. Too fast would send her flying and too slow would get her hung up on the rocks. Next, a tight switchback to the left before a drop off. It would be vital to maintain a good speed through that section to avoid disaster on her landing. Finally, it would be smooth sailing as fast as wheels would allow to the finish.

BEEP.

The countdown had begun, bringing her back to the present.

BEEP.

With one deep breath of crisp, clean air, she gripped the handlebars tight.

BEEP.

Another breath, as she steadied her right foot atop the pedal. Every muscle tensed in anticipation of their imminent explosion.

BEEP.

Her eyes snapped open, locking in on their target—the first turn of the winding singletrack ahead.

BEEP.

Silence engulfed her mind. No more time for contemplation. Her mind and body became one, ready to react to whatever the track had in store.

BOOOOOOP!

Powerful quads exploded into action sending her rocketing down the mountainside. Dirt, rock, and roots passed by in a blur, pushing the limits of how fast her wheels could spin. Two knobby tires mounted to a frame of aluminum moved as an extension of her being, obeying every command with delicate precision. The bike shuddered with vibrations from the earth below, reverberating through her bones. Foam and plastic were all that protected her body, yet she fearlessly carved through turns, conquered rocks and flew off jumps without concern, loving every nail-biting moment.

Never one to settle for second, Sierra pressed harder and harder. Eagle-like focus read the terrain ahead. Black and red painted finger nails dug into their grips as her thunderous heartbeat silenced the whistling of fans perched along the trail. Every muscle worked the bike to keep as much speed as possible through each obstacle encountered—a tenth of a second here, a thousandth there—they all added up.

Brakes were not an option. Not today.

Wisps of jet black hair mingled with fiery red strands blew wildly from under her helmet as the wind whipped against her face. This was what Sierra Cody lived for—this controlled chaos. She thrived on the thrill of adrenaline and the challenge of claiming the podium.

It was a good run. She could feel it.

Last turn up ahead—a little gravel and a high banking. Easy-peasy. Been there, done that a million times before. She was dialed in. Could victory be within grasp?

Hitting the banking full steam, her overly-aggressive entry threw her weight forward allowing the back tire to slide. Fast as lightning, well-trained reflexes kicked in, adjusting the bike seamlessly back on course. The top of a boulder exposed from previous rides, however, refused to be denied. The front wheel caught, bringing the Gambler to an abrupt halt. Headfirst, Sierra punched her ticket to a one-way flight over the handle bars.

"Shit!"

Every inch of ground passed in slow motion as she rapidly approached her destination—the three-foot-wide trunk of a century-old Western Red Cedar. On instinct, she threw up her shoulder and rotated her torso, hoping to strike something less vital than her head. Upon impact, a loud thud echoed through her ears accompanied by a sharp pain that pierced her left shoulder and forced the air from her lungs. Sierra's limp body bounced off the trunk and crashed in a heap at the base of the giant tree. Ringing. Gasping. So much gasping as she fought to recover her breath and her wits.

"Son of a..."

Every inch of her body spoke to her. Some parts hummed with a numbing tingle, while others screamed. Nothing responded to her command to move as she lay in the dirt for several long seconds. Finally, the haze cleared, but the stinging pain lingered.

How bad is it?

A moment of paralyzing fear struck Sierra as she considered the real possibilities that might lie ahead. Never one to sugar coat things, it was time to take stock of body parts.

First things first, she looked at the upside. *I'm alive. That's a win.* Now, for the downside. *Okay. Let's start with my neck.* She carefully flexed and then rolled her neck. It was sore, but seemed fine. *Arms?* "Owww, shit!" The left one was angry as hell. *Finally...legs?* Their lack of immediate response sent her into a panic, but seconds later, they were good to go.

Thank God! That could have been bad. So very bad.

As she struggled to sit up, the medics arrived. A hand to her sternum kept her still as they performed a swift, methodical assessment. This was the part no rider ever wanted to deal with and Sierra Cody was known to be more cantankerous than most.

"Really guys, I'm fine. Nothing I haven't done before. Just a little separated left shoulder, I think."

Again, she attempted to get to her feet, but they were having none of it. A clean cut, dark-haired medic named Derrick pulled out his penlight and checked for equal and reactive pupils, while an older, bald medic, Joe, asked questions. "What's your name? Can you tell me where you are?"

Casting a sideways glance and wearing a deep frown, she gruffly answered, "I'm Sierra Cody. This is the Bend stop of the Genesis Pro Downhill Series. And that, my friend, was an epic fail."

The medics laughed and carefully helped Sierra to her feet. Derrick smiled. "Glad you're all right, but you know we have to take you to the care center for a full check-up." He held up his hand as she opened her mouth. "And before you say it, Sierra, we know how you are, but it's the rules. Please don't give us a hard time, okay?"

With a defeated sigh, she nodded and made her way slowly to the truck with her injured left arm tucked into her side. The crowd cheered and she threw them a wave to let them know she was fine. Taking a seat in the truck, Sierra stared out the window and cursed herself for being so reckless.

That should have ended so much better, but I screwed up. Again.

"Damn, that was a ballsy ride, girl! One hell of an endo too. You must have caught at least six feet of air to reach that tree," Joe gushed. He was as much in awe of the crash as he was the ride.

"I hate to be the one to tell you this, but you had Ronni at that last split." Derrick laughed and gave her a pat on the back.

The only thing Sierra hated more than losing was being on the receiving end of a sympathy pat. Ronni Demartini may have been her roommate and best friend since childhood, but they had one hell of an intense rivalry. "Yeah, I guess she takes this round. I'll get her next time though," she grumbled, sinking into the corner of the backseat.

Over and over, the fateful error replayed in her head. Ronni had warned her about the rock. It had become more and more exposed over the weekend and could have been avoided had she not insisted on holding the tight line she had chosen. The high line would have taken a split second longer, but she would have finished her ride instead of getting a personal escort to the care center.

"Dumbass." Sierra muttered to herself. Dejected, she leaned forward, perching her right elbow on her knee, and pressed her face into a gloved hand. *Why do I always have to be so damned stubborn?*

CHAPTER TWO

Standing silently in the doorway of the care center, Sierra held her left arm against her body and took a casual look around. The drab gray walls and stench of menthol mingling with antiseptic made her skin crawl. Though downhill mountain biking was a dangerous sport, she'd been fortunate enough to have avoided too many visits.

People milled about the large open area, some giving care, some receiving. Still others hung out to watch the live race coverage. With the event nearly over, the staff had already begun packing the empty tables and left over supplies, leaving the place with a ransacked look about it.

Her visual tour came to a halt at the sight of a rider on crutches carefully making her way out the door. Keri wouldn't be back on a bike for weeks. Sierra thanked the heavens she had avoided that fate. She'd rather injure an arm than a leg any day. Not being able to ride for an extended period would drive her mad. Luckily, she tended to heal fast. While that had not been an issue in quite some time, her luck may have finally run out. There was no telling what the final verdict would be on her left shoulder and the uncertainty of her future had her on edge.

All right, let's get this over with. Being here is making me antsy.

Sierra's fidgeting ceased when her gaze was drawn to the graceful glide of an approaching woman. She was tall with an elegant demeanor and athletic build, her attention focused on the clipboard held in strong, yet slender hands. Her auburn hair was styled in a spiked pixie cut in the back, while bangs hung choppy in the front. The pressed navy polo with gold embroidering over her left breast spelled out the name "Dr. Davies." The doctor looked extremely put together, quite the contradiction from the rag-tag crew that usually worked the downhill events.

Still streaming thoughts from whatever she had been finishing, the doctor pulled the pen from behind her ear and made notes, humming as she went. Without a glance, she offered a greeting, "Hello. I'm Doctor Davies. Please follow me."

Walking side by side toward the exam area, a brief second passed before the doctor lifted her head and turned her focus to her new patient. Sparkling sea-green eyes met Sierra's as she offered a polite smile. "Sorry. I needed to finish that note while it was fresh in my head. What's your name?"

Sierra's impatience from moments ago eased away as she took in the sight of the woman before her. She may have been in a hurry to get the annoying formalities of this visit over with, but a beautiful woman, or a hot bike, would always earn some patience in her book. If there was a hot bike in the room, she sure as hell hadn't seen it, because good god...was this woman ever a beauty. Not supermodel beautiful, but more real, as in the girl next door with an irresistible smile and a little something extra that hit Sierra dead in the chest.

Sierra stared wordlessly—seemingly star struck—missing the smile spreading across Dr. Davies' face. Quickly realizing her behavior, she shook her head and apologized. "Uh, sorry. I may have hit a little harder than I thought. I'm Sierra Cody."

Dr. Davies offered a reassuring smile, seemingly unfazed by the open admiration. "It's all right, Sierra. It happens all the time after a crash." An easy silence followed as her eyes slowly drifted down Sierra's tight-fitting jersey, pausing when she reached her breasts.

Sierra smiled inwardly. They were certainly her most popular feature and it gave her a bit of ego boost to have drawn the doctor's attention.

"Okay, so...um..." Dr. Davies squared her shoulders and pulled her eyes back up. A light pink tinged her cheeks, but she was right back to business. "What did you do to yourself?"

"Well, the course wasn't quite challenging enough, so I decided to take on a tree," Sierra replied with a cheeky grin, still enamored with the doctor.

Dr. Davies chuckled before she said, "Please remove your jersey so I can get a better look at your shoulder."

She turned and pulled the divider closed for privacy, allowing Sierra time to appreciate the way the doctor's tan, form-fitting slacks complemented her lean, athletic physique...Especially from behind.

"So, you're the one who launched herself over the handlebars?"

Not the impression Sierra had wanted to open with, but she would own it like a champ. "The one and only." Now, if she could just get her arm out of her sleeve.

"You had one hell of a ride going before you decided to pick a fight with that tree. Whatever did he do to piss you off?" the doctor asked with a sly grin.

"Yeah, well...we go way back." Sierra laughed as she finally pulled her injured arm out of the tight jersey, noting some scratches along the bike chain tattoo that wrapped around her right wrist. "I'm usually known for my epic saves, but I guess I lost one of my nine lives today. Really, I'm fine. This kind of thing happens all the time."

"Well, it's my job to make sure you're all right. I'm going to assess your shoulder and neck first, and then rule out a concussion. A few of the exams may cause pain, but I promise to make it quick."

Sierra nodded her understanding. "Whatever you need to do, Doc. But I gotta warn you, I'm an adrenaline junkie and I'll need to feed my habit again soon. So, fix me up stat!"

"I'll do my best." Her smile was sincere and she oozed confidence. After visually scanning her patient's body for any signs of damage, Dr. Davies paused to make a few notes.

What happened next shook Sierra to her core. When the doctor's bare hand finally touched her skin, it was unlike anything Sierra had experienced before. Scintillating. Electric. Her touch brought Sierra's numb nerve endings back to life and erased the pain on contact. Closing her eyes and relishing in the feel of warm fingers on marred flesh, Sierra bit her lip and hoped Dr. Davies hadn't noticed the flush rushing across her skin.

Damn! How hard did I hit that freaking tree?

Sierra's eyes popped open as a piercing pain ripped through her. "Ouch! Shit! That hurt!" On instinct, she tried to pull her left arm back, but the injured limb was locked in the doctor's grasp. *Weak ass,* she chided herself. That was not the impression she had wanted to leave. "Sorry for the language."

Unaffected by the outburst, Dr. Davies offered a sympathetic smile and continued her exam, taking the various body parts through ranges of motion and making mental notes. For the most part, her palpations were more a caress than a move to provoke pain. Sierra would swear those hands lingered a bit longer than necessary a time or two, though the doctor was never unprofessional. Not for one second. Still, the feel of the woman's expert hands on her skin evoked not-so-innocent images of the goddess in a polo shirt running those hands all over her naked body.

An uncontrollable groan of pleasure freed itself without permission, bringing Sierra back to the awkward reality of curious green eyes studying her with concern.

"You okay?"

"Huh? Umm...yeah. Sorry. Just ready to get this over with. I haven't spent much time in these places." Apparently, hitting a tree revved up her libido. That never needed a boost. She needed a distraction. "How long have you been doing this?"

Dr. Davies paused to write in the file and then replied, "This is my second mountain biking event. They recruited me to help since the sport's grown so much. I've worked other events though." She returned to work through the rest of the exams, the Glasgow Coma scale, balance and reflexes, before returning to the left shoulder. As she traced over the darkening skin of Sierra's shoulder, the doctor's firm touch softened and her hands slowed. The word "amazing" was murmured in awe.

Sierra glanced over her shoulder, grinning seductively as she caught a look at the doctor's beet red face.

"I mean..." The previously stoic professional faltered for a moment, then cleared her throat. "I can't believe you're A-C joint wasn't separated after a blow like that. It seems you'll only have bruising. Just amazing." The flustered doctor turned away, returning to the safety of her notes.

Sierra didn't want to come off as cocky, but there was no way she could leave that comment hanging. It wouldn't be her. With a confident smirk, she said, "I love it when women tell me I'm amazing."

"I'm sure you do." Amusement sparkled in the doctor's words.

"Well, Doctor Davies, I would be happy to fill you in on my diet and training regimen sometime. You know...so you can see what makes me tick." Arching a brow, Sierra watched for any reaction whatsoever. It was a sincere offer that also included the intended innuendo, should the doctor decide to take up the offer. The fact that she didn't have much of a regimen was irrelevant. She'd wing it if the opportunity arose.

Was that a hint of a smile working at the corner of the doctor's mouth as she finished her notes? The possibility of the subtle response gave the Sierra hope of a late-night rendezvous, but that dream came to a crashing halt when the physician fell right back into full doctor mode once again.

"Your neck is out of alignment after that shot you took and your gleno-humeral joint is jammed. With your permission, I'm going to provide some gentle manipulation to help return them to their natural place and allow the body to heal itself. Have you ever been adjusted by a chiropractor?"

"No, can't say that I have. Usually, I get some meds or a shot for the pain. Like I said, I heal quickly."

"Sorry. That's not what I do. My job is to put motion back into the joint and allow the body to do the rest. If pain meds are what you want though, I can refer you to one of the MD's, but I promise I'll be quick and gentle."

"I don't mind a little rough here and there."

The comment had the desired effect as the doctor fought a grin, but the corner of her mouth hiked up anyway. She refrained from a retort and continued on topic, "You need to ice on and off for the next forty-eight hours, but I expect you'll be good as new before you know it."

"That's what I like to hear."

The exam had long since ended, yet the doctor's hands remained on Sierra's shoulder. A wicked grin curled as she formulated a plan. Lying back on the table, she figured she'd give it another shot, maybe wear the woman down. "Well, if you decide you want to know how this superwoman maintains her indestructible body, let me know. There is an open invite for you to do a little research." Sierra broke out the infamous "Cody smile" that left the girls swooning and faked a stretch that accentuated her breasts.

This time, the doctor's professional persona broke and a laugh poured out. Tiny gold flecks danced in her eyes like the sun danced on the ocean, dazzling Sierra and commanding her full attention.

Dr. Davies smiled warmly, took Sierra's arm, and began to manipulate her shoulder. "Well, I do like research." Her strong, confident hands moved with precision and speed.

In a matter of minutes, Sierra had been pushed and pulled and squished and twisted, or "adjusted," as Dr. Davies had called it. Whatever it was, it had worked wonders. She sat up and moved her neck and shoulder. There was much more freedom throughout the range of motion. Pleasantly surprised with this newfound treatment, not to mention the treating physician, Sierra remarked with awe, "You're really great with your hands."

Dr. Davies rolled her eyes and laughed. "Thanks. I think you're all good now. Follow up with your primary physician if you experience any lingering effects and be careful out there, Ms. Cody."

The use of a formal name was a mood killer. The doctor may have been into her breasts, but apparently, that was all. "Thanks Doc, but I'm not making any promises." As she slipped her jersey back on, with only minor soreness, a whooping and hollering called out from the entrance.

"What up everyone? Ronni D is in the house! Where's my girl, Wiley? Wiley Cody?"

Sierra's best friend had dubbed her "Wiley," as in the coyote, years ago. She didn't love the nickname, but that damn cartoon coyote was determined as hell and that was something she could relate to.

She peeked out from the curtain to find Ronni fist bumping everyone in celebration of her victory. Her old friend was tall and lanky, but strong as an ox, and not to mention, fast as all hell. Never one to be lost in a crowd, she was always sure to stand out, both in attitude and attire. This weekend was all about orange—orange hair, orange shoes, orange jersey, orange bike. Ronni was definitely one of a kind and apparently, a marketing gold mine.

"Over here, Ron." Sierra waved from the back of the room.

Taking time to greet every person in the room, Ronni made her rounds until finally reaching the back, her hand raised high in wait for Sierra to return her five. Her eyes drifted toward the corner and one Dr. Davies, who had begun packing up. Looking the doctor up and down, Ronni nodded approvingly and winked before letting out a wolfish whistle. "Damn, Wiley! I'd bet if you knew the doctors here were this hot, you would've taken a header a lot sooner."

Sierra cringed and shook her head. Subtle, her best friend was not. Had there been any sliver of a chance left with the doctor, it was certainly gone now. Shooting a look of disapproval had little effect, but that was no surprise. Glancing over her shoulder in hopes of offering an apology, Sierra's heart sank. The doctor had already made a quiet escape.

"Dammit, Ron!" It was a hushed whisper followed by an elbow to the ribs.

"Ow! What? Oh wait, were you trying to hook up? Shit. I'm sorry. Where'd she go? I'll fix it."

Looking back over her shoulder again, Sierra said, "No. No. You leave it alone. She's not interested. But you made it weird."

"Okay, well, she's hot for sure, but seemed a bit uptight. I mean, I'd bet her panties were perfectly pressed too. Am I right?" Ronni laughed.

Sierra palmed her face and shook her head. Thanks to Ronni, she was imagining the doctor in several varieties of underwear, the pictures flashing through her mind like a lingerie catalogue

Ronni squeezed Sierra's arm, pulling her attention back as her smile faded and concern took over. "You okay? I don't like to win that way."

"Fine," Sierra grumbled. "Indestructible as always." Her shoulder was already feeling better, but her desire to spend more time with the doctor had her more worked up than usual. She could definitely use a drink. "Let's go celebrate."

"Now, that's what I'm talking about." Ronni thrust her fist into the air in victory. She smiled as she caught sight of the doctor again and called out, "Hey, Doctor McHottie!"

Sierra whipped her head around. Ronni's attempts to fix things had never worked in her favor. She dreaded what might come out of her friend's mouth next. It appeared that Dr. Davies was every bit as frightened as she side-stepped behind a large storage container in a failed attempt at hiding, looking as though she'd been cornered by a Rottweiler. In a sense, she had been.

With a "trust me" wink that failed to soothe Sierra's fears, Ronni continued, "Everyone's headed down to Taco'd Brewery. You should join us. Drinks are on me," she sing-songed the last two words. "Cause I'm the winner, bitches!"

The few stragglers remaining in the room roared their approval and Ronni flashed a championship-worthy smile.

Dr. Davies' eyes popped wide. Her hands gripped the box she was holding hard enough to crease the sides. "N...No," she stuttered. "I don't think so. I have a lot to get done here, but thank you and congratulations on your win." She turned her attention to Sierra. "Ms. Cody, don't forget to ice."

Ronni's brows jumped up and her lips pursed. "Ms. Cody?" she whispered. "Ouch." With a sympathetic pat on the back, she added, "Better luck next time, Wiley," and then meandered toward the exit with much fanfare.

Count that as my second crash and burn for the day. Go me.

Sierra signed the release form and lingered near the back of the pack as the last remaining riders cleared the care center. Her pride had taken a hit today and as easy as it would be to walk away and drown her sorrows in alcohol, there was something about Dr. Davies that wouldn't let her accept defeat.

Before the doctor could shut the clinic door, Sierra stopped and turned back around. With all the pomp and circumstance of the event over, the two of them were alone. Standing face to beautiful face, Sierra was struck with something she was not at all accustomed to—nerves.

Trying not to appear too anxious or desperate, she smiled and sputtered, "I uh...I wanted to thank you. I'm feeling much better already."

"You don't have to thank me. It's my job."

"I know, but still, I appreciate you. And we'll shut Taco'd down tonight, so please feel free to stop in, even if it's not until later. I'd love to buy you a drink to thank you. Plus, I can fill you in on my superpowers," she finished with a wink.

Dr. Davies shifted awkwardly and gave her a tight smile. "I appreciate the offer and I'll think about it, but I have a lot of packing up to do and an early morning. Please enjoy your evening. I'm sure I'll see you again sometime, especially the way you ride," she teased.

Though Sierra had expected the letdown, it didn't hurt any less. Deflated, but determined not to show it, she reached out to shake the doctor's hand. On contact, she was once again rendered awestruck. There was something about the woman that had her desperate for more time together. Unfortunately, it seemed it wasn't in the cards tonight. She pulled the doctor close and leaned into her ear. "You can bet on it, Doctor Davies."

The doctor's face was unreadable as she replied, "Have a good night, Ms. Cody."

Again, with the shifting to a formal name. For a moment, irritation began a slow, steady pick at Sierra's ego. Times when her persistence failed to pay off were far between. Resigned to the fact she wasn't going to get her chance tonight, Sierra turned to leave, but not before flashing one more knee-weakening smile for the doctor to remember her by. Her first impression may not have been the best, but she was going to try her darnedest to make the last one leave a mark.

CHAPTER THREE

Thanks to the race, the crowd was larger than normal at Taco'd Brewery, even for a late-summer Saturday night. While Bend, Oregon had no shortage of amazing breweries to kick back in and enjoy a pint or two, most fat tire fans chose the one with the bent bicycle rim logo. The appeal of Taco'd was much like any old pub with hardwood floors and a long antique bar, but what clinched it for Sierra and her friends was the collector's delight of all things bicycle that hung upon the walls. The owner, Axel, was a local pioneer of the sport. He'd been carving up the mountainside since long before manicured trails and full body padding. On any given night, he could be found regaling the patrons about the good old days of biking.

Axel's first mountain bike, Betsy, a blue and white bike he had built from spare parts, hung proudly over the bar. His other pride and joy, his father's bike, sat in the corner behind a velvet rope. The 1930's Schwinn, one of the first fat tire bikes ever produced, had been restored to perfection. Some joked his collection was the reason they held so many races in Bend. Never mind the fact that the trails were among the tops in the nation and the town was a dream destination for any outdoor enthusiast.

Many nights, patrons would be treated to great musical talent, but every night, the food was not to be missed. Weekly specials featured new dishes from around the world as well as old staples done to perfection, such as burgers, wings, and nachos. Of course, a big reason for visiting a brewery was the beer and while Axel and his buddy, Cal, had brewed their own award-winning IPA beers, they prided themselves on a magnificent selection of alcohol from around the globe.

Folks would come from all over in an attempt to get through the entire alphabet. The few persistent and hardy enough to make it through the list received a Taco'd t-shirt that said, "I drank myself around the world and all I got was this lousy t-shirt." It seemed to be a great marketing ploy, because the place was always hopping.

Sierra tipped her bottle of Bottomed Out Stout to Axel. The sixty-something year old man with long, white hair pulled back in a ponytail smiled and gave her a wave. As a local herself, she'd spent plenty of nights here shooting the breeze and laughing over Axel and Cal's tales from their youth.

To her right, a swarm of riders cheered. She turned to find Ronni standing on the edge of the bar doing shots and beer chasers from her first-place cup—a tradition born of a spontaneous joke between the two friends before they were even old enough to drink.

Ronni scanned the room, acknowledging many of her friends and stopping when she had found her intended mark. "Yo, Cam! Suck it, Bi-yatch!" She flipped her red-headed rival the bird as she nearly fell off the bar in drunken laughter.

Camryn O'Reilly gritted her teeth and returned a middle finger of her own before she downed another shot. Second place was as good as last to her when she finished behind Sierra or Ronni. The long-legged rider was a loner with piercing hazel eyes and some serious attitude.

Camryn turned to her teammate, Kourt, one of the veterans of the sport. She whispered something that made them both snicker, no doubt a derogatory remark pointed at Sierra and Ronni.

Sierra laughed it off. She preferred to do her talking on her bike and Ronni had never once been fazed by Camryn's attempts at intimidation, no matter how hard the woman had tried. Ronni climbed down from the bar and perched on Sierra's lap, holding onto strong, sober shoulders to steady herself. The light haze of alcohol had begun to set in her eyes, which meant she was ready to ramble. Ronni was a talker, even more so when she had a few drinks in her.

"How you feeling?" Ronni asked. "That was quite a blow you took. And by that, I mean both the tree and the way the Doc McHottie shot you down. Damn sure wasn't for lack of trying though." She laughed and then continued, "For what it's worth, I think she was interested. Probably some code of conduct thing or something. She seems like the stickler for rules type—which I may point out—you are not." She had that cocked eyebrow thing going, something Ronni did when she already knew the answer, but wanted you to say it out loud.

Sierra's face lit up. "I don't know...She is just...I don't know. She's definitely hot, but it seems like there's a lot more to her." Her smile spread upward from her cheeks to her ears thinking about the woman. "I mean, yeah, of course I want her, but I also want to know more about her."

"Wait, what's with the emotional stuff? I thought you'd given up on all that love at first sight crap? Now it's just hit 'em and quit 'em."

"I did, but—"

"Damn, girl. How hard did you hit that tree anyway?" Ronni shook her head and downed another shot.

"When she touched me...I can't even explain it. I mean, maybe it was the shock of the blow I took, but it felt so real and I think she felt it too. Doesn't matter though. I doubt she'll show up tonight. Even if she did, she was pretty clear. I'm sure she has her reasons. We'll see what happens if she's at another race." The words were easily said, but there was a drive inside her to pursue the doctor— something she had never had before.

"I know you don't give up easily, but it's probably for the best. You travel a lot and you promised yourself no distractions this season. So, don't get all emo on me. I need you focused, killer," Ronni said with a pumped fist as a sign of strength. "Find some chick here tonight that can scratch that itch and then get ready for the next event."

With a laugh and a nod, Sierra sipped her beer and returned to enjoying the party. Ronni was probably right. Hell, she usually was anyway. Tonight, Sierra would wallow in self-pity and indulge in her friend's victory celebration. Tomorrow, it was back to business.

***

As she set the last box of medical supplies down beside the back door, Dr. Davies overheard several staff members talking about the brewery. Seemed it was a ritual of sorts. She had worked many other events and couldn't recall a time when a group had spoken so adoringly about a place of business, but those events had been much larger and more commercial. Maybe it was due to the close-knit biking community that everyone sounded so familial. Either way, she was intrigued, though she had no plan to see it for herself. At least, not tonight.

When she turned to gather her belongings, the racing association director, Martin Dearborn, smiled and waved her over. The director was a distinguished-looking, forty-year-old with slicked back salt and pepper hair who towered over everyone with his lanky six-foot-seven frame. "Doctor, thank you for your work today. I hope it was enjoyable."

"Very much so. Thank you for having me." She always enjoyed the challenge of working on-site, but one rider had made her day more interesting than usual.

"We're all done now." He set his large hand gently on her shoulder. "You should come join us for a drink. It would be a terrific way to get to know everyone since you'll be with us now on a regular basis."

Kara was tempted by the offer, even more so by the possibility of seeing Sierra Cody once again. The woman was a pure seductress on two wheels. She toed the line between butch and femme and carried herself with a swagger that surely left many ladies swooning. As much as Kara would love to see her again, she was in no place to entertain such thoughts. Heading home and burying herself in work would be the smart thing to do.

"Thank you for the invitation, but it's been a long weekend and I have an early morning." Hoping to smooth over any hard feelings for declining she added, "I've enjoyed working with everyone here. What a great group of people. Everything flows so smoothly. Really a pleasure. I look forward to many more events with you all."

"Come now, Doctor Davies, I won't take no for an answer. Your talents may be in demand by many, but you must eat and take some time to relax. It's my treat." He lifted his bag over his shoulder and with a confident smile, he motioned to the door. "Shall we?"

With no way out, she nodded and grabbed her jacket. "Very well then. I suppose it would be good to relax. Thank you," Kara replied, although she was certain the evening would be anything but relaxing. She had maintained her resolve against Sierra's earlier onslaught, but wasn't so sure she'd survive a second wave.

Maybe she'd be able to steal a few glances without being seen or find out a bit more about the rider from the staff through casual conversation. Yes, just some easy, emotionally unattached conversation, like a patient exam. One thing she was good at was getting information. Questions were the key to piecing together any puzzle. But there was one important question she couldn't honestly answer herself. Was Sierra Cody a puzzle she wanted to solve?

The ride to Taco'd was filled with her own thoughts. She enjoyed the scenery and pretended to listen as Martin spoke of epic battles and champions. He loved the sport and was passionate about his role in shaping its future. She wished she was more interested in listening, but all she could think about was the feel of Sierra's smooth, creamy skin beneath her finger tips and how she hadn't been able to take her hands or eyes off her the entire exam. She was frustrated by how unprofessional she had been, but there was something magnetic about the woman.

That behavior would never fly in her office.

Kara scolded herself again for being so reckless and begged her inner desires to go back into hibernation. Still, she couldn't help but feel excited, and nervous, and a thousand other feelings, at the possibility of seeing Sierra again.

She couldn't seem to stop her knee from bouncing or her usually steady-as-steel hands from fidgeting. She needed to get out of the car and have a drink. "How much farther?" Kara asked, unknowingly cutting off Martin mid-sentence. "Oh, I'm sorry... I didn't mean to interrupt." She covered her face in embarrassment.

Martin laughed. "It's ok. I've been known to spout off at the mouth. Not sure I've ever had anyone ready to bail out of the car before." He glanced over at the red-faced doctor and laughed some more. "Although, I may have been told a time or two that my ramblings make people want to jump ship." He chuckled again.

Relaxing back into her seat, Kara forced her knee into stillness and gave him a gentle smile in thanks for dismissing her rudeness. "I'm sorry. I'm not usually like that. I think the exhaustion of the last few weeks has set in. I don't usually take time to relax. Thank you for freeing me from myself for a few hours."

"I'm glad I could persuade you to join us then. It's just up ahead."

A deep exhale of relief flowed through her lips, but her stomach was still twisted like a towel with a loose thread caught in the washing machine. Having no idea how the night would play out was as exciting as it was nerve-racking. Kara was used to being in control of everything all the time. A strict schedule with specific goals, she had learned, was the secret to success. Her chiropractic office, sport science research, and meticulous patient care plans were all organized and well planned down to the smallest detail. Even her day was timed to within a fifteen minute window—breakfast, lunch, dinner, patient slots, work outs, experiments, bed time...everything.

Running through her daily schedule, she came to the realization that there was never a spot for relaxation. *My god I've gotten boring*, she mused as she stared at a bent bicycle rim sign adorning the rooftop of the brewery. Of course, her ex-girlfriends had always underlined her rigid routine and lack of playtime as primary reasons for breaking up with her, but until now, she hadn't taken stock of the fact that she was truly all work and no play. She wasn't even sure how to socialize anymore.

Feeling out of her element, the reserved doctor took a deep breath as she exited the car, forcing the most natural smile she could muster. *It's only drinks and conversation for crying out loud. Pretend you're talking to patients.* She steadied herself and followed Martin inside. He pointed to a table near the bar, directing Kara to the rest of their group. She nodded and followed slowly behind as her eyes scanned the room for a certain intriguing rider. To her dismay, her efforts proved futile. The bar was beyond packed.

Shoving her hands down deep into her pants pockets, Kara repeatedly coiled and uncoiled her fingers, releasing the pent up nervous energy that coursed through her veins. *Why am I so interested anyway?* Something about Sierra Cody had gotten under her skin and while she might be emotionally unavailable, she couldn't deny the physical attraction to the cocky, yet beautiful, rider.

Sierra's free-spirited confidence had piqued her curiosity. There was definitely more to her than a burning need to get an adrenaline fix. As her thoughts continued to swirl, a light smile replaced the tight-pursed lips she had worn mere moments ago. Although socializing wasn't in her list of favorite activities, Sierra was one person she wouldn't mind chatting up. Seemed Sierra was a puzzle she did want to solve after all.

She was even curious about the tattoo on her right calf, a crankset with a heart in the center. Such a unique design, obviously inspired by her love for biking, but how did the idea come about? Were there more tattoos besides the calf and wrist? She longed for any little detail that hinted at what made the woman tick. But her quest for knowledge would have to wait. Unfortunately, it was Martin and the rest of the staff she would be mingling with tonight, instead of the mysterious woman who had captured her attention.

Kara was pulled from her thoughts by Martin's hand on her arm. He pointed to the end of the table. "They saved us seats over there," he said, speaking above the bustle of the crowd.

As they weaved through the swarm of bodies on the way to their group, Kara's hopes fell flat as another quick survey of the room came up empty. *At least there will be more races.* The attempt at soothing her disappointment was not as effective as she had hoped. Her eyes narrowed as it occurred to her that she couldn't remember the last time she'd been so curious about someone.

"What would you like to drink?" Martin asked, cutting off the search through her memory banks.

A drink would surely help her relax. Three or four would help her forget, but she wasn't lying when she had said she was tired and had an early day tomorrow.

"A glass of Riesling, thank you." Kara greeted the others with a friendly smile and claimed one of the empty chairs. Sitting back with one ear on the conversation, she couldn't resist the urge to search out the woman with streaks of red burning trails through wild, long, dark hair.

CHAPTER FOUR

Sierra's spine tingled with a sixth sense. Whipping around, she expected to find someone sneaking up from behind, but there was no one. Something was off. She could feel it. Her gaze skimmed across the crowd and around Martin Dearborn standing near the doorway, finally landing on a familiar and extremely welcomed face. Those pressed pants and tightly tucked shirt made Dr. Davies stand out as sorely as a sleek, sporty road bike among a trailer full of rugged, knobby tired downhill frames.

The beat in her chest picked up speed, pounding hard against her sternum. A wickedly seductive grin commanded her lips at the sight of the doctor and she whispered to herself, "It is *so* on."

She slipped behind her group of friends to watch from afar, studying every nuance as the doctor made her way toward the crowd—the uncomfortable fidget of hands, the shift in weight, and the subtle smile that disappeared almost as soon as it had appeared. What had brought about the brief moment of happiness? A small glimmer of hope had Sierra wishing it was the thought of seeing her. Not a second later, she mulled what could've possibly wiped the smile away. Did the doctor not like Martin, or perhaps the staff? Did she not want to be here? Was the place beneath her standards?

The straight-laced professional looked even more out of place jostling amid the bodies of tattooed, endorsement covered, adrenaline junkies than she had standing alone in the doorway. Like a tiger awaiting its chance to pounce, Sierra stood stock still, barely managing a breath, until Martin had led the doctor to their seats. Her gaze never wavered from her mark, even when Martin headed to the bar, obviously on a mission to secure drinks. A smile tugged at the corner of her mouth as Dr. Davies attempted a casual glance around.

Sierra was on to her now. The doctor was most definitely searching for her. Her gloating was rudely interrupted by Martin's return, extending a glass of white wine to the doctor. Sierra chuckled and shook her head. *Oh yeah. She definitely looks like the wine bar type.*

"Hey, Wiley? Why ya hiding back there? I never took you for a wallflower. And why aren't you out 'getting to know' Doc McHottie?" Ronni had blown past tipsy and was on her way to plastered. At least those episodes were few and far between these days. Even drunk though, she never missed a thing.

Receiving no answer, Ronni slapped Sierra on the leg and said, "Earth to Sierra. Get your ass over there already. She looks bored anyway. Or maybe that's how she always looks. Who knows." She continued to ramble, "It's not like you to wait so long to pounce. You sure she likes women? You're ogling her like you're already in love. Geeze, you don't even know this chick. I need another shot." She spun around and nearly fell over as she called out, "Bartender!"

"Ron!" Sierra scolded her best friend while taking care to steady her. There were three things Ronni was good at—drinking, downhill, and running off at the mouth. "Good god, will you relax? I'm not in love. I'm just scouting. You know, making a plan." She nodded as if to convince herself of her own reasoning.

"She's not the type I usually pick up and I seriously doubt I'm what she usually looks for. I mean, look at her. I can't go over there with some cheesy pick up line. She's too sophisticated for that. She's drinking white wine for goodness sakes! And I don't want to wham-bam thank you ma'am her either. I have to do this right." Sierra exhaled and took another sip of her beer. This was indeed new territory for her, but she was never afraid of trying.

After all, nothing good ever happened if you never left the starting gate.

Ronni pretended to gag, then rolled her eyes and shrugged. "Whatever. Just be careful with that one. She seems frigid. She's already turned down two potential suitors and isn't doing much talking. If you need me to help break through—"

"No! Thank you." Sierra's hand shot up in protest. "I'll handle this myself. The last time you helped me you started a brawl." Sierra side-eyed her best friend.

"Yeah. Good times, bestie, good times." Ronni slapped her on the back and staggered to her feet. "Well, if you change your mind, I'll be with Blake and Harley getting my drink on." She chucked her thumb up over her shoulder.

Blake Volden, the owner of Team Traxx, raised his beer to her. He was a well-dressed, meticulously-groomed gentleman with light brown hair and a drop-dead gorgeous smile. Sierra's ex, the dirty blonde spitfire named Harley, waved them both over.

On many a night, Sierra would've accepted the offer, but tonight she preferred to continue her pursuit of the doctor who had already turned down several drink offers. That was one of the reasons she had to do this right. Another reason was that the doctor deserved better than some ridiculous, overused pick-up line. A plan took shape in her mind. Now, all she had to do was figure out how to get her alone so she could make her move.

As soon as the question was posed, an answer presented itself. The doctor excused herself from the table and headed toward the ladies room. Sierra was quick on her feet, searching out a willing accomplice to help get her foot in the door. After a stop at the bar for two bottles of beer, she approached one of the male rookies on the tour, Rob. He was handsome, with dusty blonde hair and crisp blue eyes and had enough of a buzz going to agree to a favor for a free beer. When the doctor returned, Sierra pointed her out and Rob set out to intercept his target.

Anticipation bubbled in Sierra's chest. "Perfect," she whispered as she followed a few feet behind him, but was careful to remain hidden.

Thanks to the crowd, the doctor was held up at the far end of the bar. Rob approached from behind and when she was forced to stop, he leaned in and said, "Excuse me. I'm Mr. Right. Someone said you were looking for me."

Not again. Kara rolled her eyes and took a deep breath. Never one to be rude, she had a polite turn down on the tip of her tongue as she faked a smile and spun around.

"Thank you but...Sierra?" Startled to find the object of her infatuation rather than a mystery man, she quickly glanced right and left in confusion. "I didn't expect to see you there. I mean...there was just a guy..."

Sierra smiled seductively and took a step closer. In a husky tone, she replied, "Yeah well, I told him if anyone was buying the smoking hot doctor a drink tonight it was me. I hope that was all right." She looked down and picked at the label on her bottle before meeting Kara's shell-shocked stare once again. "But..." She shrugged. "If *he's* more your type, then I can get him right back here."

Long, dark lashes framed Sierra's light amber eyes which shimmered like gold. The touch of black eyeliner accented them to perfection. Mesmerized by the way they sparkled back at her, Kara stood speechless, motionless, frozen in an imaginary tractor beam that kept pulling her closer to the other woman until Sierra's warm breath tiptoed across her skin. Goosebumps blazed a trail from her collar bone to her scalp. A shiver swept over her. Unable to form words, Kara finally gathered the strength to look away, dipping her head and blushing furiously. Sierra Cody had the power to render her speechless and it was unsettling.

With the stunning woman out of her field of vision, Kara's short-circuited nerve endings began to fire anew, allowing her to put syllables together in a coherent manner. "That won't be necessary, but thank you," she said with a shy smile. She was no stranger to being on the receiving end of flirtation—which she always declined with ease—but with little to no effort, Sierra had managed to put everyone else she had ever encountered to shame. Saying no to her was about as easy as fighting gravity.

When two men vacated the stools beside them, Kara wasted no time claiming one and inviting Sierra to join her on the other. Realizing she had finally gotten her wish, Kara now had no idea what to do next. She truly had no intention of hooking up—that wasn't her style— and she wasn't in the market for a relationship. Her life was already complicated enough. *What am I doing?*

Sierra slid her stool closer. The way Sierra's eyes analyzed her every move was both nerve-racking and the ultimate compliment. Afraid she might give into her desires being in such close proximity, she shifted away.

Taking note of the discomfort, Sierra graciously slid back, an apologetic smile on her lips, offering more space until Kara relaxed again. When Axel hustled past, she flagged him down. "Axel, whiskey please, and the lady will have...white wine?" Her brow arched.

Kara flashed an amused smirk. "Riesling, please." As Axel took his leave, Kara's curiosity had her burning with questions. "So, you know what I'm drinking. Lucky guess or have you been spying on me tonight?"

There was a gleam in Sierra's eyes when she replied, "I wouldn't call it spying. You may find this hard to believe, but you're very hard to miss."

Looking to the ceiling, Kara let out an uncomfortable chuckle and decided to shift the conversation. "Well, thank you for the drink, but you really didn't have to. How are you feeling?"

"Why Doctor Davies, does the doctor in you never shut off?" She sucked her bottom lip between her teeth. "But to answer your question, I'm feeling very well, thanks to you. May have to get that done more often. My neck feels better than it has in a long time. You're amazing."

Kara rolled her eyes and laughed. "I do love it when women tell me I'm amazing." An easy smile took shape as she returned the familiar phrase.

"Touché." Sierra let out a melodious chuckle as she pulled out a twenty for their drinks.

Axel slid the glasses in front of them and gave Sierra a wink before quickly slipping away.

Feeling her confidence grow, Kara sat upright in her seat and met Sierra's amused grin with her own. "Thank you for the drink. I'm glad you're feeling better. And, yes, I can shut it off, once in a while. Since we're not in the clinic anymore, please call me Kara."

"Kara. I like that. So, is this your first time here? It's my favorite place in town." Sierra discretely slid closer as Kara turned and reached for her wine.

With her fingers around the delicate stem, Kara slowly brought the wine glass to her lips for a sip. She paused a moment to savor the dry, fruity flavor before turning back to answer. "I've been to Bend several times, but this is my first time at Taco'd."

Sierra's smiled in response and in the silence, Kara found her gaze drifting, starting at the black Fox brand ball cap turned backwards and covering dark hair that was neatly tucked behind Sierra's ears. Then down, following the tan skinned trail laid out by her revealing dark gray V-neck. Unlike her, Sierra was comfortable in her own skin. She was certain the woman knew how to use her charms for good, or for evil.

"Oh?" Sierra leaned in closer, allowing Kara a better look. "Do you live nearby? Or only travel here for work...or maybe pleasure?"

Kara quickly returned the glass to her lips, relieving her now parched throat with another sip of wine. Trying to maintain her composure, she deflected to her comfort zone—the topic of work. "I'm not too far. That is, the company I do research for is not far. Sometimes I stop through when I work there. I love McMenamin's. Having a beer while kicking back on a sofa in an old Catholic school auditorium is one of a kind."

"It really is. It's also unique with all the old school photos and the tiny elementary school-sized toilets." Sierra chuckled.

"Very true," Kara agreed with a grin. "But I do like this place too. The staff is wonderful, very friendly. I'll have to come back." She retreated to the safety of her wine glass while eyeing the dark-haired seductress.

Unfortunately, the heady mixture of entrancing eyes, abundant, unabashed cleavage, and alcohol were making Kara lightheaded faster than usual as blood rushed to places other than her brain. Distant places that had her wanting to do crazy, impulsive things.

"If you're a chiropractor, then what kind of research do you do? And if it in any way involves needing test subjects to get some free treatments from you, I'm in." Sierra touched Kara's leg playfully as she laughed. This time, she didn't flinch at the invasion of personal space and Sierra's eyes sparkled.

Kara's heart leapt into a full gallop, which only served to increase her feeling of unsteadiness. "Appealing to my scientific nature?" She raised a brow in jest. "I do actually have projects that could use a few more pro athletes. Measuring reaction times and gauging the effects on proprioception and mechanoreception in the cortex and cerebellum during sports related movement pre and post manipulation. Maybe I could help you shave a little off your time."

Sierra's eyes lit up and she grinned wildly. "I don't know what the heck you're talking about, but if you can help me win, I'm all for it."

"I can't make any promises, but every little detail helps. I'll get you the information and put you on the list." Kara indulged, downing the rest of her wine and then glancing around the bar in a poor attempt at avoiding Sierra's gaze. The woman's excitement had added to the shimmer in her amber eyes, effectively taking Kara's breath away.

That might have been the worst idea she had ever had, but Kara couldn't deny that she was equally as excited. And scared. And aroused. And...she would have to search a thesaurus later for more words, but basically, their working together could lead to any number of things happening and not all were good. The scientific possibilities had clouded her mind every bit as much as the desire radiating off of Sierra. Seemed work's foothold in her cerebral cortex was getting some competition from the most beautiful woman she had ever laid eyes upon.

As the evening wore on, Kara enjoyed learning more about the nuances of the sport, which would help her create more precise tests, not to mention some tidbits about Sierra. She had come up with the crankset tattoo on her own. Having gotten the ink after her dad had passed a few years back, she said it "just made sense." Downhill may have been her passion, but he had been her heart—a daddy's girl to the end.

Following her third glass of Riesling, she became acutely aware of Sierra's close proximity as the subtle brushes against her skin left her flushed from head to toe. The light mandarin orange musk overwhelmed her senses. It was a unique scent, not like the oft used vanilla or flowery perfumes. And it was subtle—very unlike the woman wearing it. Rather than be caught staring, Kara fought to focus on Sierra's words, nodding when it seemed appropriate and smiling even though she had missed what had been said.

"See that girl over there?" Sierra pointed to her Aussie rival, the angle forcing their shoulders to meet.

"Mhm." Kara swallowed hard. It was taking an iron will to follow the line of sight rather than admire the sculpted profile of the woman leaning against her.

"That's Camryn. She seems to think she can scare people off by giving them 'the look'. It's supposed to put fear into her competitors and knock them off their game or something." Sierra shrugged indifferently. "Hasn't worked on me or Ronni, but a lot of the newbies sure do get rattled. She can be cool too, but you never can tell what you'll get with her. The woman to her right, the one with straight black hair and way too much jewelry, that's

Evie. She owns Team Comp and acts like she owns everything else," Sierra said in a tone that clearly stated how irritating she found the woman.

They both laughed. Kara gave in to her urge, shifting her gaze from the women across the room to the one beside her, landing on a smile directed at her that was brighter than all the oversized diamonds on Evie's fingers combined. Kara bit her lip and returned a beaming smile of her own. She marveled at the way Sierra's eyes lit up at the gesture. No one had ever looked at her that way—so honest and without intention. There was plenty of desire flickering in those sparkling eyes, but also the truth that Sierra simply enjoyed spending time with her. It was easy and fun and quite uncanny, considering the almost stifling amount of sexual energy keeping her on edge.

Having gotten the scoop on several of the other riders in the room, Kara returned the conversation to Sierra in an insatiable need to learn as much about her as possible. "Well, there is certainly an interesting collection of personalities here. What about you? How did you get started in downhill?"

"I did it to piss off my mom," Sierra said with a laugh.

Kara smiled. "Why doesn't that surprise me?"

Sierra shrugged and took a sip of her beer. "I can't imagine."

They shared a glance and then Kara dug a bit deeper. "It is dangerous. I can see why she wouldn't approve."

"It wasn't that at all." Sierra paused, seemingly drifting to another time and place. "She wasn't around much, but when she was, she had a dream for a perfect little socialite princess. That was never me, as much as she tried. Anyway, when Ronni's family started mountain biking, my dad got me a bike so I could go with them. It didn't take us long to become hell on wheels." A fond smile shaped Sierra's lips.

Kara's eyes were once again drawn to that amazing smile—her heart making a quick skip as she laughed. "Oh, I have no doubt and how old were you?"

"Twelve. We didn't start riding downhill until we were about...fifteen. But I was instantly hooked the from the very first trail ride. The freedom, the speed, the exhilaration, the oneness with nature. There's nothing quite like it, whether you're out for an easy ten mile an hour ride or screaming down a mountain."

The fondness with which Sierra spoke of her sport was endearing. Kara could relate. That was how she felt about chiropractic and research. "Then, that begs the question, what team do you ride for?"

"No one. I ride for myself," she responded with pride. "Many riders are just like me, finding a few local sponsors while working a job to fund their dream. It's hard, and there are a lot of women who either don't make it or they are forced to cut their race schedule down. I'm lucky. My job giving mountain bike tours is flexible and I've been placing well enough to garner attention. People say they love my 'reckless abandon and epic saves', or whatever." A wide grin took shape, but then fell away as she continued, "There are only a few big teams that will pay you to focus on riding, but there's always a catch. My goal is to win a championship and then become a World Cup contender."

Kara nodded her understanding. Female athletes always had to work so much harder than men's, even though the talent was equally as strong. Of course, they had come a long way, but there was so much farther to go and she admired those who kept pushing their sport for bigger prize money and contracts. Yet, it didn't seem like that was what Sierra was after. "But it sounds like you don't want one of those teams."

An impressed grin formed on Sierra's lips. "Ya got that, did you?"

Kara nodded again.

"I've been approached and after some soul searching, I decided no, that wasn't what I wanted. Ronni rides for Team Traxx and keeps nudging me to sign on. Sometimes they lend me some parts in a jam. It would make life easier for sure and I'm definitely grateful they're here. We need big money teams to keep building the sport and giving women the chance to compete, but," she shook her head, "I want to create my own success, my own brand. One of these days I'll stand on top of the podium at season's end as champion and I'd have done it my way. No one telling me where to be, what to do, or how to do it. Reckless abandon, epic saves, and all." A laugh escaped, but determination burned in her eyes.

"I have no doubt you'll succeed."

"Thanks. Maybe your help will put me over the top," Sierra said.

The statement was laced with hope, but not pressure, and Kara found herself wanting it to be true. She wanted to help this woman achieve her dreams and for the first time in her life, she wasn't just thinking of what her research meant to her. Kara felt as if she were a partner in this endeavor, even though she was keenly aware no such relationship existed. Still, if she could help Sierra improve her times, then she would have used chiropractic research for something more than a professional journal entry. Instead of numbers as proof of success, she would have a real-life success story for a very deserving woman.

"Hey Sierra."

An overly-sweet, honeyed voice was all it took to pull Kara from deep thought. She turned toward the sound to find an attractive blonde with silvery-gray eyes laying her hand on Sierra's arm. She didn't like it. The sight gnawed at her gut and bristled her cheeks, but she swallowed it down. She had no place.

"Hi, Harley," Sierra responded. Their interaction spoke of an intimate familiarity.

"What're you doing over here?" Harley looked Kara up and down in a less than friendly way before turning her attention back on Sierra. "Why don't you come back with me and I'll buy you another round?"

"I'm fine right here chatting with the new clinic doctor. Harley, meet Doctor Kara Davies."

Harley gritted her teeth and politely shook Kara's hand. "Pleasure," she said with a snake-like smile and then immediately turned back to Sierra. "So, you coming back with me?"

Sierra gave her the stink eye. "Uh, maybe later. I'm quite comfortable here. I'll be back in a little while."

With a huff, Harley stomped back to her table.

"Don't worry about her. We dated for a while and now she acts like we're mated for life." Sierra chuckled, trying to lighten the mood.

Kara shifted in her seat, trying not to seem too interested in the ex-girlfriend, but couldn't help herself. "You could do better." There was no mistaking the hint of jealousy in her voice.

Sierra smirked, but withheld a response. The women locked eyes. Kara was the one to break the stare, opting to finish her wine, then she stood to leave.

"Thank you for an interesting evening, Sierra, but I must be getting back. I have a long day tomorrow." She pulled out a pen and scribbled a phone number on a napkin. "Here's the number to the lab. Call me and I'll get you started. Try to take it easy tonight."

"I'll do my best. Thank you for an enjoyable evening. And I gotta tell you, when you geeked out about your work, it was a total turn on." Sierra flashed a stellar smile and bit her lip.

Kara's body responded. She needed to get away before she did something she would regret, like sending the wrong message. "Good night, Sierra. See you soon."

"Have a good night, Doctor Davies. You'll most definitely be seeing me again soon."

Kara's stomach fluttered at the thought as she took her leave. Shaking her head as she pushed out the door, she had no idea what she was in for, but given Sierra's persona, it was bound to be one hell of a ride.

CHAPTER FIVE

Monday morning arrived and Sierra wasted no time picking up the phone. By nine o'clock she had already made an appointment with Kara at the research facility. Excitement bubbled in her chest and trickled down into her legs. The same wonderful twitchy feeling she would get before a race. Not only would she see the doctor again, but she could possibly unlock the key to winning a championship, though she was cautious not to get too wrapped up in the latter. Winning the title took season-long mental stamina and a bit of luck here and there. Then there was the dedicated training and diet regimens, which she had been skimping on. Still, she had spent Sunday resting and searching the internet for information on the benefits of signing up for such an endeavor.

Apparently, sports science was a popular thing. Many of the greats around the wide world of sports had signed on, anxious to have their every move analyzed in the pursuit of maximum performance. Her head had spun at the complicated medical jargon, but she did get the gist of it all, and it was amazing the things they were learning through the scientific measurement of movement and reaction times.

This step made Sierra feel like a big dog. She was going to take her game to the next level, like the millionaire football and baseball players. Sometimes, all it took was hitting a tree to open a world of opportunity. Only time would tell, but meeting Dr. Kara Davies might have been the best thing that had ever happened to her...in more ways than one.

With jacket in hand, Sierra bounded down the steps from her room and headed to the kitchen. "Hey Ron, I'm headed to the lab to check it out. Wanna come with?" As confident and excited as she was, there was also a brontosaurus-sized ball of nerves twisting in her stomach. Trying to woo someone was not her usual style. Usually they came to her.

Receiving no response, she glanced up from pouring her coffee. Her best friend was camped out in her gaming chair wearing pajamas, immersed in a session of *Assassin's Creed*.

"Ron," she called out again, louder this time.

With a groan, Ronni hit pause and looked up with a contemplative expression. "Hmmm...and watch you fawn over Doc McHottie like some tween Bieber fan? I'll pass. It might ruin the image of the bad ass Wiley I know. Besides, I'm saving the world right now. This is some serious shit," she said as she resumed her game.

Sierra abandoned her coffee and positioned herself in front of the television screen. A look of ire blazed from her best friend. Giving the best pouty look she could muster, she kneeled down and pleaded, "Come on Ronni, please? I need your insight here. I'm into her and I think she's into me, but I need your help in this. It's been a long time since I've tried the 'get to know you' thing."

"True. Your time with Harley could hardly be called 'getting to know you.' Unless you were talking about in-depth knowledge of one another's lady parts. I was starting to think you'd give up racing and become a gynecologist."

Sierra rolled her eyes, unamused with the brutally honest relationship assessment. However, it only served to validate her request. "First off, gross. Second, you see? That's why I need you."

"Ugh. Since you're wanting my expertise in the matter, I can't see how I can say no. You're gonna owe me though." Ronni frowned, then pushed up from her chair and stomped toward her room shaking her head. "I still don't know why you're so obsessed over this one. She's got a hot bod, sure, but she's as cold as my pint of mint chocolate chip and way too vanilla for your appetite."

Ignoring the negativity, a brilliant smile lit up the room as Sierra rushed over and wrapped Ronni into a big hug. "Thank you. You're the best."

"Don't you ever forget it," Ronni choked out, breathless from the force of the bear hug.

"Never." She kissed her on the cheek and then shoved her through the door. "Now hurry up and get dressed."

***

The address led them up Highway 126 toward Redmond. Sierra veered her blue and black, partially restored, 1970 Plymouth Barracuda off the exit for Smith Rock. As they approached the entrance of the large, modern building framed with reflective glass, steel beams, and white concrete, she read the sign out front and frowned.

Volden Research and Development. A division of Traxx Industries.

"Why didn't she tell me she worked for Traxx? Is this some ploy to get me to join your team? Did you know they had this?" Sierra asked, her anger beginning a slow boil. She was no one's puppet. If this was an attempt at manipulating her, the doctor, and Blake Volden, would be severely sorry.

Quick to exonerate herself of suspicion, Ronni answered honestly, "No. I've never heard anything about it. But I warned you about going gaga over a woman you know nothing about."

They climbed out of the car and made a slow track for the front door. Sierra's thoughts flew a mile a minute, filled with questions and accusations. She stopped outside the front door. Her brow furrowed. Her heart teetered on the verge of breaking at the thought of being misled. Part of her wanted to give Kara the benefit of the doubt. Their evening had felt genuine, honest. Kara had even admired her need for independence, which had only made her crush harder on the doctor. But the other part of her, the hot-headed part, wanted nothing more than to march in there and give Dr. Davies a piece of her mind for leaving out such an important detail.

Ronni gave her a once over and then pushed the door open. "What's the worst that could happen? It's not like they're going to turn you into some mutant like Dead Pool." She chuckled and slapped Sierra on the back. "Let's go check it out."

A slow breath fell from Sierra's lips, more an attempt to calm herself than one of surrender. With a fiery look in her eye, she strode up to the front desk, ready to hear Kara's explanation. A caramel-skinned receptionist with pale green eyes greeted her with a predatory smile that made her uncomfortable.

"Welcome to Volden research. I'm Christie. Do you have an appointment?"

"Yes, with Doctor Davies. I'm participating in a project. I'm Sierra Cody." Her fire fell away and now all she wanted was to escape the voracious eyes of the receptionist.

"Of course." Christie made no bones about her open appraisal. "I'll page the doctor. Please, have a seat." A provocative smile followed her words.

"Ok, well um…" Sierra was used to being physically appreciated, but something about this felt all wrong. She slowly backed away, cautious not to send the wrong signal. "Thank you." There was only one woman in this building she was interested in and it wasn't Christie.

As Sierra slid down into her seat making herself as small as possible, Ronni snickered at her dilemma. "Damn girl. You are some kinda sex magnet."

"Dammit, Ron! I can't help the way I look," came her retort, her voice hushed to avoid attention.

"True, but you didn't have to wear the skinny jeans and V-neck."

"That was for the doctor's enjoyment, not the woman visually raping me with her crazy eyes."

"At least you wore your Converse sneaks. That girl's eyes would explode if she saw what boots did for your ass." Ronni had to rub it in.

"Stop. You're creeping me out." Her body shivered, and it wasn't the pleasurable kind she had experienced the other night with Kara.

"No question she would like to do some research with you and she does *not* look vanilla. Just saying." Ronni's mischievous laugh filled the quiet room, earning an evil eye from Sierra.

"I'm here for Kara, not some random roll in a workplace closet. And stop calling her vanilla," Sierra fumed. "Besides, maybe someone less colorful is what I need in my life."

"If you kept the girls under wraps a bit more, you might be able to avoid some unwanted attention. They scream 'look at me' every time you walk into a room," Ronni explained.

"Noted." Sierra sighed and slinked further down in her chair. "I wanted them to catch Kara's eye."

"I have no doubt they will. Oh, speaking of vanilla, here she comes now. Damn, she even presses her lab coat. Let the fun begin. Wait. Does she even know what fun is? This is gonna be a long day," Ronni teased while elbowing Sierra gently, oblivious to the wide smile on her best friend's face as Dr. Davies appeared in the hall.

There were definitely questions that needed answering, but the only thing occupying Sierra's mind right was how amazing Kara looked in a form-fitting lab coat.

Kara made a stealthy approach, shooting a quick glare at Christie, whose eyes were still burning a hole through Sierra to no avail. Sierra's focus was solely on her. A warm smile formed on Kara's thin, shapely lips as their eyes met. "Hello, Sierra." She lingered for a moment before adding, "And Ronni, I don't think we've officially met, but I'm glad you came." Her greeting was professional and to the point.

"Wouldn't miss this for the world."

Sierra was familiar with the sarcasm of her best friend, but her using it on the woman she was desperate to get closer to grated her nerves. She shot Ronni a glare that said, "don't be an ass," which resulted in a smirk and a shrug. As usual, Ronni had found a way to rile her up, but Sierra needed her focus elsewhere.

Looking up at the patiently waiting doctor, whose eyes shone with more interest in her than a research subject, a warmth filled her chest, swallowing up all of life's little annoyances.

"Care for a tour?" Kara asked, looking between the two friends. If she had noticed the friction between the two of them, she didn't show it.

"Please." Sierra stood and moved toward Kara with a graceful sway of her hips, flashing a blinding smile that widened when the doctor's eyes took a quick detour south. *Mission accomplished.* Sierra would even admit to feeling pleasure at the way Kara had been annoyed by Christie. Depending on the answer to one extremely important question, this could be an interesting day.

Kara cleared her throat, regaining the professional composure reminiscent of their first meeting. "All right then..." she trailed off and led them away, but not before casting one last glare at the receptionist, who quickly righted herself and slung her eyes in the direction of her computer screen.

As they strolled the long white halls, Kara chanced a quick glance at Sierra. "I'm glad you decided to do this."

"Me too. I hope it's okay I brought Ronni along."

"No problem at all. You told me she was your best friend, so I sort of expected her to come with you," Kara replied with a soft smile. "Over here." She directed their attention to the right. "This is where they input all the data. They make charts and graphs, so we can easily compare the tests and their parameters."

They continued through the corridors, getting acquainted with the many facets of the facility. Research was only one piece of the pie. There was also a top-of-the-line training, rehab, and tech development. The doctor brought them to a stop outside a glass window. Inside, a couple of men wearing headsets played tennis without a ball. Their bodies were covered with colored stickers and wires.

"So...this is crazy weird looking. What's this all about?" Ronni inquired with curiosity.

"Well, Ronni, this is one of the things Sierra will be doing."

"Whoa Doc, Sierra is no good at tennis. Believe me," she scoffed.

"Hey now, at least I'd look good in the outfit." Sierra smiled and winked at Kara, loving the blush that raced into her cheeks. That was all the confirmation she needed to know her intended visual had hit its mark.

Kara dropped her eyes to the floor. "I umm...didn't mean that she would play tennis," she chuckled lightly, regaining her poise. "She would be on a bike. The headsets are virtual reality simulators and the pads are sensors that read body movement, enabling us to measure reaction times to stimuli. We can also measure the accuracy and control of body positioning. Part of my platforms with Sierra will include spinal manipulations to measure how it affects her responses. I hope to track the differences between outcomes among various regions of manipulations within the same test."

Kara turned to face the women. "Well, that concludes our tour. Did you guys have lunch yet? We have a wonderful café."

"I don't know about you guys, but I am famished," Ronni exclaimed with Meryl Streep-like dramatics. "Any chance lunch is on the house for your tour guests?"

"Ron! I can't believe you. Please ignore her, Kara." Sierra covered her embarrassment with a well-placed hand.

Kara dismissed the comment. "Actually, Ronni, the food is free for employees and participants. I'll make sure yours is taken care of, but maybe you'd like to join one of our studies?"

"Well, Doc, that depends on how good the food is."

"It's pretty good."

"We'll see about that."

Sierra and Kara chatted casually while Ronni enjoyed multiple servings of the free food. The mood was relaxed and comfortable and though Sierra wanted to ask deeper questions, she tried to keep it light. "You mentioned you also have a practice. How does that work? I mean, doing research here and seeing patients over there. Wherever there is," Sierra queried, hoping to learn a bit more about the doctor.

Kara clasped her hands together on the table top and took a deep breath. Her eyes grew large with barely restrained enthusiasm as she launched into an explanation. "My business partner, Nicole, and I co-own an office. We were friends long before we went to chiropractic college. After graduation, we decided to open an office together. She's good at the business part, as well as an excellent doctor. I enjoy helping patients live a healthier life, but I've always been drawn more to finding out why things work as they do and the effect that our treatments have on patient function. I like seeing measurable differences and validating the work we do. So, I set up small test groups in our office."

After a quick pause for a sip of water, Kara continued, "That grew into treating high-level athletes and measuring changes in performance. I had been working on research grants when Mr. Volden came to recruit me. My scientific mind couldn't say no, so we hired on an extra doc at the office and here I am. Besides, my work brings recognition not only to my profession, but also to our office, so it's a win-win."

Sierra's curiosity had been piqued. "Wow, okay. So, what exactly will you be studying in my project?"

"Several things actually, but we'll start with a baseline of reaction times and measure your efferent and afferent signals through a series of actions." Kara's eyes were bright and her hands animated, as she spoke about her work. "Each time, you'll receive spinal manipulation and we'll run you through the same tests to note the changes. Though we're doing similar tests with different sports, we're hoping to see that manipulating certain spinal levels will cause an increase or decrease with specific times and kinesthetic abilities...." She trailed off, realizing Sierra was staring at her in silence with a goofy grin fixed upon her face. Then there was Ronni, with her mouth agape and a healthy scoop of pudding frozen in mid-air.

"Sorry, I tend to get excited about my work."

"No, Kara, it's fine. Endearing, actually. I kinda like it when you ramble on with all those sexy medical words," Sierra joked. The shy smile she received in return was exactly what she had hoped for, but she wasn't prepared for the rush of warm tingles that rolled through her body in response.

"That was intense. I don't know what you said, Doc, but you got a big ole brain on ya." Ronni shook her head and shoveled the spoonful of pudding into her mouth.

The confident physician was uncomfortable with complements, blushing and ducking her head. Sierra found she rather enjoyed seeing that side of the woman and made a mental note to instigate such responses as often as possible. Even though she hadn't asked her all-important question, she decided it would be impossible to not see Kara again. She was already too smitten.

Clearing her throat, Sierra made her move. "So, um, I don't know what you're doing this weekend, but Saturday we'll be taking our motorcycles out for a ride. We always have breakfast at this nice little diner called Viv's before we head out. Why don't you join us for breakfast? And you're welcome to hop on the back of a bike if you'd like."

Ronni shot her a look. Sierra ignored her and said a silent thank you that Kara had been too lost in thought to notice.

Kara smiled and stood to collect the plates. "Since there's no race this weekend, I was planning on staying in town and getting things set up, so...breakfast sounds nice. Thank you."

They stared longer than necessary for the hundredth time in the last two hours, broken only by Ronni coughing. Sierra glared at her friend, who offered no apology for ruining the moment.

"We should get you signed up and we can get started on your testing later in the week." Kara nodded over her shoulder for the women to follow.

"It'll take about forty-five minutes or so to fill out the paperwork and consent forms. I'd like you to start Wednesday, if you could. Ronni, I think I may have something you'll like as well. How about testing out some high tech virtual reality games while you wait?"

"You're not going to hook any electrodes to my brain, are you? I mean, that free lunch didn't imply that I'm a lab rat now, did it?" She stepped back and wrapped her arms protectively around her waist.

"Guess you didn't read the fine print, huh?" Kara's expression was unreadable and Ronni's eyes grew wide. "No." Kara relaxed and laughed. "Nothing like that. Part of this facility is involved with the gaming industry. They use data and biomechanics from our athletes to design more realistic gaming experiences. You can try them out and leave feedback while they're in development."

"Whew! You had me there for a second." Ronni blew out a sigh of relief, ignoring Sierra's laughter. "Really? No strings?"

"No strings."

"I'm in." Ronni bounced with excitement. "When can I start?"

"Head right through there and tell them I sent you. Sierra can come and get you when she's done."

"Sweet, Doc. You may be vanilla, but you sure know how to treat a gal." She gave Kara a friendly punch to the arm, then yanked the door open and rushed inside.

"Um...thanks, I guess."

Laughing at Ronni's exuberance, Sierra joked, "I don't think you realize the trouble you just got yourself into. She'll be here every day playing those games and eating the food."

Kara laughed heartily. "I know the way to a woman's heart is through video games and good food."

"Yeah well, you do have a big ole brain, Doctor Davies."

"That I do. You ready?"

"Yeah, but can I ask you something first? It's kind of important."

"Of course. What is it?"

"I'm happy to be your lab rat and all and I hope you can help me improve, but I have a sneaking suspicion that this is some kind of an attempt to get me to join the Traxx team. I was a little upset you didn't tell me you worked for them." As the last words fell out, Sierra eyed Kara carefully.

Turning to face Sierra fully and meeting her eye to eye, Kara said, "I apologize if you feel deceived in any way. Yes, I am employed by Traxx in a roundabout way, but what I do here has no bearing on your contract status. I'm allowed to work with you and in return, your data benefits us. We work with athletes from all sports, from all around the world."

Kara began walking again and Sierra followed alongside. "I just started here a few weeks ago and I've only worked the two races, so I'm not yet familiar with all the people or divisions of the company. I'm sorry if you felt betrayed. That was never my intention." She glanced over and offered a soft, apologetic smile.

Basking in the honesty of ocean green eyes that screamed for forgiveness, Sierra returned the smile and then sighed out, "I'm sorry for jumping to conclusions, I just…" Her head swiveled left and right before she continued, "I get tired of everyone trying to get me to choose a team. I choose my team. Money is great and all, and I do want to be the best, but I really just love to ride. Mountain biking is my passion and I don't want anyone ruining that joy by having someone telling me what and when to do things."

Having thoroughly vented, she took a deep breath and relaxed, followed by the realization that she had dumped everything on Kara, who had only meant to help. "Sorry for the rant." She ducked her head. A tight, sheepish smile took shape.

Kara's hand slipped onto her arm. Her bare skin was warm and soothing, bringing Sierra an instant calm. The rider known to command rigid wooden trails to bend to her will was suddenly putty under the doctor's gentle touch.

"No need to apologize. It's my mistake. You'd stated that plainly the other night, but I didn't realize this might be a problem or I would've been more upfront." Kara's look of concern melted into a reassuring smile as she reached for the door. Holding it open for Sierra, she added, "This is my first time with a big company. I'm also used to being my own boss. Unfortunately, in research you need money to advance the science, so here I am."

"So, you pimped yourself out for science, huh?" Sierra's left brow rose into a perfect arch as she fought to contain her smile.

"Mmm yes," Kara replied with a roll of her eyes and a cheeky grin that dimpled on the right. "And you're my next John."

The reference effectively lost the battle for Sierra as her smile widened until it was all teeth. "I think you mean Jane," Sierra corrected and then suggestively waggled her brows.

They shared a laugh, followed by a comfortable silence, until Kara asked, "Are we okay?"

"Perfect."

Kara nodded happily. "See you soon then?"

Sierra walked through the open door, turned, and then flashed her most swoon-worthy smile as she replied, "Very soon, Doctor."

CHAPTER SIX

With a hot green tea in hand and a certain woman on her mind, Kara moved slowly through the long winding halls toward her office and the growing piles of data awaiting her review. Dressed in her work attire of tan khakis and an embroidered navy polo, she felt at home, even though she was still getting accustomed to her new surroundings.

This was her dream, running her own experiments on a large scale to prove the efficacy of chiropractic manipulation in every way imaginable, and she was ecstatic. There had been months of prep. Long days filled with painstakingly scrutinizing the details of each and every experiment to ensure the tests would render valid results. However, the two days since Sierra's visit had passed in a blur.

While the many projects she had going continued on task, her ability to focus on analyzing the results had been virtually non-existent, resulting in scattered stacks across her usually neat and tidy desk. If she was being honest, she found her lack of productivity irritating, unprofessional, and extremely out of character. Still, she surrendered to a smile as her thoughts drifted to her upcoming appointment with her newest participant.

Aside from getting to spend time with Sierra this week, the only thing that had pleased her had been her ability to make it through their Monday meeting without staring at the other woman's breasts the entire time. If she hadn't already known Sierra was prone to flaunting her form, she would have sworn it had been a challenge. While she may not have aced that test, she had definitely managed a solid B+. She laughed at the thought. Never in her life had she been proud of a B+, yet this seemed like a monumental achievement.

Not a moment later, her smile faltered. One single word had circulated through her consciousness for the last two days. *Vanilla*. That was the way Ronni perceived her. And the way it was used, as if it were some kind of deficiency that Ronni took pity on, had been grating her to no end. What made it even more aggravating was that she cared.

As she rounded the final corner, she shook her head to purge the negative thoughts. With her office door in sight, she took a sip of tea, hoping the calming properties of soothing heat would quiet her mind and allow her to get some much-needed work done.

No such luck.

Kara had never been one to concern herself with other people's perception of her. She had been called cold, boring, workaholic, uptight, and most anything else along those lines. Oh yes, she was acutely aware of what others thought of her, but none of that had ever been as important to her as the satisfaction she received from her from work. She wouldn't be where she was today professionally, had she given in to the demands of her previous girlfriends to "live a little."

So why did it bother her now?

That answer escaped her keen diagnostic abilities at the moment. There was something about Sierra Cody that stirred her from within, and not just her sex drive. The woman dominated her thoughts and challenged her to step outside her comfort zone. But did Sierra also think of her as vanilla?

Slipping into her large leather office chair, she stared at the stack of files on her desk. Her brow furrowed in thought. Clearly, Sierra was used to associating with more colorful people, but just because Kara enjoyed working, didn't mean she never let loose.

Her lips curled into a devious grin as a thought came to mind. At breakfast Saturday, Sierra and Ronni would get to see a whole other side of Dr. Kara

Davies—one that has not come out to play in far too long.

"Vanilla," she scoffed. "I'll show you."

"Dr. Davies? Ms. Cody is here for her appointment," Christie announced over the intercom.

Kara flinched at the verbal intrusion, spilling tea onto her desk. *Shit!* Thankfully, it had missed her reports. "Thank you. I'll be right there," she replied and then quickly jumped into action wiping up her mess.

Once she was sure she had gotten it all, she tidied the papers, arranging them back into the orderly piles to which she was accustomed. The simple feat helped her regain some semblance of control. This was a professional visit after all, and Kara wanted...No. She needed to maintain her poise in the presence of Sierra.

She rose from her chair and walked to the door, taking one last look around before grabbing her white lab coat and slipping it on with care. The cotton garment was more than a designation of rank, so to speak. Sure, the navy embroidered name on the upper left told everyone she was a doctor, but it was more like her superhero cape. The lab coat represented Kara in her element—calm, composed, and in control. In the coat, she made a difference. Her choices were sound. The coat was how she wished she could live her entire life, personal and professional, but her life out of the coat lacked control.

Her personal life was messy, a continuous string of missteps that she seemed doomed to repeat. She had hurt people, unintentionally so, but pain had been caused nonetheless by her insistence on choosing the life in her coat over all others. Today would be no different.

A deep breath fortified her for the day ahead. Before stepping out, she made a stop at the mirror. First, she looked over her slacks, then her hair, and finally, her lab coat, whose collar she adjusted until it was perfect. Now she was ready. Dr. Kara Davies was prepared to take on the world.

As Kara reached the edge of the lobby, her steps slowed. Sierra was a sight to behold, quietly thumbing through *Outdoor* magazine, bathed in the late morning sunlight falling through the large glass pane windows. The bright blue long-sleeved shirt clung to her breasts and her well-tanned, muscular legs filled out the cuffs of her black baggy riding shorts. She was clearly uninterested in reading, but rather using the glossy pages as a shield from the receptionist's insistent stares.

If Kara's lab coat made her feel like a superhero, then Sierra was proving to be her kryptonite, stripping away her powers of levelheaded professionalism and leaving her helplessly swinging on a pendulum of emotions. The blood coursing through Kara's veins grew hotter and hotter. She thrust her hands into her jacket pockets, hiding them from the world as they balled into tight fists. Staring at the receptionist, her lips curled into a sneer. Christie's behavior was going to end right now.

There was a fine line between exerting her professional authority and bringing personal issues into the ring, but in this case, the receptionist had pushed both boundaries. Kara's legs carried her quickly toward Sierra. The steely glare she threw Christie on the way past was deadly enough to make the woman recoil and bury her head behind her computer screen. Kara held her laser-like focus on the woman, begging her to lift her eyes once more, but she didn't dare.

Satisfied her point had been made, Kara refrained from uttering a word and instead, veered left toward Sierra. Coming to a stop three feet away, she stood in silence as her mind stumbled through an array of possible greetings. A simple, "Good morning. Nice to see you again," would have sufficed, but no words came out. Instead, she basked in the beauty of the woman, as if standing before the Mona Lisa for the first time.

Sierra peeled her eyes from the behind the safety of the magazine, looking up with blazing eyes and a smile as blinding as ever. Kara's tensed muscles released their hold, relaxing the stern frown that had fixed itself upon her lips, freeing them to assume a more pleasant form. Her entire body seemed to smile from the inside out.

"So nice to see you again, Doctor Davies." Her hair was different—a touch shorter, darker, and no longer streaked with red.

Kara took a moment to admire the new look and decided it suited Sierra nicely. Finally, she regained her senses, cleared her throat, and returned the greeting. "Nice to see you as well, Sierra." With her hands still buried in her pockets, she motioned her head back toward the corridor and asked, "Shall we?"

Sierra nodded and rose to her feet, pausing a moment to stretch her legs before taking stride. She brushed lightly against Kara's shoulder as she passed, then glanced back over her shoulder with a wicked grin, clearly pleased with herself. When she reached the first hallway, she stopped and turned around.

With Sierra's expectant gaze upon her, Kara realized she had not yet taken a step. Worse yet, her jaw was slack, her lips partially agape, and her mind void of thought. A rush of embarrassment swept through her at having been caught in Sierra's thrall. Composure. She needed some stat.

Kara took a deep breath and shoved her shoulders back as she finally moved forward. Her body willed itself to pass within Sierra's orbit, the gravitational pull between them too strong for Kara to fight. She would have to do a hell of a lot better than that if she was going to stay focused on work.

It was going to be a long day.

***

Sierra sat quietly as a lab tech took her vitals. The young man with a buzz cut and dark glasses was quick and methodical about his work. Her gaze drifted across the room to the doctor diligently setting up shop. Wires, computers, a mountain bike on a stand, and an adjusting table like the one from the clinic, had her curious as to how this would all work. Mostly, her questions revolved around the woman in the pressed lab jacket secured around her torso like a coat of armor. Much to her dismay, not many words had been exchanged as they made their way from the waiting room to the lab. She had also noted the distance Kara maintained as they navigated the long halls.

Had she overstepped her bounds? This was Kara's workplace after all.

"All done here, Doctor Davies," the lab tech called out as he unwrapped the blood pressure cuff from Sierra's arm.

"Great. Just need one more minute," Kara replied over her shoulder, her eyes glued to a computer screen as she typed at a feverish pace.

The longer Kara typed, the wider Sierra's smile grew as inappropriate thoughts clouded her mind. *Damn, look at those fingers go! And I already know she's good with her hands.*

"Ms. Cody?"

The lab tech tapped her on the shoulder. The firm contact was enough to pull her from her musing. Having lost track of time and space, she glanced around in confusion and mumbled, "Huh?"

"The doctor is waiting on you. You all right?" An analytic eye scoured her blank expression for answers.

"Oh. Right. Yeah, I'm fine. Thanks." Catching a gleam in Kara's eye, she knew she had been caught staring yet again. There was no point in making excuses, so she dropped her head, fought a grin, and ambled over to the testing area.

How was it that Dr. Kara Davies had so easily taken up residence in her mind—a place that had previously allowed only the singular idea of winning a championship? The sudden change in thought process was sure to have negative effects on her performance, but she was helpless to change a thing.

"Do you think you'll be able to concentrate on the tests, Ms. Cody, or are you still experiencing the lingering effects of hitting that tree?" Kara managed to keep her snicker to a minimum, but her smug grin was on proud display.

"Ha ha. I'll be fine. Thanks for your concern, Doctor." If it had been anyone else, Sierra would have let her hot head prevail over a comment like that, but she enjoyed the playfulness. The back and forth between them had been hot and cold. When it was hot, she would take all she could get.

Kara's smugness faded into an easy smile as she motioned to the bike. "Very well, then. If you'll climb onto the bike, we can get it fitted for you."

"Sure. How's this going to work?"

"Once you're all set, you'll put on the virtual headset and I'll attach a few electrodes to your body. A video of a downhill course will play and you'll ride as if it were a real race, responding to what you see. Your goal is to get the best time possible."

"Then what?"

"We'll adjust a specific region of your spine and run a new race, comparing reaction times and the force of muscle output in your legs. We will do this over the course of eight sessions, as your schedule allows."

"And this will help me?"

"That's my hypothesis, but I can't promise you how much it will affect this season. It will take a few sessions to get a baseline of how you respond. Then we learn from that. Also, I have to complete the eight sessions without deviation, or else it will invalidate the results. But after that, we are free to experiment with other possibilities. Any other questions?"

"No. I don't think so. At least, not right now."

"Okay, but feel free to ask if one comes up. I want open communication between us. Also, let me know if the virtual reality makes you feel woozy. I don't want that to affect your times. You ready?"

"Every second of my life. Let's do this."

CHAPTER SEVEN

Saturday morning, Kara slipped one foot into her black leather Dainese riding pants, then the other, and then pulled them up—a tricky thing to do when you were sweating like crazy. Nerves had gotten the better of her somewhere around the time she had pulled up to her house in Eugene last night.

It had been a quick in-and-out stop, grabbing clothes, loading her black and gray Ducati Corse 1199 Panigale onto her bike trailer, and then hitching it to her Grand Cherokee. She was gone in less than half an hour, not even stopping by to see her best friend and business partner, Nicole. That had not been one of her smarter moves. Nicole would have been the voice of reason reminding her why this was a bad idea. Or not. More likely, Nicole would've encouraged her.

There were so many little reasons why Kara should strip off her riding pants, put on her khakis, and go back to the lab. So many...not to mention one really big one. She needed to grow a pair and deal with that sooner than later, but burying herself in work was so much easier. At least it had been, until she met Sierra. No matter how hard she tried, she couldn't seem to say no to the woman, even though she knew she would only end up hurting her. Work would always win in the end.

Kara picked up her phone and mulled over a quick call to Nicole, but the idea of cancelling on Sierra made her chest tighten, resisting expansion as if someone had screwed a vise down onto her sternum. She could practically see the sadness in those damned expressive eyes.

"Dammit," she muttered and tossed the phone back on her bed. She fastened her pants button and patted herself on the back for having kept such a strict diet and workout regimen. She hadn't worn the pants in two years, but they still fit perfectly. Black riding boots and her black leather and fabric jacket were next. Finally, she made her way to the mirror and smiled. Kara missed this. Not only had she lost girlfriends to work, but she had lost riding as well. This was one thing she would have to get back to, starting right now.

With her backpack fastened in place, she walked out the door of her Bend apartment—a perk from her job—and stared at her bike. She had kept it well maintained and had run it around the block here and there, but today, she was going to let her Ducati stretch its legs.

"Let's do this," she said and then swung her leg over

her bike. The engine turned easily. The soft purr brought a smile to Kara's lips as a deep satisfaction filled her. Yes, she had missed this—a lot. Her hand slid down to the fuel tank, lightly caressing the paint as if taming a feral cat. "Time to let you run wild."

***

The parking lot at Viv's was nearly full when Sierra pulled in on her old-school, flame painted, 1947 Harley Knucklehead chopper with straight pipes and a bitch seat. She was dressed to impress a certain doctor, wearing her favorite low cut black leather vest with matching jacket and chaps over her tight black pants and boots. If this look didn't have Kara doing a triple take, then she'd be severely disappointed.

No sooner had Sierra dismounted before Ronni roared in on her custom-painted pink and black Suzuki Hayabusa sport bike, taking the spot beside her. She removed her pink helmet adorned with a black mohawk and shook out her freshly-dyed platinum blonde hair. As usual, her attire matched her bike, with a pink riding jacket, white tank top, black leather riding pants, and tall lace up boots with black and pink laces.

Ronni chomped on her gum, appearing uninterested in her surroundings. "I bet she shows up in something pressed," she spouted out of the blue. "There is no way anyone that uptight is going to ride on the back of a motorcycle and get her pants creased."

"I don't know. Maybe," Sierra replied, trying to stymie the possibility of disappointment. "But I can't help feeling there's something else to her. All I do know is that she is delicious when she is in doctor mode." Just the mere thought brought a wide smile to her face.

"Who we talking about, ladies?" Randy Burns, an old friend and fellow rider on the men's downhill tour, intervened. The thirty-something year old with scraggly red hair and a deep voice was known as "the old man" of the group and joined them from time to time on a ride.

Ronni piped up teasingly, "Sierra's in love with the new clinic chiropractor, Doctor Kara Davies."

Sierra huffed, her hands moved to her hips as she challenged, "I'm not in love with her. I just think she's interesting."

"Don't forget 'delicious,'" Ronni added with air quotes and an eye roll. "She actually said that, Randy."

"Yes, she is. She is delicious and the way she recites all that medical jargon is as sexy as…well, as sexy as speaking a foreign language." She drifted off with a goofy grin.

"It is a foreign language. Its Latin," Randy returned matter-of-factly, causing Ronni to snort with laughter.

"See? Sexy." Sierra smiled and smacked Ronni on the shoulder. "Besides, you love her too since she fed you and let you play video games all day."

"Love? Sure. The woman gave me of my two favorite things in life, and I must admit, it was kinda cool of her. But in love? No. That, my dear, is you going all googly eyes every time you see her."

Sierra crossed her arms and pouted, unable to deny her best friend's assessment, although it was far too early to say she had feelings for Kara. She was merely a smitten kitten.

"Well, ain't that something now? Ole 'never to be tamed' Wiley is into the domesticated, uptight doctor type. That explains why you haven't taken me up on any of my generous offers. I'm not straight laced enough for you," Randy teased.

"I'm sorry to inform you that there are plenty of reasons why I've not accepted any of your offers, only one of which is that you're a dude. Besides, there is nothing straight about Kara," Sierra smirked. "Can you all give her a chance, please?"

"Sure, sure. I want you to be happy, but I worry about you. You've never jumped off the deep end like this before. I mean, you and Harley were hot and heavy for a bit, but you weren't all O.C.D. like you are with this chick. You got Doc-on-the-brain, twenty-four-seven." Ronni draped her arm around Sierra's shoulder and smiled as she pulled her close. "I'll be here to help you any way I can and I promise not to be too snarky."

"Thank you, Ronni." Sierra bumped her best friend with her hip, then turned to Randy. "What about you?"

He groaned and frowned, then burst into a smile. "Okay, I'll bite. This could be entertaining, but the second it gets boring, I'm outta here."

The alluring sound of a speeding motorcycle drew their eyes to a shiny black and gray Ducati weaving with precision through traffic. The rider veered into the lot and pulled into a space three spots down as they all watched with rapt attention.

"Sweet bike," Ronni and Randy gushed in tandem.

"Never seen that bike around here. Wonder who it is?"

The rider's lithe body dismounted gracefully. The group stared at the rider's back as the helmet was removed to reveal short auburn hair, spiked in back.

"Is that...?" Sierra trailed off, noting the familiar hair style. It couldn't be though, could it?

The rider pulled off her gloves, stuffed them into her jacket pocket, and then turned around. There stood Kara, staring back at them with an amused grin. She secured her helmet to her bike and then made a slow approach, her eyes meeting Sierra's before moving to Ronni and Randy.

"Holy...No way! Doc McHottie?" Ronni fell back against the hood of the nearby car as she pretended to pass out.

"I guess it's not just her foreign language that's hot, huh?" Randy laughed wildly as he reached over to pick Sierra's jaw up off the ground. "Don't drool, Wiley. It's embarrassing."

"K...Kara? Um...err..." Sierra stammered having fallen under the doctor's spell. She had been right. There was more to Dr. Kara Davies than met the eye and she couldn't wait to find out what other surprises were in store.

"Hey guys. Sorry I'm late," Kara offered nonchalantly. "I hope it's all right that I brought my own ride. She hasn't stretched her legs in a while. Shall we get a table? I'm starving." She breezed past them with a long, confident stride, headed straight for the entrance.

Sierra stood transfixed, still unable to form words after that wet-dream-worthy entrance. The nickname "Doc McHottie" was more than fitting today.

Randy leaned into her ear and whispered, "This is going to be a ton of fun. I can feel it." He gave her a wink and skipped off to catch up with Kara.

Ronni picked herself up and grabbed Sierra's arm, leading her toward the diner. "Wow! That was like, sex dream hot. You all right?"

Sierra had yet to say a word. Her focus was set on putting one foot in front of the other in proper order.

"Jeeze, Wiley. Be cool. You don't want to be all blubbering idiot when you get inside. Now c'mon and let's grab some grub."

When they arrived at the booth, Randy and Kara were engaged in lively conversation. Kara appeared relaxed with a genuine smile. Sierra was happy to see her having fun, but a flash of anger struck upon seeing Randy occupying the spot beside her. She had hoped to recreate the close proximity from their evening at the brewery. With a heavy heart, she slid across from Kara, whose smile brightened and green eyes shimmered at the sight of her and suddenly, she wasn't upset with Randy anymore.

Breakfast flowed smoothly as the group filled themselves with pancakes, eggs, bacon, and coffee. Sierra had been more quiet than usual as she painstakingly chose her moments to engage with Kara. Her hesitance, however, didn't prevent her from stealing glances or blushing profusely whenever she caught Kara doing the same.

"So, Doc," Ronni broke the food-induced silence. "How long you been riding?"

After swallowing her mouthful, Kara gazed wistfully up at the ceiling in thought, then lifted her coffee as she answered, "Most of my life, actually. I did a little motocross when I was younger. I looked up to my older brother growing up. He was passionate about it, so naturally, I wanted to do it as well. It was a great bonding activity. He taught me everything I know. I enjoyed it, until I broke my back. I had time to kill during recovery and fell in love with science and the brain-body connection. Seeing it for myself as I went through rehab was just amazing. After that, everything else just sort of fell by the wayside."

"That's cool. I mean...it sucks about your back, but you found something you love."

"I did. Now I have a question for you." Kara leaned forward and narrowed her eyes at Ronni. "Why do you keep calling me, Doc McHottie?"

Everyone laughed as if it were the most ridiculous question ever posed to mankind, causing her to frown and pull back.

"Seriously, Doc?" Randy asked, his head shaking side to side in disbelief. "Have you not seen you in a pair of pants?"

"Yeah, I mean, you definitely have a rockin' bod," Ronni agreed, then followed with a wolfish whistle.

"Oh lord!" Kara's face flashed beet red, her hands quickly serving as a shield.

"What? I mean, I'm not into the gentler gender, but anyone can see the gods gave Sierra some rockin' boobs, you a rockin' bod, and me? I'm all-around awesome," Ronni gloated.

"True," Sierra was quick to agree while Kara chuckled, still red with embarrassment.

"Sorry to bring this exercise in modesty to an end, but it's time to get this show on the road. I've got a hot date tonight with three lovely ladies and I don't want to keep them waiting."

The three women grumbled as they collected their things, muttering their opinions of his evening plans.

"What?" He asked, his voice rising two octaves. "I know at least two of you are jealous." His quip resulted in both Sierra and Kara breaking out into guilty smiles while shrugging. "See? I know women, regardless of who they're attracted to."

"All I'm saying, is that three of anything sounds like a lot of work," Ronni grumbled.

"Then you're doing it all wrong," Randy quickly returned with a mischievous smirk.

The brash rider's mouth opened and closed before she could muster the weak defense of, "I've not been doing it at all."

Sierra roared with laughter. It was a rare sight to catch Ronni red with embarrassment, much less to see her flustered. She was the queen of snark.

"Ah, well then, you don't know what you're missing." He leaned in and gave her a suggestive wink. "You should broaden your horizons. Dudes, chicks, whatever pumps your tires, Hon."

"So, uh," Sierra cut in for the save. "We better get going. It's getting late."

"Yup," Ronni agreed, her eyes rising from the table to let Sierra know her assist was appreciated. She scooted free of the booth and headed for the door.

Randy trailed, followed by Kara, with Sierra bringing up the rear so she could enjoy a certain view. Breakfast had been all she had hoped for and then some. They may have had a day of riding ahead of them, but Sierra already wanted her time with Kara to stretch into the night hours. The question was how?

Their few meetings had proven that Kara wasn't impulsive like her, so pushing the issue would get her nowhere. Kara wasn't about to jump quickly into anything, even if she had shown some signs of interest. Her finger tips twisted the edge of her leather jacket back and forth as she quickly devised a solution

As they reached their bikes, Sierra piped up, "Hey guys?" Her heart raced as the question lingered on the tip of her tongue. *What if she says no?*

All three turned with a questioning stare. Like that first turn out of the starting gate, there was no going back now. She took a deep breath and held on tight as she asked, "What do you say to drinks at Taco'd when we're done with our ride?" When the last word was out, Sierra was proud that they had flowed so smoothly and confidently despite the giant knot in her belly, and it wasn't from the huge stack of chocolate chip, pecan pancakes she had eaten, either.

Her eyes tracked around the group. Ronni agreed. She was always up for a party. Randy gave her a fist bump. He never turned down a beer. The wild card, and the only one whose answer mattered, was Kara. A momentary pause, which felt painfully long for Sierra's bated breath, preceded a nod of approval, followed by a sexy half-grin and sparkling eyes, as if Kara knew exactly what she had planned.

A rush of relief brought much needed air back into Sierra's lungs. An overwhelming and unusual bashfulness swarmed over her, forcing her to look away from the pair of beautiful, suspecting eyes. Receiving a positive response sent the pounding thump in Sierra's chest into a thunderous vibration that rivaled a ten thousand horsepower nitro funny car.

She lifted her eyes as Kara turned and walked a few spots further to her Ducati. Sierra's eyes darkened and she couldn't help her infatuated grin from spreading ear to ear as her focus fell to Kara's ass while she mounted her bike.

Kara turned knowingly, catching her lustful stare and hungry eyes. "Hey Sierra," she called out. "You're going to have a tough time staying on the road if you're busy staring at my ass."

Cocky Kara was quite the turn on, as was every other version so far. No longer feeling shy, Sierra shot back a sexy smile of her own as she answered, "Maybe. But if it's the last thing I ever see, I'll die a happy woman."

CHAPTER EIGHT

As the evening wore on, Randy left for his date and Ronni met up with Blake, leaving Kara and Sierra alone. Sierra took notice of a couple vacating the sofa in the quietest corner of the room and suggested they move. With beers in hand, they settled side by side into the comfy worn brown leather couch. Kara tucked one leg under the other and turned her body to face Sierra, who smiled and mirrored her position, their knees nearly touching.

"I don't usually drink this much," Kara stated with a slight slur, feeling the room spin.

"Oh? You mean Dr. Davies doesn't do Jägerbombs on a nightly basis?" Sierra teased, seemingly unfazed by the amount of alcohol they had consumed.

"Nooo." Kara fell into a fit of laughter. She dug her elbow into the top of the sofa and propped her head against her hand. "I think I'm drunk," she mumbled with a sigh and closed her eyes.

"I concur." Sierra's head fell back with a raucous laugh as Kara scrunched her face and sunk deeper into the cushions. "However, in my professional opinion, Doctor, you should let loose more often. It's a beautiful sight to see." Leaning in closer, she pushed a rogue strand of hair from Kara's brow.

Sierra's hand lingered and Kara's eyes fluttered open. Sierra was so temptingly close, causing Kara's heart to skip a beat. A million "what if's" flooded her cloudy mind. What if she lunged forward and tasted those luscious full lips? What if they got lost in one another for a night? More than a night? There was such a strong attraction to the woman seated so agonizingly close to her that she could almost let herself go, but she couldn't indulge in her desires right now.

Her body tensed, winding tighter until she could barely take a breath. Kara's "what if's" that had nearly grown into a "why the heck not" faded into "not going to happen."

"You okay?" Sierra asked. She placed her hand on Kara's knee and squeezed.

"Good question." A soft, appreciative smile took shape. It was nice to have someone concerned about her well-being. "It's been a long time since I was this adventurous. I'm sure to pay for it tomorrow." Kara's eyes cast down at the hand on her knee. An unusual sensation coursed through her, a rush of warmth that washed away the tension that had wound every muscle to its snapping point, setting her at ease.

Was it Sierra or the alcohol?

The answer was irrelevant, for in that moment, the old "lowered inhibitions" won out. Unable to curb her craving to reach out, her hand mingled with Sierra's. Kara closed her eyes again and luxuriated in the soothing comfort of their interwoven fingers. When she blinked open, she was met with a pair of smoldering eyes that danced with wonder as they skimmed the features of her face, pausing more than once at her mouth. She could lose herself in those eyes. They simultaneously turned her legs to rubber while giving her the strength to race to the peak of Mt. Everest. Kara's heart pounded like crazy, accentuating her dizziness. Desperate fingers dug into the couch, attempting to steady herself, even though she knew it was useless.

Sierra leaned in closer. She trailed a finger lightly along Kara's jawline, causing a soft gasp to escape at the touch. "You're so beautiful," Sierra whispered and ghosted her lips over Kara's.

The sensuous contact had Kara quivering. She desperately wanted to kiss Sierra, to taste her lips, but she couldn't. Not now anyway. Every bit of willpower was called upon to strengthen her resolve. Her hazy thoughts became clear and she pulled away. "I can't." It was barely a whisper. "Not right now. Not like this. I'm so sorry."

Sierra slouched back into the sofa. "No, I'm sorry. You're right." Her attempt at hiding her hurt failed and Kara couldn't bring herself to meet Sierra's gaze.

"I uh...I couldn't help myself and I moved too quickly. I hope I didn't offend you, but I felt like you...Never mind." She sighed and brought one hand up to forcefully rub her forehead.

"I did," Kara rushed to undo the damage, hoping it wasn't a breaking point for them. "I do. I mean..." She shook her head as a frustrated breath of her own flowed out. "It's complicated...my life, right now. I like you, Sierra. I do, but I don't want to hurt you and right now things are just..." In that moment, the spin of the room went from a slow carousel to full on carnival ride. "Can we maybe talk about this later when we're not so inebriated?"

"Umm...yeah. Sure." The ease between them was gone, replaced by awkwardness and uncertainty. The light in Sierra's eyes dimmed. She cleared her throat and then called out to Axel. When he turned around, she swirled her index finger, to which he nodded and picked up the phone.

She turned back to Kara. "I think it's time to get you home anyway. We can leave our bikes here tonight and take a cab." Despite the look of indecision upon her face, she stood and extended her hand.

Kara stared for a long moment before accepting the assistance. As she got to her feet she said, "Thank you. I like your chopper. Did I tell you that?"

"Thanks," Sierra replied with a wide grin that finally chased the darkness from her mood. "It was my dad's. He did all the custom work himself. I like your Ducati. I've always wanted to ride one."

Seeing Sierra smile made Kara feel things. Overwhelming things. Things she could almost let herself admit she wanted to feel more of. "Maybe next time we can trade for a bit?"

"Deal."

As they made their exit, Kara bumped into the door frame and nearly fell over. She cracked up as Sierra steadied her. Even through her ever-growing intoxication, she didn't miss the return of the warmth that spread throughout her limbs and into her heart. The scientist in her would argue that she had discovered the answer to her earlier question—it had been Sierra and not the alcohol—and she should immediately seek more contact to see if it would yield the same results.

Instead of acting on her impulse, however, she blurted out, "Hey Sierra, did you know alcohol not only affects your cerebellum, which controls coordinated movements, but also increases norepinephrine, leading to decreased inhibitions?"

The drunken babble lead to a full out laugh as Sierra chortled, "Wow! Drunk Kara is kind of a nerd."

"Yeah well, sober Kara is pretty nerdy too," she shot back, followed by a snort.

"Just so you know, I find nerdy Kara unbelievably sexy—drunk or sober."

The color was quick to fill Kara's cheeks and she laughed to cover her nervousness.

With a shake of her head, Sierra snickered. "You, my dear, cannot hold your liquor." She helped Kara toward the curb where an old green van with a taxi sign had pulled up. "Now," she opened the door. "Have a seat and please don't vomit."

The ride to Kara's was short and after serving her two glasses of water, Sierra tucked her safely into bed. She then set two aspirin and a Gatorade on the nightstand and perched herself on the edge of the bed. "Anything else I can get you?" She reached up and brushed Kara's bangs away from her eyes.

"No," Kara mumbled. She was numb and no longer affected by Sierra's touch or proximity. "Thank you," was the last thing she uttered as she drifted off to sleep.

"Sleep well, Doctor Kara Davies."

Sierra watched Kara adoringly until she had begun to snore. Placing a kiss upon two fingers, she pressed them gently to Kara's lips before slipping off quietly into the night.

CHAPTER NINE

For Sierra, Sunday morning couldn't come soon enough. The hope of seeing Kara again had made sleep difficult to come by, but she had awoken with a start at eight a.m. Unfortunately, Ronni was not an early riser. Sierra needed a ride back to Taco'd to get her bike and after considering the idea of calling a cab or another friend, she opted for a workout to burn off some excess energy while she waited for Ronni to wake.

When they finally arrived at the brewery, it was nearly lunchtime. Sierra's heart dropped at the absence of Kara's Ducati. She should've gotten there earlier, but that didn't deter her from the idea of going to see her later. She now knew where Kara lived, after all. But first, a stop in to say hello to Axel, who'd be gearing up for the afternoon rush.

The moment Ronni opened the door, she gagged. "What the hell are you cooking, Axel? It smells like sweaty feet in here." Ronni pulled her shirt up over her nose in disgust.

"If you must know, it's an old Scottish dish," he huffed. "I've been craving it, so I decided to try it as the special today."

"Well, the smell makes me want to rip my nose off. Sierra, I gotta cut out before I pass out. Catch ya later," Ronni yelled as she high-tailed it out the door.

Sierra laughed at Ronni's dramatics. She had grown accustomed to them over the years. "It's not that bad, but it's not the most appetizing thing I've ever smelled."

"You're welcome to try a bite," he offered with a proud grin. Axel dipped the spoon into the pot and held it out, only to be met by a hand waving him off.

"No, really, but thank you. I'm a little hung over and I'm pretty sure that's not going to help."

"Your loss." Taking the spoon into his mouth, Axel rolled his eyes in ecstasy. "Perfect."

"I'll take your word for it."

"So, how's it going with that woman you've been drooling over?"

Shock poured across Sierra's face. Her hand fell to her chest. "I have not been drooling over her!" Had she been that obvious? Is that why Kara had gotten cold feet?

"Oh really?" Axel let out a cackle as he slapped his thigh. "I have never seen you so awestruck. You are positively infatuated with her. And if I may say so," he added, "you have good taste."

A pink flush swept up her neck to her cheeks. That was new. Since when was she so shy? "I definitely like her a lot, and thank you. Kara's smart, sexy, fun, and good with her hands," she beamed and then wiggled her brows suggestively, before turning contemplative. "Now, if I could just get her to let me in."

"She's definitely interested. That much was obvious both times you've been in here. She lights up when you're around. Be patient. All good things are worth waiting for." He gave her a supportive pat on the shoulder.

"Thanks. I'm going to head over and check on her. She was pretty trashed last night. You should've seen her in drunk nerd mode. So cute," she gushed and then rushed off.

"Ah, young love." Axel propped his elbows on the bar and rested his chin, drifting off to another time and place.

As Sierra reached her bike, her cell alerted her to an incoming text. She pulled the phone from her back pocket and smiled like crazy when the display beamed Kara's name. Her fingers couldn't work fast enough to open the message, but her bright smile faded as her eyes skimmed the black and white words etched in simple Arial font.

Thank you for taking care of me last night. I promise I don't usually get that drunk, but I enjoyed spending the day with you and your friends. I have a few things to take care of today, but I will see you again soon.

An ache seeped into Sierra's chest. She had really been looking forward to seeing Kara again soon. But at least she had gotten a text. That meant Kara had thought enough to reach out to her. Sierra smiled as she read the words again, chuckling that the message was so grammatically correct. After careful consideration, she typed out an equally precise reply.

You are most welcome. I'm happy to have you back among the living. I enjoyed spending time with you too and look forward to doing it again soon. Don't work too hard.

She paced, killing time in hopes of a reply. What she was hoping to achieve beyond more contact, was unknown, but she couldn't help the pull she felt toward Kara. Five minutes and no text. Sierra came to a stop. How sad was she? A few weeks ago, she would've been happy with a quick fling and now she was wearing a circle around her bike in an empty parking lot, chewing her fingernails to the bone.

Sierra was never one to sit and wait. Perhaps she had come on too strong last night, but when she wanted something, she went all out. First thing tomorrow, she would head to the one place she'd be sure to find one Dr. Davies—the lab. There might still be many unknowns about the doctor, but her passion for work was not among them.

With a plan in place, Sierra straddled her chopper and fired it up. The roar of the engine brought her back to life. It never mattered if her bike was powered by motor or pedals, the one thing that could always chase away her blues, was a ride on two wheels.

***

The next morning, Sierra hopped into her car and headed to the lab. Upon arriving at the desk of the creepy, ogling receptionist, she was shocked to find the workaholic doctor had taken the day off. Deflated, she stepped outside and dialed Kara's number, but was sent straight to voice mail. She left a brief message to give her a call back, but as she hung up, worry set in. What if something was wrong? Was there anything she could do to help? Facing Christie again was not on her wish list, but unless she wanted to wait it out, she had no other choice. Sierra was good at many things, but waiting was right at the bottom, next to following rules.

Sierra steeled herself for another encounter with the woman who simply would not take a hint, but this time she'd play it to her benefit. Sauntering back to the desk with her famous smile on wide display, she leaned on her elbows and gave the woman a magnificent view of the feature she couldn't seem to peel her eyes from. "Dr. Davies said she'd be here all week," she stated in her sexiest voice. "Any idea when she'll be back?"

Unable to stop staring at the soft swell of flesh before her, Christie mumbled, "Said she needed to take care of some things at her clinic. She'll be back in a day or two." She licked her lips without shame and met Sierra's eyes. "You sure there isn't anything *I* can do for you?" There was nothing professional in her tone or demeanor.

"No thanks, but if you talk to her, be sure to tell her Ms. Cody came by." Sierra turned and high-tailed it out the door, anxious to put miles between her and the lecherous receptionist in a hurry. Maybe she would use that memory as motivation on her next race start. That would surely get her out the gate in a hurry.

When she had reached the safety of her car, she released a heavy breath and considered her next move. Kara had mentioned her clinic and if she recalled correctly, it wasn't too far away. She yanked her phone from her pocket. Her fingers moved with precision as she pulled up a search for "Dr. Kara Davies, Oregon chiropractor." She waited, not-so-patiently, chewing on her lip as the screen loaded.

Seconds later, the corner of Sierra's mouth tugged up into a grin as the location of Kara's clinic popped up. Eugene was only a couple hours away, and the McKenzie River mountain bike trail was nearby. The perfect cover story. If she left now, she could grab her bike and get there by lunch. There was no way she could wait a few more days to see Kara. The woman had invaded her entire being, filling her with a desperate ache to be near her again and Sierra was never one to deny herself.

***

Kara entered her clinic for the first time in weeks and smiled at the familiar face standing behind the front desk reviewing a claim. The woman dressed in gray slacks and a black polo was a good six-foot tall with fine features that never failed to turn heads. The fact that she was a fitness nut with the body of an Olympian didn't hurt either, but she was more than just physically strong. There was no one in Kara's life with more character than her best friend and business partner, Dr. Nicole Miles.

"Hello, Nic."

The doctor swept her long chestnut hair back over her shoulder and then glanced up. Her blue eyes widened in surprise. "Kara? I didn't expect to see you back this week. How's everything going at the lab?" Her modest southern accent carried like a melody.

"Actually, really well. The place is a dream come true for a nerd like me."

"Oh, come now." Nicole circled the desk and headed toward her. "You're brilliant and this world wouldn't be nearly as interesting if it wasn't for nerds like you making cool stuff." A teasing smirk followed her words.

Kara rolled her eyes. An amused laugh trickled out. "Thanks. I just need to grab a few things and take care of something at home. Looks like everything is running smoothly here. You don't even miss me."

Nicole swung her arm around Kara's shoulders and gave her a firm squeeze. "Of course we miss you, but you're usually holed up in your office anyway. The new doc we hired is doing well, so you can relax and enjoy your research while we handle the patient flow. Oh, and Jamie has been asking for you incessantly. Are you guys still on a break?"

Avoiding eye contact, Kara glanced around the office as she admitted, "That's the main reason I'm here. She'll be coming home at four and I want to officially break it off. It's not fair to her and I'm...well...I'm not in love with her anymore. I'm not sure if I ever was. I know that's sounds horrible."

"I'm so sorry, Kara." Nicole's long arms pulled her in for a hug. "She'll be heart broken, but if you're not all in, then you're doing the right thing." Pausing for a moment, she pulled back and studied Kara carefully. "Pardon my asking, but is there someone else?"

Dropping her eyes to the floor was a dead giveaway and Kara hated that she had such an easy tell. "There wasn't, until the other day." Slowly, she raised her eyes, which glimmered with hope and fear. "I knew I hadn't been feeling it with Jamie. That's why I asked for the break. But you know me, I preferred to focus on getting set up in the new lab and enjoying all the places this new adventure would take me professionally, rather than dealing with a break up."

"You prefer work to anything relationship related, my dear."

Kara glared, but couldn't argue. After their many years of friendship, Nicole had seen all her failed relationships and she had spoken the truth. "Until I met her. God, it was like, wow! I can't even explain it," she gushed. "But I knew it was something I never had with Jamie...with anyone, for that matter. I even took a Saturday off."

"No!" Nicole blurted out, shocked.

"Oh yes," Kara answered, a laugh flittering through her. "And before you ask, no, we haven't done anything, but I had to fight like hell not to. That's when I decided to get up here and end it. I won't be known as a cheater."

"Well, you're trying to do the right thing. I'm sure it'll all work out in the end. I cannot wait to meet this woman."

Hearing the front door open, Nicole swung around intending to greet their guest, but the athletic-looking woman with dark-hair and tattoos standing in the entrance had her eyes glued to Kara.

"I bet she could take your mind off work for a while." Nicole snickered under her breath as she nudged Kara with an elbow.

"Huh?" With no idea what Nicole was talking about, Kara turned her attention to the entrance and fell into instant paralysis. Her jaw fell slack and her face froze somewhere between horror and the best surprise ever. Sometimes there was a thin line between the two.

There stood Sierra, with those gorgeous golden eyes and that damned haunting smile that made Kara melt like chocolate on a hot summer day. "Shit," Kara muttered under her breath.

"What's shit?" Nicole whispered back, confused as to Kara's sudden change in mood. "What's wrong?"

"That's her, the woman I mentioned. That's Sierra."

CHAPTER TEN

Kara never would have taken Sierra for the stalker type. She appeared to be too much of a free spirit for that kind of behavior. Nicole cleared her throat and only then did Kara realize she and Sierra had been wordlessly staring at one another for an unknown amount of time. Sierra had a way of rendering her dumb. That hadn't been their first awkward moment and she was certain it wouldn't be their last.

"Sierra? What are you doing here? Is everything okay?"

"Yeah. Everything's fine. I uh…" Rapt attention had dissolved into something akin to embarrassment as she spoke low and soft. "I'm sorry. This was stupid. You probably think I'm a creepy stalker or something." She folded her arms tight to her chest and shifted her eyes to the floor. "I should go."

Despite the weirdness of the unexpected arrival, Kara was happy to see her. The timing was just so wrong. Kara stuffed her fidgeting hands into her pants pockets and shook her head. "Don't be silly." A light chuckle fell out to disguise her distress, while a slew of thoughts flashed through her mind. *How did she know I thought she was a stalker? Thank goodness Jamie isn't here. What time is it anyway?*

A gentle nudge from her best friend broke Kara's loop of internal monologue. Her best defense against life in general had always been doctor mode, so she stood taller and centered herself. "It's nice to see you again." Kara invited Sierra to approach the desk. "This is my business partner, Doctor Nicole Miles. She runs the clinic while I'm off being a research geek."

"Nonsense, Kara. You're a fantastic doctor who happens to enjoy the science behind the adjustment, that's all. If not for people like you, who would advance the world of chiropractic?" Nicole's pride was unmistakable. "It's a pleasure to meet you, Sierra. What brings you to our neck of the woods today?"

Sierra relaxed and let her hands fall to her sides. "Nice to meet you too. I was headed to McKenzie trail for a training ride. I had stopped by the lab to ask Kara if she had any tips after last week's tests, but she wasn't there." She turned her focus to Kara. "Christie said you were here. I hope you don't mind that I looked up the address?"

Kara bristled at the mention of the lab receptionist. She was certain that visit had also included an obscene amount of unwanted sexual advances on Christie's part. While the lack of professionalism alone was a huge pet peeve of Kara's, this instance struck her on a deeper level. Could she truly be jealous? She hardly even knew Sierra.

"Not at all. You just surprised me. I mean, it's not like I'm hiding out here. We want people to find the clinic." Kara laughed awkwardly. "I have to finish a few things in my office, but then I was headed for a bite. If you'd like to join me, we could talk then."

"That would be great. Thanks."

"Okay, well, I shouldn't be long. Please feel free to have a look around while you wait."

Sierra beamed that gorgeous bright white smile and then leisurely strolled off. Kara could get used to having that smile directed at her, a little fact that brought her back from fantasy land and into the reality that she had a break up to deal with in a few hours.

Dragging Nicole by the hand, she led them to her office and shut the door securely behind them. Kara fell back against the door fame, let out a deep breath, and shook her head. Her pensive expression drew a laugh from her partner, which earned Nicole a set of glaring eyes and a stern frown.

"That's what you said no to the other night?" Nicole asked. "Kudos for your willpower, Kara. After being on a break for three months, even I would've had a tough time saying no, and I love my husband to death."

"Thanks...I guess." Kara dropped her head and ran her palms over her face as she mumbled, "But this is bad, really bad." Already exhausted from the drama that had become her life, her arms fell limp against her sides and she looked up at Nicole. "I'm here to end things with Jamie. I like Sierra, but I don't need this distraction right now. Tonight is going to be bad enough without me having to keep myself from jumping her this afternoon." Sighing deeply, Kara shook her head. "I have never lacked control the way I do around her, Nic. It's quite disconcerting."

"You? Out of control? I never thought I'd see the day."

Kara rolled her eyes, not at all amused. She was seriously stressed, and aroused, and worried. What if she messed everything up before it even got started? Should she dare give in to this growing impulse to be with Sierra? "I don't know what I'm doing. I'm way out of my element here, so a little help would be appreciated."

She had never put herself out there before, not even with Jamie—a thought which filled her with shame. Jamie was smart, pretty, fun, and loved her, but they never had that ease between them. It always felt stressed, even though they mostly seemed happy. Work had been the sticking point. Jamie had always complained that work was Kara's wife and she was her mistress. She told Kara that until she found someone who could compete with her passion for research, she would never have a real chance at a relationship.

Could Sierra be that woman?

After just one week, Kara had come running home to turn the never-ending break into an official split. That had to count for something, didn't it? The fact she had taken time off work to see Sierra and to finally deal with her least favorite thing in the world, drama, just to open the possibility of dating her...That counted for far more in her book.

It should be so simple, yet Kara was scared to death. She had spent her entire life avoiding these moments. Sex was fine. Dating, not too bad. But to feel so much for one person? Insanity! Chasing love, in her experience, was a sure-fire way to end up with nothing—unless misery counted. If she chased Sierra, misery would be her future. She could feel it in her bones. But she was powerless to stop.

Kara's breaths grew quick and shallow, a sign of an impending anxiety attack. Nicole had witnessed that look twice before. After a quick and careful analysis of Kara's predicament, Nicole took her hand, calming her as she said, "Look, I know you always like to have a plan, so go have a casual lunch and keep it business. Just riding and results. Don't get close enough to tempt yourself. Then send her on her way. You can make a date for later in the week if you feel like you're ready for that step. Afterward, you go home and settle things with Jamie. She still thinks you two can work things out, you know? It won't be pretty, but be honest. How does that sound?"

Kara nodded quickly. Long, deep breaths served to clear her head and slow her racing pulse. "Yeah. Okay. I can do that. Thanks."

"Good." Nicole wrapped her in a strong embrace and then made her way to the door. She stopped and turned on a heel, then added, "Oh, and Kara? Remember I'm here if you need anything." With a supportive tip of the head, she walked away, leaving Kara to ready herself for what lay ahead.

Kara had intended to go straight to lunch. She honestly had. But, not expecting Sierra to show up, the box of files she had brought with her was sitting on her kitchen table. Sierra followed Kara's Jeep in an old black

Subaru Outback with her bike mounted to the roof. When Kara parked outside her two-bedroom townhouse, she silenced the engine, sat back, and took a deep breath.

"Quick in-and-out. No problem," she mumbled. She could do this. She stepped out of her car and walked over to Sierra, who had parked behind her and was waiting patiently with her window down.

"Nice house."

"Thanks," Kara replied. Her lips pressed thin into a forced smile. This entire situation had her neurons in a steady state of hyperactivity. "I brought home some of the lab results to analyze. Let me grab them and then we can get lunch."

"Great." It was one word that could be uttered a million different ways, but the sparkle in Sierra's eyes when she dipped her dark Oakley sunglasses spoke volumes.

Yet again, Sierra had managed to send Kara's heart to the races. Her enthusiasm was contagious, causing her tightly pressed lips to ease into a warm smile. Three steps toward her house, Kara stopped, looked back, and offered as casually as she could, "You can come in if you'd like."

What am I doing? This was not the plan.

Sierra's grin widened. With a bounce in her step, she was out of the car and hot on Kara's heels in a second flat.

All concerns were tossed into the wind. Feeling free and easy with Sierra by her side, Kara unlocked the door and shoved it open. No sooner had they walked through the door than Kara stopped short, sending Sierra crashing into her back and nearly knocking her over.

"Jamie? What are you doing here? I wasn't expecting you until four?" It was only one-thirty and yet, here was Jamie standing with a bouquet of roses awaiting her arrival. Moments earlier, her heart had raced with the prospect of spending time with Sierra. Now it pulsed erratically with the dread and anxiety of the shit show about to unfold.

How am I going to fix this mess?

"I didn't think I needed an appointment to see my own girlfriend, but apparently, I should've checked your book since you appear to be occupied," Jamie snarled, directing her eyes around Kara to cast a heinous glare at Sierra. She was half-Hispanic and that fiery temper reared its head as she moved with slow, steady steps, closing the gap between them like a tiger on the hunt.

Kara wanted to step in, but her mouth had gone dry and her voice was non-existent, as if a giant hand had wrapped around her throat, suffocating her.

"Girlfriend?"

The hurt in Sierra's voice hung heavy in the air. Kara was glad to be facing Jamie so the look on Sierra's face wouldn't be burned into her memory. Her chest ached for causing such pain, but her blood boiled at the sadistic smirk occupying her soon to be ex-girlfriend's face. Kara turned, ready to face the music and explain everything, but Jamie grabbed her wrist, demanding her full attention.

"What the hell, Kara? I've been waiting for you for weeks and you're out with another woman?"

"I'm not *out* with anyone. I'm allowed to have friends, Jamie."

Searing dark brown eyes looked Sierra up and down with blatant disgust. "Yeah, she looks like your usual type of friend. When did you start slumming it, Kara?"

"Bitch! I don't know who you are, but that shit won't fly," Sierra growled and tried to push past Kara.

Stuck between the two and desperate for a resolution, Kara spun and pushed Sierra back by the shoulders. Sierra's eyes never left Jamie's. Her fists balled tight as she continued to try and bull her way through. She was strong, damned strong. Kara had to widen her stance and brace her core to keep from getting run over. An image of the running of the bulls flashed through her mind. Good thing she was fit, but she couldn't keep this up all day.

"Please, Sierra, this is between me and Jamie. I'll handle it."

"Fine." Sierra relented and stepped back abruptly. Kara nearly fell to the ground as the brick wall of a body she had been fending off moved away. "Don't worry about me, Kara. I'm fantastic. Enjoy your time with your precious girlfriend," she spat and rushed out the door.

The screech of tires on pavement sent Kara's heart plummeting through the floor into the basement. *Stupid. I told Nicole I was out of my element.* The plan had been food and research. Kara was a smart woman. She could have come up with something to tell Sierra instead of bringing her to her house. Now, there was more drama she had to deal with, but that couldn't be her focus. She had to settle things with Jamie first.

Love's imminent cascade of misery had begun.

"She seems pretty upset for someone you're not doing anything with," Jamie remarked accusingly before walking to the fridge and grabbing herself a cold beer.

Jamie was angry. She should be. She had been on a break for what felt like forever with little to no communication from her. Kara had thought some time apart would make her realize how much she missed having Jamie around, but she didn't miss her at all. It came as only a small surprise that she already missed Sierra. The fact would've been more shocking had she not already accepted that the woman had a vise grip hold on her.

Sierra. Was it too late to go after her? Yes, it was. Besides, she needed to turn her focus on the woman burning a hole through her with bitter disdain.

Avoiding her girlfriend's glare, Kara walked to the kitchen, pulled a glass from the cabinet and filled it with water. Already exhausted from the last few minutes, she sighed and gathered her resolve. It was only the two of them now and there was much to be said.

"She's a rider I treated at the last race. I recruited her to participate in one of my research projects. I haven't been *doing* anything with her."

Jamie's brow arched. "Seriously? Look Kara, when I told you to take all the time you needed I never expected you to be out hooking up with patients."

Still ignoring the set of blazing eyes staring her down, Kara made her way to the dark leather sofa in the living room and replied with sarcasm, "You've caught me, Jamie. That's all my projects are, one good fuck after another in the name of research." She plopped down onto the cushions and propped her feet up on the cherry wood coffee table.

"Fuck you, Kara. I deserve better than this."

Kara's frustration grew. Jamie did deserve better. That was what she had come home to tell her, but the woman didn't want to hear the truth. Kara's head lolled back against the top of the couch. She may as well have slept with Sierra. It would've been so easy. Well, that part would have been easy, but this day would've been a whole lot uglier. The last thing she needed was even more reasons for everyone to despise her.

When Dr. Kara Davies did something, she went big. Today was no exception. She had managed to turn both her break up and her attempt to move forward with Sierra into epic disasters. Was there any kind of Guinness Book achievement for failed relationships? Had other people failed as miserably in similar feats? Surely, she wasn't alone in sucking at relationships. Hopefully, when she returned to Bend, Sierra would let her explain. Then maybe there would be a chance to give a relationship a try. That was, if she could even handle dating again when it was all said and done.

She rolled her eyes, unable to believe she was in the middle of calling it quits with her current girlfriend and all she could think about was Sierra. If she had given Jamie as much thoughtful consideration, they may have been a happy couple. But there was a reason it hadn't worked out. Jamie wasn't the one for her. Kara had long come to believe that there would never be any person she would care to spend copious amounts of time with, but one interaction with Sierra, and that hypothesis was blown to shreds. Now, only one person stood between her and the woman who might possibly be her future. It was time to move on.

Kara lifted her head and regarded her girlfriend, who had taken a seat at the other end of the couch. There was a time she had enjoyed running her hands through those short, honey-brown curls that framed searching, deep brown eyes. She had gotten lost in the sensations that talented curvy mouth could dish out. But that seemed like ages ago and even then, it was on a whim and not filled with the need to connect with a lover. With a deep breath, she released the words she'd been holding in for far too long. "I'm not happy. I haven't been for a long time."

"What? Kara, I—"

"No." Kara tore her gaze away from the tears welling up in Jamie's eyes. If she crumbled now, she would never get the words out. "You're right. You deserve more, Jamie, but I can't give it to you. We aren't right for one another."

Jamie slid forward, her hands finding a soft landing on Kara's knee. "Kara, I know we've had our problems, but we just need to spend more time together to get back to where we used to be." Jamie fought back tears as she pleaded her case.

Kara shook her head. More time together was not the answer. As much as her heart was breaking at the distraught look upon Jamie's face, she otherwise felt nothing. If more time had been all they needed, she was certain she would've felt some kind of twinge or nudge to try again. But there was nothing. Her heart only ached for another. "That won't help and you know it."

"It's that woman, isn't it?" Jamie sat back. Her eyes swirled with pain and betrayal—a heady mix that would often send a person off half-cocked. "You needed a romp on the wild side. Now that's out of your system and I forgive you."

"No!" Kara shouted, desperate to make Jamie understand. "It's not about her." A little lie. It was, but their relationship had been over long before Sierra had ever entered the picture. She was merely the catalyst Kara had needed to grow a set and make the change. "And I haven't slept with her. I haven't even kissed her. I haven't done anything with anyone, Jamie. There is no reason other than I don't want to be with you anymore."

Ouch! That had come out more harshly than intended.

Jamie's eyes bolted wide open. Her body flew back hard into the corner of the sofa as if a superhuman kick had struck her dead in the chest. "But I love you, Kara," she whispered, realization finally taking hold.

"And I did love you, Jamie, but this isn't working anymore and it's not fair to either of us. I'm sorry, but we're done.

CHAPTER ELEVEN

Knocking on Harley's door was a return to the cycle of shame that would leave Sierra hating herself later. She knew it. She had done it before—three times, actually. Four, if she counted the one when they'd broken up and then had sex an hour later. Yet, she couldn't find the strength to break herself of the habit. Ronni would have some choice words for her later and deservingly so, but none of the negative after effects were enough to deter her from repeating the mistake.

There had been assorted reasons over the years for Sierra's trips to Harley's to screw herself happy, but of all of them, this one had hurt the most. More than the time she was passed over for a team endorsement. More than when that other chick, whose name she had since forgotten, trashed her bike because Sierra told her she wasn't looking for a girlfriend after they had spent two days shacked up together.

No, this one ached deep into her bones. She had fallen for Kara and fast. She had trusted her. She had even been ready to try the relationship thing again—something she had sworn off for good. With Kara, she had wanted to reach for that happiness so many people bragged about having.

She knocked again and then leaned wearily against the deck railing. She wiped her lip and winced. The pain from her bike crash a few hours ago was setting in, but the scrapes and bruises were no match for what Kara had done to her heart.

Harley opened the door in a sweat-soaked pink spandex tank top and a matching pair of tiny compression shorts, looking none too pleased to see her. She looked Sierra up and down and shook her head. There was no concern for her injuries. A labored breath escaped her lungs and she wiped her brow. "What the hell, Wiley?"

"My bike and I had a disagreement." Sierra shrugged with indifference and moved into her personal space until mere millimeters separated them.

"Since you're at my door," Harley began unfazed, "I'd say the disagreement wasn't just with your bike. I told you I wasn't going to do this anymore."

Sierra ignored her protest, answering with a light peppering of kisses down her neck. "Come on. You know you want to, for old times' sake." Her finger followed a drop of sweat as it tumbled free and easy from Harley's chin, down her neck, and into the valley between her breasts. She continued her path around a spandex covered nipple that was quick to stand at attention.

A guttural growl rumbled through Harley and Sierra smiled in victory before ending the standoff with a ferocious kiss. Succumbing to the advances, Harley parted her lips and deepened the kiss. Her hands slid down to squeeze a nicely-toned ass as she pulled Sierra in tight. There was no passion between them, no worshipping of flesh, only raw carnal lust as they ripped the clothing from one another's body, leaving a trail from the deck to the bed.

Sierra moaned with pleasure, but silently cursed herself once more for running back to her ex. Why did she feel the need to punish herself even more? Was the pain of crashing her bike and careening twenty feet off the side of the trail not enough? She had done nothing wrong. It was Kara who had lied, but she was the one crushed and miserable. She needed to forget, to feel numb, so she shut down her thoughts and let the physical pleasures serve as an escape—however brief it may be.

The moment they finished, Harley rolled out of bed, walked across the room, and slipped on her robe, never once looking at Sierra. "Feel better?"

There was something in her tone that cracked open a world of realization for Sierra. Feelings were at stake.

Feelings she never knew existed. What a jerk she had been. How had she never known? "Harley..."

"No. I'd kept hoping you'd change your mind, but...I just...I can't do this anymore." She paused, half-turning as if tempted to catch one last glance of a naked Sierra lying on her bed, but then mustered her strength and strode away.

Lying alone in a room still awash with the thick scent of sex, a wave of shame crashed over Sierra, leaving her flailing among a sea of tears to catch her breath. She had screwed up in so many ways. She felt bad about what she had done to Harley, she truly did, but mostly, she hated that she had taken the leap and put her heart out there for Kara. No wonder she not only threw herself down the mountain, but doubled up the shame spiral with sex with an ex. Sex that also made her ex feel like shit.

That would never happen again. It was time she found a new outlet for life's disappointments. Heartbreak would not be one of them though. As of this moment, her heart was officially on lock down.

She quickly dressed and rushed out without so much as a word. Sierra knew she had to make some changes in her life, and she would, but right now she wanted a shower, a beer, and a good, long sleep.

***

Slamming the front door behind her, Sierra muttered one profanity after another as she limped up the stairs to her room. She was so done with this day. Her bed would be her salvation. No sooner had her body hit the mattress than Ronni burst through her bedroom door.

"What's all the...Whoa!" She stopped on a dime. Her eyes widened at the cuts and scratches adorning Sierra's arms and legs. "Oh shit. You all right?"

"Fantastic."

"What the hell happened? You wrestle a mountain lion at the trails today?"

Sierra groaned and shut her eyes tight. She wasn't in the mood for a trip down memory lane. Ronni slid into bed and brushed away the wild hair covering Sierra's eyes, refusing to let her hide.

"I was jonesing for a rush. Guess I lost control and it ended badly. At least there's no dead bodies." She let out a gingerly chuckle.

"Looks like you tried pretty damn hard though. You want to tell me what really happened?"

Sierra sighed deeply and considered her options. Ronni would never let her rest if she held out. Her only choice was to spill her guts. Then she could hole up under her covers for the next eight hundred years or so.

"Kara has a girlfriend." Saying the words aloud brought a lump to her throat. Tears nipped at her eyes and emptiness consumed her heart and mind.

"Wait, what?"

"She has a girlfriend," she repeated, feeling the hurt burrow even deeper into her heart.

"I knew she was bad news. She tried to buy me with video games and free food. I should have given her the speech."

"Not the speech, Ron." Sierra opened her eyes, fixing Ronni with a hard look. "Threatening people is not the way to wingman me." She shook her head and then stared up at the ceiling.

Sometimes her best friend could be a little overwhelming to new comers. So far, Kara had handled her well, and that was one more reason Sierra had become so enamored with her. Kara had an easy confidence when dealing with people, even if she was a bit socially awkward.

"So, there was a little anger in there with that adrenaline rush, huh? You didn't go running to Harley, did you?" Ronni asked casting a sideways glance, but her furrowed brow and growing frown said she already knew the answer.

Sierra remained silent and refused to meet her stern gaze.

"Dammit, Sierra!" Ronni shoved her shoulder hard in frustration. "You know that only makes you feel worse."

"I know," she muttered. "I know."

"How did you find out about the girlfriend?"

Sierra pushed herself up to a seated position, resting her back against the large aspen headboard. She quickly detailed her day, how she drove to Kara's office, and how their stop at her house turned into a lovely stroll through a hornet's nest. Even hours later, the stingers were still stuck dead in her chest, burning her insides with each breath.

Ronni stared at the wall and pondered the new information in silence. Sierra knew the drill. She folded her arms across her chest and awaited her opinion, because Ronni *always* gave her one. And she was usually right. *If only I had such clarity of mind.* But she didn't.

Camryn, in all her wisdom, had once said that Ronni had an old soul, that she was wise for her age, even if she was a "massive bitch." Sierra smiled at the memory of a drunken evening with their biggest rival.

The bed shifted as Ronni slid up beside her and relaxed back. Sierra braced herself. It was time for some sage advice on stalking, or relationships, or whatever.

"Wiley, I love you. I really do. And I love how passionate you get. While I've never seen you so passionate about a person, I am glad you're evolving. I want you to find your happily-ever-after. With that said, I can see you're hunkered down for my mom speech, so here it goes..."

Ronni turned to face her fully. She took Sierra's hands in her own and gave them a squeeze of support. "You may have been a little umm...scary, finding out where she was and showing up at her clinic. I mean, you just met. But I know these feelings are new to you. Still, it seemed she took it well. I do think she likes you, but Sierra, you got to give a girl some space. You have no claim to her. You haven't even gone out on a date. And what did she say when you almost kissed? Something like 'she couldn't right now,' right? For all you know she may be single again. Of course, you could chalk it up to infatuation and find someone new."

Sierra shook her head adamantly. "I don't want to find someone new. She makes me feel something. She makes me want more. I've never had that before. It was always just sex. It's like she ruined me and we haven't even had a date yet."

Ronni nodded her head in understanding. "Then you need to talk to her. As much as I hate to take her side, I don't think she meant to hurt you. Take the time to clear your head. Think things over. If you like her as much as you say you do, then you have to give her a chance to explain. Only then can you decide if it's something you can move past or not. But, and I am only going to say this once, you had better not go running back to Harley if you guys don't work out. You got it?"

Rolling her eyes, Sierra said, "Don't worry. I'm done with that."

"I've heard that before." Folding her arms across her chest, Ronni looked less than convinced. "That's all from mother-knows-best tonight. I'm off to meet Blake and the gang. Why don't you come with? Drown your sorrows, or who knows, maybe find someone to take your mind off her."

"I don't know, Ronni. I just want a hot bath, a beer, and some chocolate," Sierra whined.

Ronni hopped to her feet and towered over her. "That's a big negatory, Wiley. As your best friend, it is my job to keep you company during the hard times. I will not allow you to wallow in self-pity right now. So…" She reached down, grabbed one arm, and pulled. "Up and at 'em. Get cleaned up and meet me downstairs in fifteen." With a quick once over at Sierra's shoddy appearance, she added, "I better give you twenty."

"Gee, thanks." Sierra huffed.

Words couldn't express how much she didn't want to go out, but maybe Ronni was right. Maybe, being alone wasn't a good idea. Silence would give her thoughts a chance to fester. But she would be damned if she was going to make it easy on Ronni. Sierra groaned as Ronni pulled again. She laid dead weight on the bed, making her best friend work hard to achieve her goal.

"You need a night on the town to take your mind off your lady troubles." Ronni pulled again. "Damn, you're heavy."

"You're making me feel so much better about myself."

"Shut up." Ronni snickered and yanked again, this time making headway as Sierra's body slid toward the edge. She dug in and pulled one more time, leaving Sierra's right side hanging halfway off the bed

Satisfied that her point had been made, Ronni released Sierra's arm and set her hands on her hips. "Now...whew!" She huffed and puffed with exertion. "Move it. We're gonna light this town up!" Ronni hopped with excitement, flashed a wink, and then bolted out the door.

CHAPTER TWELVE

Alone with her thoughts, Kara nursed her fourth glass of white wine. That case of Riesling she'd bought for Valentine's Day was coming in handy. The room was in a slow spin as she laid her head atop the back of the sofa and kicked her feet up on the coffee table. An empty bottle laid prone on the floor awaiting a visit from its companion, the half-empty bottle on the end table. A fuzzy version of the afternoon's events replayed in her mind on loop. She had hurt Sierra. She had hurt Jamie. She had let Jamie hurt Sierra.

How did things get so out of hand? Oh right, avoidance and stupidity.

Of course, who could have predicted Sierra would happen? Kara had never been so taken with anyone before. Sierra had hit her hard and fast, leaving her reeling in a class five whitewater of emotions. Fighting the current had been impossible, so she had given up and allowed her heart to guide her to calmer water. She had finally set out to erase the one obstacle in their way, but then Sierra had struck again—like a tsunami, seemingly innocent and mesmerizing to watch, until it reached shore and plowed a path of devastation. Kara had let herself get sucked into the innocent beauty and lost sight of her purpose. Now she was left to clean up the aftermath.

Sierra...

Kara hummed and smiled. Sierra had appeared in her doorway in her baggy shorts with an air of confidence, muscled legs, gorgeous, soulful eyes, and a smile that made Kara's chest thump like a herd of running elephants. The feeling of being pursued so wholeheartedly had left her brimming with indescribable sensations, but now her chest grew heavy and her breath restricted to the point of dizziness. The thought of Sierra being angry with her was too much to bear.

Would she get the chance to explain?

No one had ever left her questioning so much about her life. Sierra brought her back to a time and place when she was unhindered by the rigid routine she had set for herself. She was free to do as she pleased. Free to live. Free to feel. And boy did she want to feel. She ached to feel every inch of Sierra Cody's toned body against hers.

"Why does she have to be so damned hot?" Kara grumbled.

The sudden realization that she was drunk and alone crept in and she criticized herself for being so pathetic. In a moment of clarity, it dawned upon her that she wasn't the least bit concerned about how Jamie felt, which made her feel a little guilty. Jamie was sweet and they had gotten along well, but they had never clicked in the "right" ways—whatever those ways were supposed to be. They had been more like close friends with occasional benefits, though it was obvious Jamie had always believed they shared something more. The desire for "something more" with another person had never been a concern for Kara, so she couldn't relate to what Jamie had wanted so badly. That is, until now.

She couldn't put a finger on when her priorities had shifted. When had she first shunned the free spirit who had raced motocross in favor of the solitude of her science? What catalyst had prompted her to shut out the possibility of emotional connections? A question better left to a sober mind, but that was non-existent tonight. Besides, there was a more pressing matter to tend to in the form of an alluring rider that had captured her fancy.

How do I fix this mess?

Fumbling with her phone, she hovered her fingers above the keys. She could send a text. A nice little "Hi Sierra" would surely clear things up. "Stttuuupid," she mumbled with a touch of a slur. Given the circumstances, that would have been pretty shitty. Sierra deserved better.

Should she call? God no! Not only could she not even fathom more drama tonight, but she was at a loss for words. And the ones she did have likely wouldn't come out clearly enough to understand anyway. With an aggravated groan, she decided to table it until tomorrow. She would sober up and then talk to Nicole.

Until then, no more thinking. There was a bottle of wine to finish.

***

With the dawn of a new day, came the vengeance of last night's binge, but Kara suffered the consequences with few complaints. Her pain had been self-inflicted. There was no one to blame but herself. By afternoon, she had managed a respectable recovery from her hangover and headed to the clinic. Nicole had requested her presence before she returned to Bend—which was a good thing, because she was in desperate need of advice.

The ride to her office was filled with much of the same self-doubt that had hovered over her since Sierra had peeled out of her driveway. She wanted to talk things out, but wasn't sure how the situation should be handled. Should she pay Sierra a visit, or give her space?

But now that her mind was clear, she was seeing things in a different light. Kara had reasons of her own to be upset. Technically, she hadn't done anything wrong. She had resisted the urge to kiss Sierra. Sure, she had led her on a bit, but she was serious in her interest and had been careful not to cross a line until after she'd had a chance to end things with Jamie. That Sierra's tone had insinuated she was a cheater had stung. They hadn't gone out on an official date. They were just two women having fun. That was what she kept telling herself, but she knew better and Sierra did have a right to be hurt.

Stepping into Nicole's office, Kara shut the door softly behind her. Nicole was diligently working on a patient file, tapping away at the computer screen without acknowledging her presence.

"So," Nicole began, still typing away. "I'm guessing from your drunk text last night things didn't go well with Jamie." Putting an exclamation point on her work with a forceful tap of the enter key, she pushed the keyboard away, looked up, and gave her friend a once over.

"That's the understatement of the year." Kara lumbered slowly toward Nicole's desk. She ran her hand over the dark wood before perching on the edge. Taking a deep breath, her gaze drifted to the ceiling as she recounted the night's events and the drama that ensued.

"I'm not sure what I'm supposed to do now, Nic." Kara's fingers rubbed vigorous circles around her temples. "I mean, yes, Sierra can be upset, but in all fairness, I could be upset that she dropped by unannounced and uninvited. Plus, we didn't do anything but flirt, so it's not like we have a claim to one another or anything. Ugh! So much distracting drama. See? This is why I stay in my work bubble," she finished with an exasperated sigh.

"Well..." Nicole released a sigh of her own. "I guess you could go back to your work bubble then. You are single again, so you can do what you want. Let Sierra go and drown yourself in what you love most—research. Maybe someday you'll want more. Maybe you're just not ready yet. Maybe you never will be. Not everyone is cut out to live the relationship lifestyle."

The last part came across as nonchalant, but it was an obvious goading in hopes of getting a reaction. And it had worked. Despite Kara's best efforts to avoid giving Nicole the satisfaction, a crease of frustration traversed her forehead as she thought long and hard.

Letting Sierra go sounded easy in theory, but the thing about theories was they were hypothetical. Even with the little bit of time they had spent together, the woman had already seeped under her skin. Kara could deny it all she wanted, there was no letting Sierra Cody go, at least not without some heartbreak of her own. She narrowed her eyes at Nicole, who sat in silence with a smug grin of victory that aggravated the hell out of her. Kara may have had a high IQ, but Nic knew people, and she really knew Kara.

"On the other hand, my dear Kara, I saw that spark in your eyes when she came in. You may have been stunned by her impromptu visit, but you were happy to see her. It would be such a shame to hide from that. You don't get many opportunities to be happy in life and you had already been going on and on about her. You're smitten."

While those words soaked into Kara's brain, Nicole stood from her chair and smoothed the non-existent wrinkles from her tan slacks as if it would somehow wipe away the mess of the last twenty-four hours. "Now, on a business note," she shifted gears, "I think we should sponsor her racing career."

"Umm...I'm sorry, what?" Kara's face contorted in bewilderment. How could her best friend suggest forming a business relationship with the woman she had just hurt so deeply? "Are you crazy? She hates me."

"Maybe. Maybe not." Folding her arms across her chest, Nicole paused with the quiet confidence one would expect of a top executive commanding a board room. "I looked her up after you left. Sierra is quite talented. And stubborn. I read she's turned down team offers before, preferring to remain independent and do things on her own terms. That choice is noble, but leaves her borrowing equipment when her aggressive style tears up her bike. We want to broaden our field in sports-related work anyway, so who better than her?"

Kara stared blankly at the wall behind Nicole. Her chest seized, allowing little air into her already exhausted body, bringing about a lightheadedness akin to high-altitude exposure. Her brain, which could quickly piece together diagnoses and treatment plans, was clueless about relationships. Her mind floated aimlessly in a sea of questions with no sign of an answer to anchor her. How was she supposed to focus on this new business venture now?

"I don't know, Nic," she answered with skepticism.

Nicole's arms fell to her sides as she walked around her desk to stand by Kara's side. "Look, Kara..." Nicole took her hand, pulling her thoughts to safety as she drew her attention. "It makes sense, business wise. You know she can be a champion. She just needs to put it all together. We can help with that. Sierra is the dawning of a new age of talent in her sport. No woman rides like her and eventually, whether she knows it yet or not, she will need some support. I would like it to be us. Plus, women supporting women...It's a win-win," she finished with conviction as she straightened her posture once again and flashed a confident smile.

Kara shook her head, apprehension etched all over her face. "Of course, you would find a way to turn this into a marketing opportunity," she said with a harsh laugh. "But I don't know if she will. Not only was yesterday a huge disaster, but she's a lot more sensitive over the team topic than you'd think. She even thought I was trying to lure her to Team Traxx with the research offer."

The veil of sadness dropped once again as she recalled that day. As tough and strong as Sierra was in all her bad-ass glory, she was also quite vulnerable. Kara kicked herself for not realizing it sooner. She never would have missed that with a patient, but in her personal life, she was as blind as the three mice in the childhood nursery rhyme. If she were to pursue anything with Sierra, business or pleasure, she would need to be more considerate in her actions.

Her eyes dropped to the floor, shifting her thoughts from her personal problems to Nicole's proposal. She had a point. Whether Sierra would agree or not was irrelevant. She was an amazing talent with a high ceiling of potential and Kara wanted to see her reach the top. Having no interest in controlling Sierra's daily activities, they could offer her stability without making demands.

"You are right though, she is definitely the future of the sport. Draw up a proposal and I'll work on it. Now, can we get back to my problem?" She arched an eyebrow in challenge.

"Of course, Doctor Davies." Nicole's hearty laugh filled the room, finally pulling a hint of a smile from Kara. "We have a tough case to solve, my good friend, but solve it, we will."

CHAPTER THIRTEEN

For the last two nights, Ronni had tried her hardest to help numb Sierra's pain, but now that she was alone and sober, Sierra was just as angry, hurt, confused, and smitten as she had been before. Partying had accomplished nothing but a hangover, loss of riding time, and a huge hole in her wallet. She groaned and rested her head in her left hand as she played solitaire on her phone at the far end of the bar. The glass of stout Axel had set beside her twenty minutes ago dripped with the perspiration of a three-hundred-pound man in Moab in the dead of summer, but she was in no hurry to put it out of its misery...or herself out of her own.

Kara had left three messages over the last three days and Sierra was at a crossroads at whether or not to respond. The hurt from being lied to was still fresh, but as Ronni had said, Kara didn't belong to her, so she should at least let her explain. Knowing a truth and acting accordingly, however, were two distinctly different things.

Widely known to act out of emotion first, Sierra had learned the hard way that a knee-jerk response only made things more difficult. In fear of being spiteful and saying something she'd regret, she chose to wait. The quiet company of her beer was much a safer bet for now.

Sierra jumped when a hand slammed down hard on the bar top beside her.

Camryn smirked at her agitated response, then prodded with a laugh. "Aww, party for one? How sad." Her thick Australian accent coated her words.

With an unimpressed roll of her eyes, Sierra returned to her beer. Usually, she would engage Camryn in a parry of quips, but she wasn't in the mood.

"What's your problem?" Camryn drummed her fingers on the bar top as she awaited a retort. "Finally get an S.T.D. from all your whoring around?"

When no response came, she mumbled to herself, then stared down the length of the bar at Axel. "Hey barkeep," she called out. "Give me something strong." She then turned back to Sierra, who refused to acknowledge her presence.

Axel slid a shot of light amber liquor toward her without a word. He picked up a towel, slapped it over his shoulder, then moved toward a couple who had taken a seat. Camryn threw it back, wiped her mouth with the back of her hand, and then occupied the stool beside Sierra.

"I love a good whiskey. Don't you?" Camryn asked as she sat staring, refusing to budge until Sierra acknowledged her.

"What do you want?" Sierra asked, her eyes still set on the glass in front of her and not on the woman so anxiously awaiting their attention. Her hands slid up and cupped the sides of the mug, the perspiration coating her palms.

Camryn shrugged. "I don't know. Guess I'm just curious."

Sierra fought her anger, refusing to give Camryn any satisfaction. Instead, she forced a sweet smile and smartly inquired, "About what? Why no one likes you, or why you can't beat me?"

A shapely lip curled upward in amusement before Camryn replied, "Aren't you cheeky?" She tapped the bar top signaling her need for another drink. "I'm curious about what put old Wiley Cody's panties in a bunch. For Christ's sakes, you're wasting a perfectly good beer. That's a sin where I come from."

Sierra turned back to her full glass and issued a sharp answer. "My business is none of your concern, Cam." Finally lifting the mug to her lips, she took the first sip of her favorite chocolatey stout. A grimace formed and she set the mug down and shoved it away. The beverage had lost it flavor in the presence of certain company.

Camryn observed with keen interest. She shifted closer as she spoke again. "Oh, come now, it most certainly is." Leaning into Sierra's personal space, her voice lowered as she delivered her taunt, "I'm going to beat the snot out of you at next week's race, make you look slower than a three-toed sloth dragging itself up a hill. And when I do, I don't want to hear the sob story about you not being in the right state of mind. Especially not over something so pathetic as a broken heart." She sat back and grinned, then slapped Sierra on the back. "So, woman up already."

The need to punch someone in the face had never surged through Sierra with as much desire as it had in that moment. Camryn's smug grin had always rubbed her the wrong way. Add words to the mix and it was no wonder they could never be in a room together for more than five minutes.

Cam's smile broadened even more, seemingly delirious with power as Sierra's eyes burned with anger. "I hit a nerve I see. What is it? Doc got you down?"

Sierra bolted from her stool and grabbed her by the shirt, her chest heaving with ragged breaths of barely contained fury.

Camryn didn't back down. She didn't even flinch. "We may not like one another, Sierra, but I promise you, we both want you to bring your A game to the mountain, so spill it." Fierce hazel eyes remained fixed with Sierra's as she tapped the bar again and held up two fingers.

Sierra slowly dialed herself down, releasing a breath as she slumped back onto the bar stool. Taking the shot handed to her, she stared at the other woman, whose features had softened as she looked at her with genuine interest. "If you start needling me, I swear to all that is holy I will punch you in the face," Sierra spat before settling in and detailing the events, including the bike crash and the pathetic hook up with Harley.

When she finished, she threw back the shot of whiskey and awaited Camryn's response. Surprisingly, she sat quietly, processing the details that had been laid out and putting real thought into a reply.

"Which version do you want, the big girl pants or the pull ups?" Camryn inquired with no expression whatsoever.

Taking a moment to consider the question, Sierra decided she didn't need any more coddling. If she was serious about making things work with Kara, then she needed it served straight up. "I'm a big girl. I can handle it."

"Don't say I didn't warn you."

Sierra groaned and palmed her face. "This was a bad idea."

"Not at all. Look, you both share blame in this one, but it's not like you had any kind of commitment. Hell, you never even had a real date, so you can't go all out bitch on the woman. I do think it's funny as shit that you wrecked yourself on some pissed off, two-wheeled, downhill rant though. Wish I'd been there for that one."

Sierra narrowed her eyes at Camryn's amused laugh.

"I must say, I thought more of you than to go running to that sad-sack ex of yours. If you ever want to make anything work with anyone then you need to put your big girl panties on and deal with shit, not go running for sex with an ex, or drowning in beer, or picking fights. You gotta deal with your shit on an emotional level and dammit, do it before the next race. That is all I have to say about that." Camryn blew out an exhausted breath and turned on her stool to lean back against the bar.

Sierra was impressed. "Wow! Who would have ever guessed you had all that insight, Yoda?" She waved at Axel and held up two more fingers.

"Yeah well, don't tell anyone or I will be forced to kill you," she stated with dry wit.

When their drinks arrived, Sierra held hers up to toast. "I still don't like you, but I appreciate your advice. Thank you. Next race, may the best woman win."

Camryn clinked her glass to Sierra's and winked. "Oh, I intend to."

CHAPTER FOURTEEN

Kara flicked on the light in her office and turned to her desk. "Shit!" She jumped back with her hand on her chest, nearly dropping her bag. "You scared the hell out of me, Ronni. How'd you get in here?"

The young woman was seated in her chair with her feet propped up on the desk. The look on Ronni's face made Kara's skin crawl. One, then the other, Ronni removed her feet and then stood. "I know people," she replied with all seriousness as she folded her arms across her chest. Her crystal blue eyes stared a hole through the doctor.

Kara was shocked at how intimidating Ronni could be. She placed her bag down, buried her hands in her jacket pockets and stood tall. "What can I do for you, Ronni?"

"What you did to Sierra was shitty." She paused as Kara shifted uncomfortably. "She fell hard for you and you screwed her over. She isn't going to do well at the next race if she's all messed up in the head over you," Ronni hissed, pointing her finger dead at Kara. "I can't say I think you're worth all the moping, but I want her to be happy, and she was happy with you. So, fix it. Either date her or clear the air, but fix it." She punctuated her ultimatum with narrowed eyes and a hard slap of her hand against the desk, causing Kara to flinch.

Kara hadn't expected to be confronted in such a manner, but never one to be bullied, she kept her steady green eyes fixed on challenging blue ones as she maintained composure. Her stance tightened as she issued a calm reply. "It wasn't my intention to hurt anyone. It's regretful the way it turned out."

Still eyeing her, Ronni dropped her arms and tapped her index finger against her chin. "Hmm, well you know what they say about regret..." she trailed off, looking to the ceiling as if searching for the right words. Abruptly, she turned her gaze back to Kara. "She's an evil bitch that never sleeps. Kind of like me," she ended with a laugh.

Kara failed to find the humor in her comment. She folded her arms and leaned against the wall as she delivered an icy glare in response.

"Ohh, stone cold. Brrrr." Ronni pretended to shake, then swept around to the front of the desk. "Okay, so look...obviously, neither one of you is equipped to handle deep emotions," she scoffed. "The question is, do you think my best friend is worthy of turning on the defroster in that heart of yours?"

Kara stood silent. Sierra *was* worth it and she wanted to give it a shot, but now she had an added concern. Would her emotional short comings be a detriment to Sierra's racing? Kara didn't want to be the reason she lost. Her job was to help Sierra get better, not worse. Kara held fast to her closed off position against the wall, her emotions warring within as Ronni patiently waited.

Finally, Kara released a deep breath and in a nearly robotic tone she said, "I've left her several messages. I haven't heard back." Steeling her jaw, she pushed off the wall and attempted an air of authority as she tried to maintain her cool, but not hearing from Sierra had been killing her and Ronni wasn't helping matters any.

In a complete shift, Ronni softened. "Sierra takes a while to process. She's passionate. Those strong emotions lead her to lash out when hurt," she explained. "She's also stubborn as all hell, which means the ball is in your court. You have to be the one to act if you want her. So, no more phone calls. I'll get her to Worthy Brewing for lunch tomorrow at noon. Be there or...well, you're already pretty square." With a laugh, Ronni walked past Kara, giving her a slap on the back as she went and calling over her shoulder, "Check ya later, Doc."

As soon as Ronni was out the door, Kara released her rigid posture. Hiding her feelings always took a lot of energy. Exhausted from maintaining her facade, she dropped her head and took a deep breath as she ran her fingers through her hair. Ronni was right. She had to fix things. She would be seeing Sierra at the races whether she wanted to or not.

Unfortunately, heartfelt apologies and the discussion of feelings were like a foreign language to her. Not knowing the language had never bothered her before, but now she hoped to speak it well enough for Sierra to understand how much she really cared.

***

The next afternoon Kara walked into Worthy Brewing as instructed. Surveying the scene, she saw no sign of Ronni, but Sierra was seated alone at the bar staring at her phone. Her beer sat untouched. Ronni had probably used the ruse of a lunch meet-up to get Sierra out, which meant her presence would be a surprise.

"Great," Kara muttered as she made a cautious approach, freezing when Sierra turned. Beautiful bright eyes spread wide as an owl at the sight of her. Was she happy to see her? Was she mad? Her expression was completely unreadable and that only amplified Kara's nervousness. If she were to gauge her anxiety on a scale of one to ten, her current spike would be well over one hundred, but those feelings paled in comparison to the erratic skip of her heartbeat caused from being near Sierra again.

Her free hand plunged into her pants pocket. The other held onto a green folder for dear life as she finally stammered, "Umm...Hello, Sierra."

"Kara, I wasn't expecting you to be here," Sierra stated with an aloofness that still provided no clue as to her current state of mind. Her eyes traveled the length of Kara's body before she turned away and wrapped her hands around her beer.

Kara would be lying if she said the lack of enthusiasm hadn't hurt. Her gaze fell to the floor. "Sorry you weren't warned."

Glancing back over her shoulder, Sierra eased her tone as she clarified, "I didn't mean it like that."

"I know." Over the initial awe of seeing Sierra again, Kara fell into doctor mode when she noticed the scratches and bruises marring what had been flawless skin. "What happened to your face? Are you all right?" She took a step forward, wanting to help ease the pain, but Sierra turned back to her drink.

"It's nothing. I'm fine."

As Kara stared at Sierra's profile, she remembered the adorable shyness the typically confident woman had exhibited when she had walked into her clinic. That seemed like so long ago now. Had Kara not been so shell-shocked that day, she might have swooped in and kissed her right then and there. No, she couldn't be mad at Sierra for following her heart, but she could be mad at herself at how she had handled the entire situation since day one. Her only defense was that whenever Sierra was near, her brain shut down. She could perform patient exams with her eyes closed, but the second her mind strayed from a practiced routine to free thought, it turned into a jumbled mess. Add Sierra to the mix and it stopped functioning all together.

The bartender's voice broke her trance, asking what she would like to drink. After requesting a water, Kara sat a few stools down and studied the woman she had been longing to see again. "You haven't been returning any of my messages," she said, her sadness evident.

"Could we just..." Sierra motioned toward the outdoor patio.

"Right...umm, okay." Kara grabbed her glass and followed behind until they reached a table away from everyone else. She paused and took in the amazing view of Mt. Bachelor looming in the distance. Taking their seats, the palpable tension was stifling as both women sat in silence.

Toying with her glass, Kara figured she should be the one to start. She looked up at Sierra with hope in her eyes as she said, "I've missed you, Sierra."

"Hmph."

The hurt she had caused put a squeeze on Kara's chest that had her gasping for breath. At least she was being given the opportunity to explain. After all, if Sierra hadn't wanted anything else to do with her, she doubted this conversation would have lasted this long. "I never meant to hurt you. I didn't do anything wrong. I never lied to you," Kara tried to reason. In her mind, she may not have been forthcoming about her relationship status, but she had also avoided crossing the line as a cheater.

"Flirting with me wasn't wrong? Not telling me about your girlfriend wasn't lying?" Sierra snapped.

Not deterred by the response, Kara refused to go down without a fight—something she never would have done for Jamie. "We hardly know one another, Sierra. I'm not one to spill my secrets to strangers." Kara paused, inhaling deeply to calm herself before continuing, "We, Jamie and I, had been on a break for three months and I had been meaning to call it off, but I guess I preferred to drown myself in work. It's a bad habit, as I am constantly reminded." She glanced down at her glass and then back at Sierra with teary eyes searching for forgiveness.

Finally showing a kink in the armor, a flash of emotion shone in Sierra's eyes as she shifted uncomfortably in her seat. "You really hurt me. I had never had such strong feelings for someone before and now..."

"I know and I'm so sorry. I didn't mean for it to happen this way. The night we stayed out after the ride...it took all I had to pull away from kissing you. I've never been drawn to anyone as strongly before either." Allowing her heart to be her guide, the words came easier than expected. She scooted closer to Sierra, trying to lock onto her gaze.

"The first time I saw you at the race clinic, I knew I was in trouble. It terrified me, but I couldn't *not* see you again. And I tried damn hard to fight it, given my situation," she said shaking her head. "Then, after our almost kiss, I drove right home. I had planned to break up with Jamie when she came back Monday night and then come back for you, only you showed up, and she was early, and now...now I've made a huge mess and I've hurt you." Kara placed her hand over Sierra's. The contact filled her with a warmth, a comfort she couldn't explain. A comfort that only seemed to come with Sierra.

"Please believe me when I say I never meant to hurt you. It's just...I have trouble thinking clearly when I'm around you. I wanted to do it right, but I screwed it up. Good intentions...Well you know..." she trailed off, exhaling deeply. "Would you please give me another chance?" She gave Sierra's hand a gentle squeeze and waited, her heart ceasing to beat until an answer was given.

It had taken a lot for Kara to speak from her soul. Sierra may not have known her well, but she did know she was guarded. Emotion was not the way Kara lived her life, unlike her. Sierra attacked life with gut instinct and little planning, happy to take whatever road it put her on, but determined to leave her own mark along the way. Kara, on the other hand, was analytical and practical and had a plan for everything. This was a huge gesture on her part, but Sierra wasn't ready to set the hurt aside so quickly. She didn't trust easily and despite her arguments to the contrary, she didn't recover easily either.

"I don't know, Kara," Sierra choked out. It hurt too much to look Kara in the eye. "I do appreciate your apology, but it still hurts. I think I need some time to process. I'm not making any promises though."

Kara's strength withered and she pulled her hand away. "Understood. Thank you...um, for listening to me." She stood from her stool and grabbed the green folder. An awkward silence fell between them once again as Kara stared at the folder and then back at Sierra once, twice, and then cleared her throat. "Sierra, umm…Could I talk to you about something else for a moment?"

Sierra quirked a brow. What else could there be to say? Perhaps something related to the research, which she would need to decide whether or not to continue. While she may not be ready to forgive yet, she was also not ready for their interaction to end. "Okay."

Right before her eyes, Kara transformed from a human full of warmth to an emotionless physician. She righted herself with rigid posture, just as she held herself at work, and pulled a packet from the folder. After staring at the front page for a long minute, she looked up and announced, "Nicole and I would like our clinic to sponsor you."

Sierra sat stunned, her mouth agape. A million thoughts ran through her head—some good, some bad. Would she want to tie herself to them with so much going on between her and Kara? Before she could get much deeper in thought, Kara interrupted.

"I know you and I are a mess right now," Kara hurried, not giving Sierra a chance to cut her off, "but this is a professional offer, regardless of what happens between us. We both agree that we'd like to be a part of your success and still allow you to keep your independence. It's not a huge contract, but it would reduce the stress of worrying about equipment and travel costs.

"Plus, we make would no demands other than you race your heart out and do one event per year at our clinic, either a meet and greet or kid's bike clinic, whichever you'd prefer." She paused before adding in an almost apologetic tone, "And you don't have to see me for treatment or the project either, if that helps your decision. We want to get you the best equipment and give you the best shot at the championship. You deserve it." Kara gave her a sincere smile. "Don't answer now. Just think about it. Okay?"

Taking in a deep breath, Sierra's eyes brightened with possibilities. There were still so many questions, so many things to consider. She had been adamant about not joining a team, but could this be the best of both worlds? She would have to sit with Ronni and read the contract.

"That's a...very generous offer. I will certainly think about it. Thank you, Kara, and please relay my thanks to Nicole."

With a nod and a soft smile, Kara remained standing as silence fell yet again, but it was not accompanied by the awkwardness from earlier. "Well, I uh...should be getting back. I have a one-thirty appointment. You can call me or Nicole with any questions," she said, handing Sierra a clinic business card. "We hope to hear from you soon."

Kara smiled again, only this time, without the weight of the world on her shoulders and it made Sierra smile in return. "Oh, and you should let someone check out your injuries, so you can heal properly before the next race," Kara remarked with care in her voice before walking away.

Sierra's smile grew. It was nice to have someone besides Ronni care about her. It may have been wrong, but she had felt some satisfaction at making the apology difficult. Kara was good at hiding her emotions and the fact that she had worked so hard only proved how much she truly did want her.

As she watched Kara leave, the shapely backside caught her attention, as it had several times before. Sierra couldn't deny she wanted to try a relationship, but first, she had to gather herself. And she would, as soon as she was finished enjoying the view.

CHAPTER FIFTEEN

Two days had passed since her meeting with Kara and Sierra hadn't done much beside ride and hide. Lounging on the couch watching Ronni play video games had served to keep her mind off important things, which was what she needed for a now. Life had been getting too stressful lately and that was something she had always made a habit of avoiding.

Sierra chuckled as Ronni ducked and moved with the action on the screen, masterfully manipulating the controller to execute pinpoint kills. As she conquered yet another level, she hit pause and let out a triumphant yell, "Take that zombies!" She set her controller down and headed for the kitchen, high fiving Sierra along the way.

"How many versions of that game are there? I know you've been kicking its ass for years now."

Chugging half a can of Dr. Pepper and slamming it down on the counter, Ronni belched before replying, "Six, so far." With can in hand, she made her way back to the living room and asked, "So, you going to go see her or what?"

Sierra groaned. Her head fell back against the sofa and she stared at the ceiling. She wished Ronni would quit hounding her. She knew what she had to do, but life was much easier inside her little cocoon, for now anyway. Taking a deep breath, she sighed out, "Yes, Ron, I will. I kind of want to wait until after this next race before I ask her out. I don't need any more drama right now."

She had hoped that would satisfy her persistent friend, but no such luck. Ronni plopped down on her lap and gave her the familiar "what the hell" look.

"I thought you guys cleared the air?"

"We did."

"If you don't want to talk to her yet, you should at least call that other chick about the sponsorship. It's a sweet-sounding deal."

Rolling her eyes, Sierra sighed again, exhausted from repeating the conversation they had had several times since she had spoken to Kara. "I know. I know. I'm scheduled to be at the lab tomorrow. I don't know if Kara is still running my tests or if she gave it to someone else, but I'm sure I can see her then."

"Okay. I'm going to take your word for it, but don't make me break out the movie quotes."

"You know I hate it when you quote movies at me." Sierra cast a sideways glance.

"Indeed, I do, but if it helps kick you in the ass a little, then..."

Sierra raised her hands in surrender. "I will, okay? So, go back to killing your zombies or aliens or whatever."

Having gotten what she wanted, Ronni kissed Sierra on the cheek and hopped up with a smile. "Okay. She'll understand, you know? She may suck at personal issues, but she doesn't want to mess with your career. That much I know for a fact. Besides, she never would've made that offer if she didn't want you to be the best...err, well, second best," Ronni said with a cheeky grin and a wink.

"Jeeze! When are you leaving for France, again?"

"Hey!"

"Just kidding." A challenging smirk formed. Sierra loved a good competition. "You know, I may be out of the running this year, but watch your little B.F.F. butt next year. I'm going to win that championship."

Ronni threw her head back with a fake laugh and then stood tall and proud. "I welcome all challengers," she announced as if it were a royal decree. "Bring it on biyatch!"

"Oh god!" Sierra crowed, doubled over in laughter. "I love you, Ron."

"I love you too, Wiley."

There were fist bumps and a hug and then Ronni proceeded to annihilate another level of her video game.

***

Arriving early for her appointment at the lab, Sierra side-stepped Christie's hungry gazes and glided down the hall toward Kara's office in hopes they could talk for a few minutes. She stopped outside the door and peered through the window. Kara was sitting at her desk entranced in paperwork. Not wanting to disturb her, Sierra took a few moments to enjoy how adorable she was when engrossed in her task. With a furrowed brow and a tapping pen, Kara was oblivious to the world around her as she read through a file.

When Kara set her pen down, Sierra saw her opening. "Hey," she whispered from the doorway, then quickly glanced to her feet in a sudden bout of shyness.

Kara's head whipped up. She appeared startled for the briefest of moments before slipping back into doctor mode. "Hello, Sierra. It's good to see you again," she said in her well-practiced, authoritative tone.

"You too." Glancing up through her lashes, Sierra asked, "I uh, know I'm a bit early, but I was hoping we could talk. Is that all right?"

"No problem at all. We can talk when we get there." Kara stood, grabbed an armful of files, and then moved with graceful precision toward the door. "Let's head over and get you started."

"Great." Sierra's lips curved into a soft half-smile as she lifted her head to fully meet Kara's eyes. Her inability to get a read on Kara's emotions made her uncomfortable, but what else could she expect? They had both admitted to their attraction and were only trying to protect themselves from more heartache. She couldn't blame Kara for being guarded when she hadn't yet given her an answer to her question.

The walk to the testing room was silent, but not entirely uncomfortable, which gave Sierra some bit of comfort. She wondered if Kara would still oversee her care. She hoped so, but would be sure to let her wishes be known, just in case.

They stepped into the office and Kara shut the door behind them. Sierra spun to face her, anxious to get the words out and officially make amends. "I'm sorry I haven't spoken to you sooner. I was trying to clear my head and figure some things out, but I'd like to sit down with you and Nicole to discuss the contract. Also, I'd like you to keep working me, if you're comfortable with that."

Kara shoved her hands into her pockets, something Sierra had discovered served as a defense mechanism. Kara gave a soft nod. A half-smile touched her lips, though she maintained her professional demeanor. "That's great, Sierra. And I would be happy to."

They shared a smile. The tension that had weighed heavily upon them dissipated, allowing Sierra to take a deep breath for the first time in days. The light was back in Kara's eyes too, causing Sierra's heart to skip with joy.

"You should start looking at companies you'd like to be associated with. Nicole is as good as a sports agent at getting deals done." Kara finally relaxed. Her shoulders lowered and her voice fluctuated with a hint of excitement for their new venture. "Also, find a bike mechanic to staff and figure out the components and such that you'd like. Call it a wish list of sorts, and then after we sign the contracts, you let Nicole work her magic."

"I can't wait," Sierra beamed, thankful to have gotten that over with, but she did have one other thing she needed to get out into the open. Embarrassed to admit it, but she owned it like a trooper, Sierra explained the origin of her cuts and bruises, leaving out her rendezvous with Harley.

Kara had a laugh when she heard the bike crash was due to Sierra's attempt at blowing off steam after she had sped away from her house. The doctor performed a systematic check of her spine and extremities for any limitation of motion as a result of the accident. Finding several areas to be addressed, Kara came alive with excitement.

Whatever Kara was saying went right over Sierra's head. The words sounded medical and boring, yet the spark in Kara's eyes and the enthusiasm with which she spoke made Sierra equally as enthused for their session. Plus, she did love to listen to Kara spout fancy medical jargon. Weird as it may be, it was an absolute turn on for her. Having been seen by doctors before without experiencing the same response, she could only credit the increase in her libido to the woman delivering the words.

"I can't wait to compare the results from other days before the crash to today," Kara spouted with passion. The thrill of science emanated from every cell of her being. "I mean, not that I'm happy you wrecked, but..." she apologized.

A hearty laugh filled the room. "I know, but you're happy I wrecked," Sierra acknowledged, not at all offended. On the contrary, she was intoxicated by Kara's honest fascination with the way the body worked. "I love it when you talk science."

Kara rolled her eyes as a light pink flush tinged her cheeks, but she couldn't stop smiling. "Normally people can't stand it, but yes, scientifically speaking, I am happy that you had an accident. I'm also very happy you weren't hurt, but now we can truly see how much difference spinal manipulation can make."

Sierra hopped up, grinning from ear to ear as she said, "Anything for science." A laugh followed her words.

Well, maybe not for science. But to see that smile? There was no imaginable limit.

CHAPTER SIXTEEN

Sierra flew down the final course of the season with pinpoint accuracy. The ride through the torturous Whistler trail was almost too easy—reminiscent of her last race descent, which had not ended favorably. A flicker of concern trickled into her mind, but she shoved her fear aside and pushed forward. She wouldn't allow the course to bite her this time. Her mind, body, and bike were one.

Drops and rocks. Berms and roots. Sierra choose her lines wisely, allowing her to remain aggressive without working too hard. As she soared over the last jump, she landed perfectly and then pedaled like a maniac through the finish line. She eased up and skidded to a halt, gasping for breath. Her legs burned like an inferno, but she had never felt better.

Had it been the treatments? The doctor? Or perhaps her contentment with the decision to sign the contract? Maybe a combination of all three. She couldn't be sure of the answer, but it was the first time she had ever felt truly at peace.

A cheering Ronni hopped out of her leader's Hot Seat and rushed up to congratulate her. "Yeah! Now, that's the Wiley I know!" She gave her a high five as Sierra slowly pushed her bike off the course. "Damn great run, girl. Not enough to beat me though." Ronni nudged her shoulder. "But I bet that time hangs on for second."

"Thanks. I felt good. Better than I have in a long time. That was a great ride to end the season too."

"Sure was. Gives you good motivation for off-season training."

"Yeah and there's going to be a lot of changes this off-season, you watch."

"I hope so. You say it every year, but this time I believe you. There's a look in your eyes today that I've never seen before. And you're so close, Wiley. If you keep this up, you'll be making my life hell every time we compete. I'm looking forward to next season. There's some World Cup in your future, girl!"

Sierra stopped and considered her friend's words. Only one thing had changed in her life since last season and it seemed the effect was even more profound than she had thought. She draped an arm around Ronni's shoulders and gave her a squeeze. "Me too. Thanks for always being in my corner, Ron."

"Always."

"Now get back in that Hot Seat. I'll catch you later."

"Go get your girl."

Sierra smiled wide. *Her girl.* At least, she hoped so. Since Kara had appeared in her life, it had been an unbelievable journey, and they were just getting started.

She couldn't wait to see what lay ahead.

After putting up her gear and throwing on her ball cap, Sierra rushed to the clinic, anxious to find a few minutes alone with her favorite doctor. Now that the season was over, she would ask Kara out on a real date and set a time to sign the contract. As requested, she had made a list of her needs for the upcoming season. Racing had a way of making her feel like a kid every day, but finally planning her future made her feel more grown up than ever before.

Two steps inside the clinic, she came to a screeching halt. Camryn was standing far too close to Kara and Sierra didn't like it one bit.

***

Kara cheered with the rest of the clinic staff that had gathered around the television as Sierra completed her successful run. A swell of pride lifted her chest knowing she had played a small part in getting the rider back into top shape after suffering two wrecks. With six riders remaining, she was hopeful Sierra would hold onto the second spot, finishing a touch under a second behind Ronni.

She wanted to stay and watch the final runs, but paperwork called and if she wanted to get finished on time, she needed to get started. Luckily, it hadn't been a busy day for crashes, but this time of year lent itself to more pre and post ride care. Stretching, ice, massage, and adjustments helped ease the athlete's aches as the wear and tear of their sport set in.

Pulling a folder of forms that needed filling out, Kara took a seat at one of the higher treatment tables within view of the television and began her work. Within minutes, a body hovered over her. She turned with a smile expecting to see Sierra, but her smile quickly evaporated as her face morphed into a look of confusion.

"Can I help you?" she asked, hoping it would be a quick question, though her gut told her that wouldn't be the case.

"I was just stopping in to visit. We haven't had a chance to meet. I'm Camryn O'Reilly." She grinned like a cat on the prowl.

"Hello, Camryn. I'm Doctor Kara Davies. It's nice to meet you. I'm sorry, but I'm trying to get the last of the paperwork finished so we can all leave on time, so if you don't require any medical attention, I do need to get back to work."

"Of course. Don't let me interrupt you. I'm just one of those friendly, chatty, gals who like to 'shoot the shit,' as you American's like to say."

A tight-lipped smile pulled harshly against the corners of Kara's mouth as she nodded. "Perhaps another time then?" Kara turned to focus on her work, praying her lack of further engagement would give the woman the hint.

In Kara's effort to ignore her, she failed to notice Sierra's arrival, but Camryn did not. Instead of moving away, she moved in closer. A devious smirk crawled across Camryn's face and her eyes twinkled with mischief as Sierra glared daggers from the back of the room.

"Sure thing, Doctor." She leaned in, her hot breath sliding uncomfortably over Kara's ear. "I wouldn't want you to consort with the unsavories in our sport. You know the type, like that Cody woman."

Kara tensed hearing Sierra's name. She wanted to pull away, to rise up and tell her off, but she refused to give Camryn the satisfaction, choosing instead to focus harder on the work in front of her.

"Sure, she's a pretty face, but she gets around. You know what she did the other day? She went on a rant after she didn't get her way, wrecked her bike, and then ran to her ex for pity sex. Pathetic. I'd hate to see someone like that trying to get her hooks in you. You are much too good for that."

"Thank you for your concern," Kara replied without looking up. "But I'm here to render medical attention, not gossip. So, if you wouldn't mind taking your leave..." She left it hanging as she pulled another sheet from the file.

"Good talk, Doc." Camryn slapped her on the back and walked toward Sierra.

Kara was startled by the contact, her head somewhere else trying to comprehend why the racer would drop such information about Sierra. Deep down she knew she had no right to be angry, but she couldn't help feeling betrayed after Sierra had made such a scene about Jamie. Was this Sierra's regular theme when things didn't go her way? Did she always run back to her ex?

"Good luck. I hope you blow a tire," Sierra spat.

Kara spun around at the sound of her voice. As happy as she was to see her, Camryn's ear worm was currently on replay, throwing her heart and mind into a vicious tailspin.

Camryn smirked as she replied, "Is that the best you could do after our little heart to heart? I'm not sure it was worth my time. Enjoy the rest of your day, Sierra." She glanced over her shoulder and threw Kara a wink.

Needing a moment to collect herself, Kara turned back around, a blank stare landing on the paper in her hand. She didn't look up when Sierra reached her side.

"That must be some riveting stuff," Sierra remarked, her voice soft, almost apologetic.

"Yeah, I was just, uh...anyway..." Kara stumbled. She fumbled with the papers and glanced up. "Hello."

A genuine smile graced Sierra's face at Kara's awkward greeting. "I had a great run. I'm still behind Ronni, but I'm hoping it's good enough to hold second place. I wanted to thank you," she said, though the excitement of a great ride was nowhere to be found.

Titling her head, Kara stared at Sierra, questioning her meaning. She didn't want to make assumptions. "For what?"

Sierra placed her hand gently on Kara's shoulder. "For treating me, and for the input from the research, of course. It helped to learn that my left leg was actually stronger than my right on takeoff."

"You did great. I watched your run. But no thanks needed. That's my job," she smiled, though it was not as bright as it usually was when directed at Sierra.

"Is everything all right?"

The expression on Sierra's face showed concern, no doubt feeling the discomfort radiating off her. Kara may not have known much about the riders on the tour, but she was keenly aware that some people enjoyed playing the instigator. She hadn't wanted Camryn's words to affect her, but they had, and now she needed some time alone to think.

"Yes, just fine. I've been a little busy today. I really am happy for you." Kara forced another smile, but she had locked herself behind her professional mask.

"Yeah well, I'll let you get back to work then," Sierra said, defeat evident in her tone. "Can I come see you at the end of the day? I'd like to talk to you about some things."

Those golden eyes blazed with hope and Kara couldn't bring herself to deny the woman her request. "Of course."

"Okay. Great. See you soon." Pressing her lips into a thin smile, Sierra dropped her head and walked away.

"Shit," Kara mumbled.

The part of her reserved for hiding in work had reared its head, threatening to send her back into hibernation. She didn't want drama. She didn't want to worry that Sierra would run to her ex every time they had a disagreement. She wanted to return to the comfort of a routine and the safety of knowing what came next.

Or did she?

The other part of her was screaming to take a chance, to remember how she felt that day with Sierra. The war within had begun again and she was running out of time to figure it out.

CHAPTER SEVENTEEN

"That sucked. What the hell? I swear I'm going to kick Camryn's ass," Sierra seethed as she marched back to the finish line. She had no idea what the woman had said to Kara, but there had been a distinct shift in mood from when they had last spoken and she was determined to get to the bottom of it all.

Camryn had no sooner cleared the finish area than Sierra was in her face growling, "What did you say?"

"Just the truth." She shrugged and brushed past.

"What truth was that?"

"Oh, you know the one where you fucked your ex, because you were mad at Kara."

"What the fuck, Cam!" Sierra roared, her hands flailing in anger. "I thought you were trying to help me. You wanted my head in the game."

With her usual cocky smirk, she replied, "I did help you. You raced. Now it's all fair game. If you thought she'd never hear about it, you were kidding yourself. Think of it as my gift to you."

"Your gift? Your gift to me?" Sierra huffed as she paced back and forth attempting to curb her burgeoning outrage.

"Yeah, my gift. If she still wants to date your sorry ass, then she gets what she deserves. Gotta say though, if she decides she's not interested, I may make a play for her myself."

Though Camryn had only been seen dating men did nothing to thwart the jealous rage from permeating Sierra's mind. As she lunged forward, she was stopped in her tracks by Ronni darting between them. With a hand on either shoulder, her lanky body gave her the much needed leverage against a very stubborn, very determined Sierra as Ronni pushed her back to a safe distance.

"You don't want to do that, Wiley. She's just pushing your buttons. Don't do anything that will cost you next year."

"Yeah Sierra, listen to your friend. I can't believe you're allowed to walk free with a temper like that. You're an unstable woman."

"Can it, bitch," Ronni bit back. "You still didn't beat her." She pointed to the board that had them tied at second.

Camryn snarled as she walked away, leaving Ronni with her hands full. Blake rushed over to help, adding his two cents. They were both in Sierra's corner, but desperate to make her understand the severity of losing her shit at an event.

They were right. She had let Camryn get under her skin in the worst possible way and her hot head had won out. That same mentality had cost her races in the past. It was one lesson she seemed doomed to never learn, but there was still time. She would try harder. She would do better. She would make it her life's work to achieve her goals so she could revel in Camryn's bitterness as she walked off with the trophy and the girl.

Yes, she would have it all.

Her will renewed, Sierra resigned herself to the fact that the best way to get back at her rival was to kick her ass on the course. She took a deep breath as she continued pacing back and forth, her steps growing slower until she came to a full stop and looked up at Ronni and Blake.

In a comforting tone, Ronni said, "Kara will be fine, Sierra. Talk to her. Tell her you're a dumbass, but you'll do better. Remember, you guys are going to start over. No secrets, right?"

"Right. Right. You're right. No secrets. I'm going to get cleaned up and then go back over. I'll explain myself, apologize, and then ask her on a proper date, if she'll still have me." Sierra relaxed. Her anger had passed and she reached deep to find the strength to grovel.

"She will, Sierra. She will. No one can resist your charms," Ronni wrapped her into a bear hug.

"Ron's right, Sierra. You got this," Blake confirmed with a nod and a pat on the back.

"Thanks guys." Sierra exhaled hard, expunging the last of her vengeful thoughts. "I am a dumbass, aren't I?" She laughed.

"Yes, but you're my best dumbass," Ronni teased, but then fell serious. "Sierra, you're one of the most amazing people I've ever known. No one tries harder to do right, even though you get a little mixed up sometimes. You've got a heart the size of Alaska, the stubbornness of a mountain goat, and the loyalty of a puppy. I don't know if she's your 'one' or not, but whoever ends up being your match, will be the luckiest woman on the planet."

Tears pricked at the corners of Sierra's eyes. She and Ronni were like family—better than family—but hearing such kind words struck her deep. She wasn't prepared for such a profound compliment. No one besides her dad had ever said such wonderful things to her before.

"Don't get soft on me now, Wiley," Ronni choked out as her own tears threatened to fall.

"Thank you. You're the best, Ron." Sierra pulled her friend into a fierce embrace. "I'd be lost without you."

"I know."

They shared a laugh before parting. Ronni gave her a slap on the ass and cheered her on, "You got this, Wiley."

"Yeah, you do," Blake added with equal enthusiasm.

Capturing Kara's heart was her goal and if there was one thing Sierra Cody did well, it was achieving her goals.

***

As the last rider crossed the finish line, Sierra celebrated her second-place finish, even if she did end up sharing the honor with Camryn. The mood on the podium was tense, but being the professionals they were, each had plastered on smiles as they shook hands and performed the required photos for fans and sponsors.

Finished with all the pomp and circumstance, Sierra once again traversed the path to the med center, but with far less enthusiasm than her last trip. She was steeled with determination to do whatever it took to get Kara to give her one date. To say her nerves were on edge was being kind. It had been ages since she had asked someone out. Flirting to hook up was an entirely different game. And to make matters even more agonizing, she really, really liked Kara. She had searched her memory for anyone who had ever made her stomach flutter the way people described in love stories and she had come up with only one name—Dr. Kara Davies.

Her experiences so far proved that Kara could run hot or cold with her, despite admitting to feeling the spark between them. Would her lapse in judgement send Kara back into the frozen tundra or would she get to enjoy a spring thaw, allowing them to see if their relationship could grow?

Time to find out.

It wouldn't be the end of the world if she turned me down, would it?

No, it wouldn't be the end of the world, but good lord, it sure felt as if the days would mean nothing without Kara by her side. She barely knew the woman, yet Kara had already managed to burrow into her heart. Insanity was the most likely explanation, but she was no stranger to that label. A person had to be some kind of crazy to throw themselves down a mountain on two wheels.

Taking a deep breath, she opened the door and scanned the room. It was empty. Her breath hitched as her heart hit the floor. Had Kara bailed without even giving her the chance to explain? The thought pissed her off. She didn't seem like the kind who'd go back on her word.

Swallowing hard, she croaked out, "Kara," and said a silent prayer to receive a reply.

"Sierra, hello. I'm in the back."

Sweet relief! The universe had smiled upon her this day. It was a good sign and all the dread that had filled her seconds ago, fell away. A smile that none could rival made a home upon her face as she strode to the back of the building where she found Kara alone packing supplies.

"Anything I can help with?"

Kara met her eyes and then drifted off. A long moment passed in comfortable silence before Kara abruptly burst out in a boisterous laugh. Immediately, she hid her face behind her hands and blushed redder than a fire engine. "Sorry."

"It's okay. What's so funny?"

Shaking her head, Kara replied, "Nothing really..."

Sierra tilted her head, questioning the unprompted outburst. "Come on, Kara," she said with a pout.

Unable to stop grinning, Kara rolled her eyes and explained, "I just caught myself geeking out during my own internal monologue." A muffled chuckle escaped. "I'm such a dork." Both hands covered her face once again as she struggled to hide her mortification at admitting the truth.

In that moment, Sierra fell a little more for the woman. Socially awkward and unknowingly beautiful—a combination unlike anyone else Sierra had ever met. She couldn't wait to learn more about her. "I'm glad you're so chipper this evening."

Snorting the last of her laughter, Kara said, "It's been a long, weird day."

Another comfortable pause filled the air until Kara turned and resumed packing. Sierra helped by handing over items, which Kara fit in a precise order into the boxes. She was meticulous and possibly a touch obsessive compulsive over the way the items were arranged, but to Sierra, it only made her even more endearing.

After sharing a few smiles and packing the last of the supplies, Sierra cleared her throat, deciding to jump in head first. "Um...I know Camryn told you some things that—"

Kara waved her off and shook her head, continuing to fiddle around inside the box. "It doesn't matter, Sierra. You don't owe me an explanation of anything that happened. We aren't together." Her eyes cast down, turning her focus to sealing the box shut.

Unsure of what to think about the comment, Sierra stood in quiet contemplation. On the one hand, she wanted to have everything out in the open. On the other, what was the point? She had no good reason and Camryn had already said all that needed to be said.

"In that case, I'd really..." Sierra hesitated, wanting Kara's full attention when she made her request. She didn't want there to be any questions or misunderstandings regarding her intentions. "Kara, could you please stop and look at me for a second?"

Kara paused. A hesitant breath passed before she placed the packing tape down with care and looked up into Sierra's soulful eyes. "Yes, Sierra, you were saying?"

A hint of nervousness tinged Kara's voice, kicking Sierra into action before any doubts could arise. She skirted around the table and captured Kara's hands in her own. Warm green eyes that made her soul float on a cloud followed her every move.

Sierra smiled like every bit the smitten fool she was as she said, "I know we've not had the most auspicious start, and this may sound like a line, but it's the truth—no one has ever made me feel the way I feel when I'm with you. Like anything and everything is possible." She swallowed hard and dug deep for the strength to continue, despite the apprehension etched on Kara's face. "I—I would love to take you out, you know...on a real date. What do you say?" Her eyes glistened with emotion as she waited for a response.

Holding her gaze, Kara's expression took a turn toward serious as she said, "Sierra, I think you know I like you."

Sierra's heart stilled, barely beating enough to stay conscious. She knew what was next, the dreaded "but," and she couldn't bear to hear the word. The single syllable that could hold pleasure or pain, in her case, would be a dagger through the chest. Her knees wobbled and she steadied herself with a hand on the edge of the table.

"I want you to know I'm only interested in a committed relationship and I need to know that you're ready for something more than sex, because as much as I want to be with you, I don't think I could stand it if you were only looking for a fling."

Long seconds ticked by. Sierra quietly analyzed Kara's response before she registered that there had been no "but" in the reply. Kara had not turned her down. Quite the opposite. She had asked for a chance at something real and lasting. For the first time since her freshman year in high school, Sierra dreamed of that happily-ever-after romance. She longed for better than the one night stands and brief relationships of the last few years.

The long silence set Kara on edge and she began to recoil. Sensing the change in mood, Sierra lunged forward and swept her into her arms, her voice cracking as she said, "I do want more, Kara. With you, I do."

The hurt that had been emanating from Kara melted away in Sierra's embrace. Her smile returned, wide and bright and lethal enough to stop Sierra's heart on the spot. With all the trauma the fragile organ had been dealt over the last few days, Sierra wondered how she had managed to survive. She also realized that even though she had been overwhelmed by Kara's words, there had been no direct answer to her question. She had to hear the word "yes."

"So, will you go out with me?" Sierra didn't loosen her hold.

Kara tried to rein in her laugh, but failed as she nodded and replied, "Yes, Sierra. Yes, I will."

Giving Kara a peck on the cheek, Sierra confirmed, "Tuesday night, then?"

"It's a date."

With her heart aflutter, Sierra skipped out of the med clinic, excitement coursing through her veins at the possibilities Tuesday held. Her pace picked up until it was nearly a full sprint. She couldn't wait to tell Ronni.

CHAPTER EIGHTEEN

The wonderful aroma of bacon wafted into her room and woke Ronni from her slumber. "I've got to be dreaming," she mumbled, rubbing the haze from her eyes. "Nobody ever cooks around here." Dragging herself from bed, she stumbled into the kitchen and her blue eyes widened in surprise. "Who are you and what did you do with my best friend?" Ronni shouted at the dark-haired woman in baggy shorts and a tank top who looked suspiciously like Sierra.

Sierra turned and laughed. "Easy there, Ron, it's just me." Seeing the stunned look on her friend's face, she shrugged. "What? I can't make us some breakfast?"

"Umm...No, because you can't cook. Duh," Ronni stated as if it were the most obvious answer ever. She perched upon the bar stool at the island and dragged her hands down her face.

"Come on now. It can't be that bad. It's only eggs and bacon." Sierra's good spirits went undeterred.

"Oh, trust me, it can," Ronni groaned. She propped her head up on her hands as she leaned on the counter top and assessed the situation. "So, uh...what's with the presto change-o?"

"What? I feel like I need to make some changes. Be more responsible, um..."

"Grow up?" Ron butted in, arching an eyebrow in challenge.

Sierra frowned as she put the finishing touches on their meal. "Okay, sure. It's just that I have that meeting later this week for my contract and a date with Kara Tuesday. I finally feel like I have some direction, something to strive for, ya know? Well, besides riding like hell and trying to become a World Cup champ. But there's more to life than that, right?"

"Yes, there is. Although, that's pretty awesome in itself."

They both agreed with a high five and a laugh.

"That's great, Sierra. I only want the best for you."

"I know." Sierra smiled and set a neatly organized plate of scrambled eggs with cheddar cheese, bacon, and wheat toast in front of her friend.

Ronni examined the contents of the plate. The expression on her face said she was impressed with the display, but not sold on the taste as she pushed the eggs around with a fork. "I'm not sure how I feel about the

Doc, but so far, she's been good for you. She better not screw you over again though," Ronni stated casually as she lifted a forkful to her nose. After taking a sniff, she placed the eggs into her mouth with caution.

"Don't worry about it, we'll be fine, but thanks for looking out for me." Sierra looked on in amusement as Ronni's eyebrows rose and her lips turned up into a grin that approved of her culinary talent.

"Wow! This actually tastes like food. Like yummy food. Why have you never cooked liked this before? Last time was an abomination to food everywhere. Can you make pancakes?"

"Gee thanks." Sierra chuckled. "And I can. I think. It's been years since I tried and the last time I was seriously hung over." She took a bite and hummed. She even impressed herself.

Devouring her food, Ronni glanced up between bites and asked, "So, where are you taking little Doc McHottie on your big date?"

The thought of starting her journey with Kara brought a giant smile to Sierra's face. "I don't know yet, but she mentioned she enjoyed the outdoors, so maybe that and then dinner."

Straight faced, Ronni quipped, "Somewhere you won't get caught having sex?"

"Ronni!" Sierra was appalled at the comment, yet excited about the prospect. It wasn't as if she hadn't thought about how sex with Kara would feel—because she had, a thousand times since first laying eyes on the woman—but she was determined to take things slow this time.

"What? Am I wrong?" With hands on her hips, Ronni dared Sierra to challenge her.

"Why do you always think I'm going to have sex right away?" She was half-offended, but knew damn well it was a reasonable assumption. That had always been her M.O.

"Ummm, because I've known you since high school. Ever since jackass Jen broke your heart freshman year, sex has been your go to. And even if you did kind of try with Harley, you were never in it to win it with her."

"Yeah well, not anymore." Sierra cleared the plates from the island. "Yes, I want her...badly, but I want more than a quick roll in the hay this time. I feel different when I'm around her. I want to be a better person." She paused at the sink as her thoughts drifted.

"Gag! Man, are you going to get all rom-com on me now? I can't have you going soft. It's not good for my rep."

Sierra returned to the here and now with a smile as she turned on the water and lathered up the sponge. Her eyes sparkled as she stepped across and wrapped Ronni into a soapy-handed hug. "I will do my best not to embarrass you, but I didn't hear you complaining about my breakfast, so maybe it's a good thing."

"We'll see." Ronni returned the embrace and then flinched as Sierra's soapy hands seeped through her shirt. "I love you, but you're soiling my designer sleep attire."

Sierra pulled back with a laugh. "Wouldn't want to ruin your boy shorts and ratty old Milli Vanilli concert tee."

"Hey! It's not old. It's vintage."

"Whatever you say, Ron."

"You need an education in style."

"And you need to throw that thing out and do some laundry. You only wear it when you're scraping the bottom of the drawers." Sierra smirked.

"Yeah well..." Ronni got up and grumbled under her breath as she trudged back to her room.

"I'm going to go for a ride. You want to join me?"

"Nah. I got stuff to do. Catch you later, Cody."

Sierra washed the plates and set them out to dry. The task was so normal and domestic and not at all as horrifying as she had thought it would be. Take out was still her food of choice, but maybe she could get used to this kind of thing, especially if she were doing it with Kara.

***

Ronni waited until Sierra had gone before getting dressed and heading out. When she was on a mission, she wasn't one to dilly-dally. She pulled up to the building, slipped a young man named Billy a twenty, and made like a stealth bomber through the halls to her destination. She had it on good authority from Billy, whom she had met while testing games, that the doctor liked to work on Sunday—every day actually—and she was not known to do much socializing after hours.

This knowledge reaffirmed Ronni's belief that Kara, despite her display with the motorcycle, was still too stiff and boring for her liking. But she wasn't the one fawning over her, so she was going to fulfill her best friend duty— the one she had solemnly sworn to perform after the "Jen debacle" in high school that left a lovesick Sierra a broken-hearted shadow of herself. Never again. Not on her watch.

When she reached Kara's office door, a quick jimmy with her credit card got her inside. It may have been a high-tech research lab, but they still had old school locks. A six-year-old could pick them. Flipping on the lights, she took a lap around the sterile office space, pausing to peruse the book case full of various kinesiology and anatomy books before turning the lights off again and settling into Kara's large leather office chair.

"So comfy," she muttered into the dark space as she leaned back and kicked her feet up on the desk. Now all she had to do was wait.

A half an hour later, Kara opened the door to her office and flipped the lights on. When her eyes met Ronni's, she jumped back against the door startled, fumbling to hold onto her stack of files before they scattered across the floor. "Geeze, Ronni! Again? Shit! You have to stop doing this." She set the files on top of her bookcase and blew out a heavy breath.

"What's shakin', Doc?" Ronni wanted to laugh, but she was here for serious reasons.

"Now what? I did as you asked. Sierra and I are good now. Thank you for arranging the meeting." Kara folded her arms across her chest and cast her a stern glance.

"First, you're welcome. Second, you did good. She's happy as a clam now, whatever that saying means."

"It refers to a clam at high tide," Kara began spouting the factoid as if it were spit straight out of a computer. "The saying originated in the eighteen hundred's. That's when they're safest from predators and their shell opens. It appears as if they're smiling."

This time Ronni did laugh. Sierra was seriously crushing on a hard-core geek. "Yeah well, it's annoying," she stated. "But thanks for that. Might help me win a bet one day." She rolled her eyes, dropped her feet and pushed up from the chair. With her game face back in place, she moved to within three feet of the doctor and stopped, matching Kara's defensive posture by folding her own arms across her chest. "You didn't let me finish."

"By all means, please finish." Kara gestured with her hand that Ronni had the floor.

Ronni got a kick out of Kara's sarcastic tone. The doctor had spunk. If she would lighten up, and not break Sierra's heart, there was a possibility they could be friends. "Why thank you. Third," she announced, "I hope you meant what you said to Sierra, because she has got it bad for you and I don't want to see her get hurt. This is new for her." Ronni eyed the emotionless doctor.

"Yeah well, it's new for me too," Kara muttered under her breath. Grabbing her files, she pushed her way past Ronni and set them on her desk.

Ronni had heard the confession, but held back a comment. The statement made her realize she was dealing with a woman who, despite her intelligence, looks, and professional façade, was every bit as clueless about relationships as her best friend. Why was she surprised? Kara's last relationship was a flop. Being a cold bitch and being cold because you're emotionally closed off were two different things. Kara was a tough read. She had traits of both, but had a warmth about her that made it seem as though she could thaw if she found the right person.

Was that person Sierra? Time would tell.

She considered going easy on Kara, but wanted her point made. Sierra wasn't just some personal research project to complete while the temperamental doctor decided whether or not she wanted to join the human race. "I wanted to say that I support Sierra in her quest to finally try a real relationship and if you make her happy, then so be it."

"But..." Kara broke in with an icy stare, her patience clearly wearing thin.

"But...if you hurt my best friend...Let's just say you'll regret it. So don't, okay?" She delivered her best and brightest fake smile.

"Fine." Kara forced a fake smile in return. "If you're finished, I have work to do. Also, I would appreciate it if you could please try to refrain from breaking into my office in the future."

"No promises there, Doc. Think I'm gonna go hit up that sweet gaming room of yours again. Want to go kill some zombies?"

"No, thank you. I wouldn't want to piss you off by kicking your ass." Kara stared her down.

Ronni could almost make out the edge of a smirk, though Kara had maintained a stone-cold expression the entire time. A little surprised by the comment, and enjoying the return of the spunk from the motorcycle ride, Ronni's blue eyes twinkled. "Hmmm...sounds like there is a challenge in there someday soon, Doc."

Ronni winked and skipped out. That was one challenge she hoped would come to fruition. If Kara wanted to take her on in a video game, she would wipe the floor with her.

CHAPTER NINETEEN

Nervous. Terrified. Uncertain if she was ready to open herself up. Those were the thoughts running through the usually calm and collected Dr. Kara Davies' highly intelligent mind as she prepared for her first date with the beautiful, infectious woman known as Sierra Cody. Could Kara avoid the same problems she'd had with Jamie? Was she long term material? Would Ronni end up kicking her ass? Worse yet, would Sierra fall back into bed with her ex?

They both had their share of relationship missteps to work through. Only time would tell if this was indeed the relationship that would inspire them to grow as people. Kara admitted to feeling different with Sierra. Something about the woman invited her to talk, feel, and touch like never before, but would it be enough? Would she be able to curb her obsession with work enough to make a relationship work?

If working extra hours yesterday to take off early for their date today was any indication, then yes. She had never done that for anyone. Maybe it was only their first date, but it was a good step in the right direction. But would the changes she was now willing to make last? Would she be able to communicate her feelings regularly and not just when she was playing a character, like she did with her motorcycle?

Kara shook her head, still unable to believe her performance that day. She didn't even know she had it in her. Hopefully, Sierra wasn't more interested in that woman, because that would only end in disappointment.

Sierra is beautiful, kind, talented, and obviously head over heels for me. Why am I so scared? It's only a date. This is a good thing.

With their date two hours away, Kara was finally able to calm herself. She was filled with a gentle humming, feeling like the girl who just got asked out by the most popular kid in school.

***

At precisely two in the afternoon, Sierra pulled her rebuilt Barracuda into an empty space at Kara's apartment complex. She turned off the ignition and closed her eyes. This was it. She was going on a date with Kara. The last time she was this nervous was her first downhill race. Sweaty palms. Heart thumping in her throat. Short, shallow breaths that left her dizzy.

"You can do this, Cody," Sierra coached herself. "This is what you wanted, remember? She likes you, so just act natural." The pep talk did its job. Sierra was out of the car and knocking on Kara's door before she had the chance think twice.

She was greeted by a warm smile. Kara looked extra adorable in her nicely-fitted navy blue Columbia pants with matching button down and a pair of hiking boots. Her aviator sunglasses hung from the buttons between her breasts. Even for an outdoor trip, Dr. Kara Davies was put together.

A lopsided grin rolled up as Sierra took in the sight of her date, beautiful as always. "Hi," she uttered with awe and smiled wider when a light pink touched Kara's cheeks.

"Hi."

Kara's gaze made a quick trek down the length of Sierra's body. Her visual journey was slow, appreciative, and Sierra enjoyed every second, even giving a slight flex to her biceps as the path traveled up her arms.

Seductive green eyes met Sierra's once again. An aura of desire surrounded Kara, though she was as controlled as ever. "I'm just about ready. Why don't you come in for a second while I grab the rest of my things?"

She stepped back, allowing Sierra to pass. "I'm going to grab my bag and water bottle. Do you need water? I can bring an extra bottle."

"Sure, thanks. This is a nice apartment, considering its lab housing." Sierra hadn't seen the place in daylight and was impressed by the modern style.

"I was surprised too, but they take good care of their employees and research participants." Kara filled a bottle with water and grabbed her bag. "So, where are you taking me?" She strode back toward Sierra. "I know we agreed on something outdoorsy or adventurous, but you've been keeping it a secret, so I packed for variety." Kara smiled wide as she came to a stop and awaited the details.

"Well..." Sierra paused, getting lost in the pair of eyes staring intently at her. Their interaction was easy, warm, like a fine summer's day. The nerves she had been battling tooth and nail finally conceded, giving way to the easy confidence she usually enjoyed.

"I figured we could ride out to the Crater Lake area, take a little hike, and then, if you're up to it, a friend of mine owns the zip line there. We could take it back down. I don't know if you're into that kind of thing, but I've never tried it. He keeps asking me to go. But if that's not your cup of tea, we can just finish the hike. Either way, we can have dinner after. How's that sound?"

Sierra hoped her plan was agreeable. She had agonized over the decision.

"Wow." Kara's eyes widened, as did her smile. "That sounds great. I've never ziplined either. How about we decide when we get there?" Kara proposed, taking Sierra's hand in her own as they exited her apartment.

"Sounds like a plan," Sierra said, staring down at their joined hands. Her belly fluttered, yet she felt warm and full as if she had gorged on her favorite meal.

Kara's stride came to a halt and her face fell to one of awe as she stared at Sierra's meticulously detailed Barracuda. "That's beautiful, Sierra. Did you restore her yourself?"

"Yeah, with some help. I always wanted one like this. My dad found this baby in some pretty sad shape and bought her for my twenty-first birthday."

Making her way slowly around the car, Kara's fingers glided baby soft along the paint, appreciating the craftsmanship. Sierra was impressed with the care in her touch. That Kara was equally as excited by her classic muscle car only added fuel to the fire. Could the woman be any more perfect for her?

"Well, it looks great. It suits you too—powerful and beautiful," Kara gushed.

"Why Doctor, are you flirting with me?" Sierra smirked as Kara scrambled to come up with a response.

Kara stiffened, but held her smile. "I do believe a car is an extension of a person's personality and I was simply acknowledging as much," she rambled to Sierra's delight. The woman was the picture of poise in her professional surroundings and Sierra enjoyed that confidence, but found her social awkwardness simply adorable.

"Relax, Kara, I was joking. And thank you, I happen to agree with you." Sierra opened the passenger door, allowing Kara to take her seat. "And for the record, I don't mind a little flirting," she added with a wink as she closed the door and walked around to the driver's side, trying to ignore the pair of eyes following her every move.

They veered onto the main highway and headed south toward Crater Lake. Hardened lava formations speckled the landscape and Kara took it all in. "I don't get out as much as I would like and the weather has been so nice. I'm glad we're doing this." She glanced at Sierra.

"Me too. I'm glad you took the afternoon off. Now we have plenty of daylight to enjoy this," Sierra agreed.

"I don't take much time off." Regret weighed on her words. Kara returned to her view out the side window.

"That makes me feel special." That wasn't just a line. It was the truth.

"Not just anyone can get me to drop work and go play outside."

Sierra pulled her eyes from the road and looked at Kara, who had turned to smile back at her. The sun's rays danced along auburn strands and illuminated her profile, making her radiant as an angel from heaven.

No other woman had ever felt so right.

Ninety minutes later, they arrived at the trailhead. The drive time had been well spent with idle chit-chat about Kara's work, Sierra's racing roots, and facts about the area. Since Sierra was a Bend native and Kara was from the rainy coast, there was quite the difference in terrain and weather, which the intellectual in Kara found intriguing. Of course, Sierra loved every second of teaching her something new and made a note to look up some trivia. Next time, she would have some impressive facts to wow Kara with.

CHAPTER TWENTY

The trail wasn't particularly challenging, allowing Kara time to do what she did best—think. She thought about work, the wonders of nature, and of course, Sierra. Her powerful command of presence as she strode along the trail was enviable...and arousing. Every now and then, Kara risked a peek at Sierra's face highlighted by rays of sun, her amazingly toned backside accentuated by form-fitting cargo pants, or her ample breasts that refused to be concealed by her short-sleeved button down. Of the three, the breasts were her favorite. She couldn't help herself. They were perfect.

Then her thoughts drifted to how Jamie had always felt the need to fill the air with continuous, mindless chatter. Rarely was there a moment of silence between them, which had always kept Kara on edge. She glanced at her watch. Twenty minutes had passed since she and Sierra had begun their hike and there had been fewer than a dozen words exchanged. The silence was comfortable and welcomed, neither feeling the need to overwhelm nature's presence with their own. What a novel idea.

Reaching a narrowed section of the trail, Sierra glanced over her shoulder with an easy smile, which Kara returned. "Watch your step. It's a little loose here."

Kara nodded and exercised caution as she navigated the path. She noted how simple it was to be with Sierra. They had so much to learn about one another, yet it felt as if she had known her forever. A few more dates and they would be finishing one another's sentences. If she had doubted their connection before, she could no longer. There was truly something special about the woman in front of her and she was determined to give this chance at a relationship her best effort.

Reaching the zipline peak, they had a lengthy discussion with Sierra's friend, Jordan, who assured them it was both safe and a thrill like none other. The view was amazing and they both liked the idea of sharing a new experience on their first date. Kara's growling stomach demanded they eat their snack beforehand, so they took a seat at the picnic table overlooking a lake and broke open the bag of trail mix.

"This view is amazing," Kara said in awe.

"It is. You should see it from a helicopter. And Crater Lake...it's so blue."

"You've done that?"

"Mhm," Sierra mumbled and nodded with her mouth full. She swallowed and took a quick sip of water, then added, "Ronni dated a helicopter pilot for a while. It was a cool experience."

"I bet. I'll have to do that sometime." The sudden realization of all she had been missing out on struck Kara like a frisbee between the eyes. She was young and healthy and lived in one of the most breathtakingly beautiful states. Why was she hiding at work all the time? And when did she become such a wallflower?

Finished with her snack, Kara brushed off her hands and jumped to her feet, determined to tackle the zipline course. She was going to start living again.

Sierra stood and stretched before turning to face her. "You ready?"

Her voice shook with a hint of nervousness that Kara found endearing. "Yup. You?"

"Of course." Her smile lacked its usual cockiness.

Kara bent down to grab her pack, nearly smacking her head with Sierra, who'd had the same idea. Their faces a mere two inches apart, Kara looked up into golden eyes that burned with desire. A rush of want flooded her body and clouded her mind. When Sierra's gaze flicked to her mouth, she unconsciously moistened her lips in response. Rapid fire images bombarded Kara's brain. Scenes from her many fantasies of the woman whose breath now danced across her cheeks flashed through her mind.

If she just leaned in...

Sierra was the one to break their trance. "We umm...should hit the zipline so we can get back to the car before it gets dark." Her voice was raspy, distant, speaking volumes of her own journey from fantasy land.

"Mhm. Sure, yeah," Kara snapped out of her daze. Sierra's cocky grin said all she needed to know. *Busted.*

Coming back to her senses, a different kind of excitement coursed through her veins. "Let's do this!"

Sierra's laugh was hearty and unmistakably happy. She picked up the pack and handed it over.

"Thank you," Kara said. She slipped her hand comfortably into Sierra's as if they had been doing it for years. It was time to embark on their first new adventure together.

Kara volunteered to go first. Jordan strapped her in and away she went. Her eyes popped wide and her heart jumped into her throat as she dropped off the ledge. Soaring high above the ground, Kara settled in and began scanning the land below for wildlife while enjoying the freedom of simulated flight.

With a quick glance over her shoulder, she caught sight of Sierra still clinging to the platform for dear life. For all her bravado on a bike, Sierra was having second thoughts about sliding down a steel cable in a nylon harness, but there was no way she would back out now. Kara laughed as the squeal of fear reached her ears from

Sierra's take off. The woman was so confident that it was hard to imagine her being afraid of anything.

Despite Sierra's uneasiness at the start, they laughed and teased at every one of the ten stops and when they reached the end of the course, Kara was waiting for Sierra with a knowing smirk.

"What?" Sierra asked, pretending as if she had been cool as a cucumber the entire time.

"Oh, nothing." Kara snickered.

Sierra shot her a look.

"Really, it's nothing. I think you're adorable when you're scared." Kara stepped closer and ran her hands down Sierra's arms in a comforting gesture.

"I wasn't scared. It just caught me off guard." Sierra stood taller, as if it would make her lie a truth.

"Okay," was Kara's response, but she knew better.

Sierra relaxed. A deep laugh rolled out as she took Kara's hand in hers and headed toward the trail head. They took turns recounting their favorite parts of the afternoon. Kara loved the fast descents and wildlife. Sierra, the rappelling and when she was safely on the ground, which gave them both a laugh.

When they reached the car, Sierra counted off their dinner options. "Since I didn't know what you liked to eat, I picked three places for you to choose from—Mexican, Italian, or burgers and wings. What do you feel like?"

Kara tipped her head to the sky in deep thought. "Hmm, what do I feel like?" she pondered aloud, tapping her finger on her chin. "As a matter of fact, I have been craving something."

Sierra smiled at the playfulness in Kara's tone. "Oh yeah? What's that?" she asked as she turned to open the passenger door.

Kara took the opportunity to sneak in behind and when Sierra turned back around, they were face to face. Kara sucked her bottom lip between her teeth, her sparkling green eyes silently debating her next move as each appreciated the soft features before them up close. The debate ended in a decisive grabbing of Sierra's shirt as Kara pulled her in close and stopped millimeters away from her lips.

For a split second, Kara couldn't believe how very "un-Kara-like" she was behaving. She wasn't known for her spontaneity, but Sierra had that effect on her. Her newfound impulsiveness might scare the shit out of her, but she was enjoying it. Nicole would have been saying "I told you so" right about now.

Kara's eyes fell shut as she reveled in the shiver that shook Sierra's body. To render such a response from the beautiful, confident woman made her dizzy with power. She knew what she wanted and this time there was nothing in her way.

Agonizingly close, that's what Sierra thought as the temptation to lunge forward and meet the object of her desire was overwhelmed by the exhilarating anticipation of soft, pink lips meeting her own. Kara's warm breath tickled her skin and the light brush of her nose teased of what was to come. Her body hummed, but a searing cold stabbed at her chest. The fear of Kara pulling away like their first almost-kiss paralyzed her. A quick prayer was sent to the heavens. She wanted this—the kiss, Kara...all of it. Her heart wouldn't survive a second rejection. Not after the amazing day they had shared.

Warm lips brushed lightly against her own in a swift reply to her plea. She trembled under the possessive hold of Kara's hands as they gripped her hips and pulled them breast to breast, before gently melding their mouths together. Her knees buckled under the power of the kiss and she wrapped her arms tight around Kara's waist to steady herself.

Fingers flitted through Sierra's dark hair, holding her head in place. To her surprise, the pace remained slow and innocent, savoring their first kiss which held steady at a gentle waltzing of tongues before Kara eased away.

Breathless and gazing into Sierra's eyes, Kara whispered, "Mexican food," before breaking out a sexy, devilish grin.

Sierra's head fell back and her body flushed as she broke into a shy smile. Kara had not only made her blush like crazy, but that kiss had melted her insides like chocolate over a flame. With her eyes alight, Sierra mused, "So, you're a dessert first kind of gal?"

"I guess I was actually craving two things." Kara chuckled low and deep, still enjoying the warm, comfortable hold they had on one another. "Is that all right?" she asked.

There was a hint of concern in Kara's voice that Sierra was quick to dispel. "It was more than all right. It was amazing. Anytime you have a craving, you feel free to fulfill it," she granted her permission with a flirty smile.

Rolling her eyes, Kara's usual self-consciousness made a return visit and she got into the car. "So, uh, about that Mexican food..."

Sierra shook her head, still shocked at the boldness of the typically reserved woman. Those moments were brief, but she loved being the one who got to experience them. What would life be like if Kara ever completely let go?

A surge of energy struck at the thought. Sierra had a feeling the surprises would be never ending should it ever happen and that would be fine by her.

"I don't think I'll ever be able to think of Mexican the same way," Sierra joked, closing the door for Kara. She trotted around to the driver's side and once seated, she risked another quick glance at the woman smiling beside her before they sped off to dinner.

CHAPTER TWENTY-ONE

Shutting her apartment door behind her, Kara leaned back against the wall and dropped her keys in the bowl. A goofy grin sprawled across her face as she took a deep breath. The date had been her most wonderful one ever. There had been no awkwardness between them or rehashing of earlier events, just the two of them getting to know one another and enjoying the feel of being together. And boy did she ever enjoy the feeling.

Not surprisingly, Sierra had been a total gentle woman, opening doors and escorting her to her apartment. Despite her sometimes-gruff demeanor, Sierra appeared to be the type that would dote on her woman, leaving no need unmet. At the front door, much to Kara's delight, they shared one more deep, longing, life-altering kiss. The taste of Sierra's lips still lingered on her own, sweeter and more addictive than she ever could have dreamed. She was hooked. No twelve-step program could ever free her from its hold. To her pleasure, reality had exceeded the fantasy—such a rare feat.

Over the course of the date, Kara had come to terms with the fact that being in Sierra's presence made her feel free and empowered. It was a bit unnerving since she was used to being calm and controlled, but the effortless way Sierra had about her made Kara feel as if anything were possible. She liked that feeling. Plus, Sierra had an infectious smile and enthusiasm that made Kara want to step out of her comfort zone, to be spontaneous, to challenge the woman's perception of her—an idea that normally made her queasy.

With so many foreign thoughts and emotions swirling through her brain, she flopped down on the sofa, tipped her head back, and stared at the ceiling. Releasing a deep breath, it was the first time in a long time she could truly say she was relaxed, and that only made her smile bigger. Instead of work and science being her overriding concern, her mind was peaceful, quiet. She felt happy.

Again, she could hear Nicole's voice in her ear whispering, "I told you so." Nicole was always trying to get her out of her shell, to "join the living and have some fun." To Kara though, every patient and every research project was a new puzzle and that was her fun. After tonight, however, she finally understood what her friend had been saying. While she may not always be so easy going, she could try harder. Perhaps she could view herself as a new puzzle to solve.

But then, that would be working and not playing.

A soft laugh fell out, filling the quiet room. Her body sank further into the sofa, her limbs grew heavy, and her mind relaxed as she slipped into a semi-conscious daze. Jamie had never made her feel this way. Honestly, no one ever had made her feel this way. From the first time she had laid eyes on Sierra, she was done. Love at first sight wasn't real, or so she had believed, but even if she had failed to realize it then, it was glaringly obvious to her overly logical mind now. She never had a choice in the matter. All she could do now was follow through and see how their journey played out.

I could also use some restful sleep, she thought as her eyelids slowly drifted shut. Spontaneity was exhausting.

***

On the drive home from Kara's apartment, Sierra was filled with an all-encompassing sense of joy. It settled in her chest and deep in her belly, making her giddy as a child at the county fair. Her mind replayed her favorite moments like a never ending SportsCenter highlight reel. She was certain her facial muscles were on the edge of exploding from the stretch of her toothy smile.

After that mind blowing first kiss, they seemed to fall right into a rhythm, natural and comfortable, as if there had never been a time they were apart. Sharing not-so-innocent touches at the table. Casting long, smoldering looks over the rim of their glasses. An unspoken challenge had been issued to see who could make the other blush more and, to that end, they had both eagerly exchanged flirtations. Being sexually confident herself, she was still shocked, yet aroused, by the fact that she had lost. Repeatedly. Seemed the reserved Dr. Kara Davies could exert quite the effect on her.

It was always the quiet ones.

If there was ever a competition to lose, however, she decided that had been the one. The way Kara's eyes had lit up, her lip curling into a deviously, satisfied smirk each time Sierra flushed red from the tips of her toes to the top of her head, was like a victory in itself. Finding a woman that could hold a flame to her powers of persuasion was hard. Finding one that could turn those same powers on her, she had believed, was impossible. Until now.

They were so different, yet so perfect together. The way their hands fit. How their bodies molded against one another like conjoined pieces of a completed puzzle. She could hardly fathom why such a beautiful, intelligent, funny woman would be interested in her—a rough around the edges, cocky, impetuous, extreme sports junkie. Kara was surprising and Sierra liked a woman who wasn't afraid of a little adventure. She also liked Kara letting go of the reins on her reserve while they were together, becoming more dominant and extroverted.

Sierra bit her lip as she wondered how that would translate in the bedroom. Kara's hands were agile and strong, having felt them during her adjustments. What could those tools of healing do in a recreational setting? *And she's definitely a skilled kisser.* A shiver of anticipation ran through her body, lighting her up like the time she stuck a knife in the toaster when she was eight. Only this time it was sheer pleasure.

Taking it slow would be a monumental challenge.

At the mercy of her memory—which held on to their goodnight kiss as if it were her last breath—Sierra was lost in the moment once again. So intense was their kiss, that even the recollection demanded the full attention of her senses. So much so, that she hadn't registered pulling into her own driveway or turning off the engine.

Their long embrace was as intimate and familiar as an old friend. Sensuous green eyes reflected the same want as her own. Sure hands glided lower than friendly, pulling their hips flush. Her own fingers traced warm, smooth skin and sifted through short, thick hair. The scent of almond and coconut surrounded Sierra as she indulged in the sweetness of Kara's lips once again. She had been dying for a second taste since the first unexpected, but lovely sampling, earlier in the day. Unlike food, however, her appetite only grew with each helping and she struggled to suppress her ravenous urges that begged to consume the woman in her arms.

Sierra asked for more, her tongue gently tracing Kara's kiss swollen lips. Entrance was granted quickly, eagerly, as velvety tongues slid together in a slow, passionate dance. The heat between them raged. An inferno of desire boiled beneath Sierra's skin, settling between her legs, sending her pulse sky high and her head spinning in the most wonderful of ways.

Even now, a long twenty minutes later, cool air had replaced Kara's comforting warmth, but the mere thought threatened to ignite the fire once again. It simmered at the apex of her thighs and reached high into her chest.

The feelings were new to Sierra. Intense. Crazy. Unrivaled. Unbelievable. Her hit 'em and quit 'em mantra had been left in ashes. She shook her head. Alone in the darkness of her car, her cheeks heated and a trail of goosebumps sprinted up her neck. Was she the only one so worked up?

No. She knew that for a fact. There was no hiding Kara's wanton desire. That had been evident in the force of her kiss, the pink on her cheeks, the desperation in her grip as she struggled to release her hold and walk inside her apartment. Neither had wanted the night to end.

How they had managed to keep their feverish passion contained would forever be a mystery, but Sierra found the slow build up a welcomed change from her usual quick hop in the sack. The oddest part, was how natural it felt—as if being with Kara was where she was always meant to be. She wasn't looking ahead to what she'd be doing tomorrow or where she might ride next. Her mind...her body...her heart...were one hundred percent consumed by Kara.

The woman has me wrapped already.

Surging with pent up energy, she wished it wasn't so late. A run was out of the question. A little workout in her room would have to suffice. Sierra skipped into the house to find Ronni watching her favorite mountain bike movie, *From the Inside Out*, and eating cereal. "Hey, Ron."

Ronni's head whipped around. The second her eyes landed on Sierra, her faced contorted as if a stranger had invaded her home. "Damn! Kara must have some wicked good lady bits for you to look like you're high...That is, unless you *are* high?" Her brow rose slowly, accusingly.

A disgusted frown erased her joyous smile. "No, I'm not high. You know me better than that. And for the record, there was no touching of bits, only lips." Sierra plopped down at the end of the sofa, returning to her happy daze as she imagined how incredible Kara's naked "bits" would feel against her own.

A pillow smacked her in the head, sending Kara's glorious fantasy "bits" back under the cover of clothing and ripping Sierra from her happy place. "Hey!" she hissed, her eyes darting to her best friend whose expression was a strange cross between appalled and amused.

"Gross! No fantasizing about that shit when you're sitting next to me." Ronni got up, set her bowl in the sink, then filled it with water to wash later. "I take it the date went well then?"

"Oh my god, Ronni!" Sierra gushed, quickly forgetting the pillow to the head. It was so easy to get wrapped up in all things Kara. She fell against the back of the couch and threw her arm over her head as a dreamy sigh escaped. "It was...it was amazing, is what it was. She is amazing. We had the best time and it's so easy being with her. I can't say that about anyone else I have ever been with before."

Sierra was beaming now and it didn't bother her in the least. "Kara is sexy and funny and..." she paused, searching for the right words. Her eyes flashed when they struck. "Quite surprising on many levels."

"Good. She better be good to you. I warned her."

"What?" Sierra bolted to her feet. "What did you do, Ronni?" Her scorching glare could melt steel.

"Nothing," Ronni brushed it off with a shrug. "I just gave her the talk. You know, the usual. Even Harley got it, which reminds me..." Ronni trailed off, offering no further details.

Sierra approached slowly, allowing her temper to cool as she contemplated her next words carefully. The last thing she needed was outside interference, even if the intentions had been pure. But she also understood her protective best friend.

"Ronni, while I love you and appreciate everything you do for me, please don't hassle Kara anymore, okay? She has her issues and I certainly have plenty of my own, so I'm sure we'll stumble, but..." A deep breath filled her lungs and a sense of peace surrounded her. Once again, her thoughts drifted to the woman with green eyes that soothed her soul like the ocean on a warm summer day. "I really, really like her, so please, please, please, don't scare her off. Can you do that for me?"

Ronni groaned her reluctance, but agreed. "Fine. But you say the word and..." She balled her right hand into a fist and punched it into her left palm with a smirk.

Sierra rolled her eyes and let out a breath. "Thank you. You are the bestest, best friend in the world." She wrapped Ronni into a vise-like bear hug and then dragged her by her hand back to the couch to sit.

"You love her," Ronni singsonged, drawing an evil, but amused look from Sierra.

Love.

The word had Sierra fidgeting in an instant. The last time she was in love, it had ended horribly. But Kara wasn't Jen. She knew that, yet the fear remained. She had kept her heart under lock and key ever since and she wouldn't give it away easily, even though the magnetic attraction between them was more intense than she had ever experienced. Their connection was special and that meant something, but love? That was a heavy proclamation not to be made after one date.

"It's too soon for that, but I definitely feel something. I can't explain it. It's...different...nice." The goofy grin returned. "We'll see."

"You know it's a real thing, love at first sight, right?" Ronni awaited a rebuttal, but received only a curious tilt of the head. "My Great Grammy Ida fell in love the moment she saw my Great PaPa Jim. They enjoyed fifty happy years together until he died. Trust me, you're in deep, Sierra, so I hope you're ready and I hope your little doctor is too."

Sierra sat quietly in deep thought. Kara's actions had spoken volumes about her intentions. If love was their destination, they would get there at their own pace. For once, Sierra didn't feel like racing.

A content smile hiked the corners of her mouth. She kicked her feet up and enjoyed the moment. No drama and no pressure. For the first time in her life, she felt...happy.

CHAPTER TWENTY-TWO

The work day had been less than productive and Kara had Sierra to blame. It wasn't that Sierra had repeatedly called or texted in a disruptive way. Quite the opposite. Sierra had sent one text that morning to say thank you for a wonderful evening and that she was looking forward their next date, which they had yet to fully plan. Not because either was hesitant, but because they had both been too stuck in their lust-filled stupor last night to manage much more than a "see you soon" as they finally managed to pry themselves apart.

Whatever it was about Sierra—her smile, those eyes, the confident aura she exuded, or the slightly masculine "take charge" manner—Kara had been lured in hook, line, and sinker. Even now, a full...she glanced at her watch...fourteen hours and thirty-six minutes removed from Sierra's presence, her heart still sped up and a smile crept its way onto her lips at the most unexpected moment. She wanted nothing more than to rush out and explore this unexplainable draw to Sierra, but there was work to be done.

Kara laughed. Since when had this ever been a problem for her? Suddenly, her chest tightened. This was precisely what she'd spent her life trying to avoid. She was quickly becoming "that woman." The one who would fall hard and lose herself in someone else, forgetting her own purpose and goals. She wouldn't allow that to be her. Even though she had already achieved most of her goals, she refused to become consumed by another person.

Another thing Dr. Kara Davies refused to be was clingy. That was a problem other women, like Jamie, had—wanting to be around her constantly. She had never understood it, never felt the intense desire to be in someone's presence all the time. That is, of course, until she met Sierra. It was exciting and infuriating and she knew she should run for the hills and bury herself in work. She felt safe there. In control. Her legs and her heart, however, refused to allow it, no matter what logic her mind presented.

The simple beeping of her cell phone, resembling a heartbeat monitor, broke through the rambling of her mind. The ringtone was enough to register an incoming call, but not obnoxious and irritating—especially when she was with a patient. Her whirling thoughts, caught in the shifting tides of the war between her desires and her fears, quieted upon the intrusion of her phone. Her mind calmed, her body filled with warmth, and she was once again surrounded by the pleasantly lingering undertone of all things *Sierra*.

"Well you sound extra perky today, Kara. Can I assume you've finally grown a pair and hooked up with that beautiful woman who's been dying to have you?"

"Just say it, Nicole." Kara sighed, but couldn't stop a slight smile from creeping onto her lips. Though she couldn't see Nicole's face, she was certain there was a feigned look of "who me?" all over it.

"I don't know what you mean, Kara."

"I can hear you smiling, Nicole."

"All right. All right. I told you so." She laughed with satisfaction. "And while we're at it, you're a highly intelligent woman, Kara. Why do I always have to point these things out to you?"

"That's why we've been such good friends and partners. My strengths are your weaknesses and vice versa. We balance each other out. Thank you for that." Kara spoke with sincerity. Nicole had always had her best interests at heart.

"Well...this is a historical moment. The ever-stoic Doctor Kara Davies has gone sappy on me. First you fall in love, next you recite Hallmark cards. I may have created a monster."

"Stop it, please. I am not in love with Sierra and we didn't hook up, but we did enjoy a nice date," Kara defended.

"Whatever you say, my dear."

"Did you kiss?"

"We did." Kara's entire body heated at the memory.

"And how was it?"

Kara paused before answering. She should probably look up an appropriate word for how fantastic the kiss was, but all she could come up with on the spot was, "Heavenly."

"Sounds amazing."

"It was," she gushed.

"I'm going to do you a favor then. I'm faxing you the contract for Sierra to review before we meet. You can use it as an excuse to see her, because if I know you, you've already talked yourself into hiding."

"I have not."

"Mhm. Have you talked to her today?"

"Only a text this morning."

"And when is your next date?"

"We haven't made a solid plan yet."

"Mhm. Stalling. Typical."

"I'm not and stop saying 'mhm.' It's annoying."

"I know this is new to you, this being in the position of wanting someone, but trust me, you don't want to ignore this one."

Words were absent, but a quiver in Kara's gut told her that Nicole was right. She had her fears and while she has fought the urge to withdraw, running and hiding had been her pattern over the years.

"Take the contract. Go see Sierra. Plan your next date. Or better yet, go on another date tonight."

"What if I push too fast? What if-"

"Kara," Nicole interjected. "After she showed up on our clinic doorstep, I doubt that would be a problem," Nicole said with a light air of humor. "Live a little. I know what you're afraid of, but I know you and that won't be a problem in the long run—not if she's the right one for you. You've worked hard. You deserve to have some fun, maybe even find someone to share your successes and dreams with."

"Now who's a Hallmark card?"

"Kara..."

"Okay, okay. I will. I'll let my hair down and go crazy."

"Don't do anything I wouldn't do. Wait. Scratch that. Go do something I wouldn't do. Stop thinking so much and be adventurous." With a wild laugh, Nicole bid her a good day and hung up.

Kara set her phone on the desk and leaned back. It was all so silly. She would never be so hesitant in any of her other pursuits, so why should Sierra be any different? There were a myriad of answers, but right now she needed food and a walk—and perhaps some chocolate. Chocolate solved all problems.

***

By five o'clock, Kara was ready to call it a day. She had managed to get on task after a short lunch break at the picnic bench outside. The fresh air and half of a dark chocolate coconut bar had cleared her head. The all-encompassing urge to see Sierra again hadn't dulled, though she had found a way to push it to the back of her mind. And thanks to Nicole's perfect timing, she was no longer trying to talk herself into hiding away at home. Not that she needed an excuse, but she now had business to justify a stop by Sierra's house.

As she packed up for the night, the butterflies in her belly circled, making her nervous and giddy at the same time. *Unbelievable.* She chuckled to herself in the middle of her empty office. Denying that she liked the exuberant feelings Sierra stirred up in her was useless. She was enjoying it immensely, feeling as light and fluffy as she had when she first learned to drive a motorcycle.

Throwing her bag over her shoulder, she continued her introspection on the way to her car. The intense sexual attraction to Sierra had created an itch that was begging to be scratched. She had never wanted anyone the way she wanted Sierra, making her thankful the woman hadn't been an actual patient of hers. That would've required ethical boundaries. Still, she might have to ask Dr. Marsden to perform the manipulations during Sierra's experiments, because touching her was wonderful torture and it clouded her mind at work. That was one thing she wouldn't tolerate. She was nothing if not a consummate professional.

Once settled in her Jeep, she turned the engine over and cranked the radio. A few minutes without thinking was much needed. Navigating the roads with ease, she sang along to every upbeat song she could find on her satellite radio, changing the channel whenever a slow ballad made an appearance—those songs didn't match her mood and she refused to have her vibe broken.

The ride to Sierra's house in the quaint town of Sisters, just outside of Bend, passed quickly—a pleasant surprise given the time of day. She pulled into the driveway and turned off the engine, but didn't get out right away. Instead, she stared at the simple tan and white two-story house that sat in the middle of the block. There was nothing fancy about it, not even much in the line of landscaping, but the grass was mowed and the two hedges were neatly trimmed. As she glanced down the road, she took notice of the fact that only a few of the homes had manicured lawns and beds of flowers. It was a quiet, low-key neighborhood that was wonderfully unpretentious, which suited Sierra perfectly.

Kara shifted her focus to the front door and her confidence waned like a torch just before it burnt out. Doubt and insecurity sidled up to her like long lost friends.

"You deserve to have some fun." Nicole's words echoed in her brain. The reminder provided enough of a kick to get her out of her Jeep and striding up to the door with the contract tucked neatly inside a red folder. As she approached, her body buzzed with anticipation. She had been dying to see Sierra again. To kiss her. To hold her. To feel that indescribable rush coursing through her body leaving her breathless and dizzy.

But would it be the same today? What if it had been the product of the buildup? What if the excitement was gone now that she had finally had a taste? What if...

There was no what if. She was an idiot and Nicole was right. *Stop self-sabotaging and see where the road goes. Have fun.*

"Have fun," Kara repeated, this time out loud. After delivering three tentative knocks on the white steel door, Kara waited. Her right foot tapped rapidly, irritatingly, though she was powerless to stop it. The nervous energy had to go somewhere and like lightning searching for ground, it had chosen her foot as its exit point. The sound of footsteps approached from inside and her folder crinkled under her grip. Nerves gave way to excitement, but when the door swung open, her excitement dwindled.

"Hey, Doc McHottie. What's shakin?" Ronni greeted with youthful enthusiasm. Her bright blue eyes brimmed with happiness, as if she had never threatened Kara at all.

Still weary from their last two encounters, Kara inwardly groaned, but schooled her features and forced a smile she was certain looked as insincere as it felt. "Hello, Ronni. Is Sierra here? I have some papers for her to look at," she explained in her best professional voice.

"No. Sierra's not here right now. Would you like to leave it with me?" Ronni replied with a mocking robotic voice.

Kara rolled her eyes. Dealing with Ronni was exhausting. "When will she be home? I'd like to go through them with her."

Ronni leaned to her left and propped a hand on her hip as she eyed Kara up and down. The gleam in her blues had since given way to suspicion. "Mhm."

Kara's jaw tightened. She was coming to dislike the word "mhm" more and more.

"You know..." Ronni glanced at the clock on her left. "Sierra should be back within a half hour or so. She went for groceries. You want to come in and wait?"

Looking back at her car and then at the woman who seemed determined to make her life hell, she exhaled in defeat, "I'll wait." *Damn libido.* Kara's drive to see Sierra outweighed her discomfort with Ronni. Her hand clutched tightly to the folder as she walked past Ronni and stopped inside.

"Don't sound so happy," Ronni muttered as she shut the door behind them. She brushed past Kara, plopped onto the sofa, and resumed her video game, leaving Kara an awkward bystander in the entryway.

Watching in silence, Kara was impressed with the gaming skills on display. Slow, quiet steps carried her to a seat in the corner, where she made herself comfortable from afar. Ronni had most likely given the guys at the lab a lot to think about during her visit.

During a break in stages, Ronni stood up and stretched, her eyes landing on Kara crunched in the distant corner chair. Her head cocked to the side as if sizing her up and she asked, "Do you play? We can play a game while you wait."

The offer seemed sincere, but Kara suspected it had something to do with the challenge presented at their last meeting. It was obvious Ronni wanted to rub her face in the dirt, but what she didn't know was that Kara was quite the skilled gamer herself. Time to educate her.

Maintaining innocence, Kara answered, "I've played some, but I don't think it would be fair."

"Aww, come on. I'll even let you pick the game. What do you like? Zombies? Hockey? War? Here," she motioned to the pile of games on the floor, "your choice."

Kara, not moving from her spot, replied with little interest, "Zombies will be fine. I mean, you've played one shoot 'em up game, you've played them all, right?"

"If you say so, Doc." Ronni set up the game and Kara took a seat beside her on the couch. Care to make a little wager?" A slight tip of the head and a furrowed brow by Kara led Ronni to reveal her proposal. "When *I* win, you'll buy me a large bottle of Buffalo Trace whiskey." Ronni smirked, confidence oozing from her pores.

It took all Kara had to contain a smirk of her own as she contemplated the question, what did *she* want when she won? "Hmm...okay. *If* I win..." Keeping with the façade of gaming ineptitude, she held a timid demeanor. "I want you to apologize for the other day and promise to lighten up. Dating is hard enough as it is without death threats." Kara waited for Ronni to respond with a nod, then quickly added, "Oh, and a six pack of Bottomed Out Stout."

Ronni's lips tensed, as if sensing something was amiss, but she was quick to shrug it off as she nodded and thrust out her hand to shake. "I hope you're ready for an ass kicking."

Kara ignored the dig and readied herself for battle. *You're going down, Ronni.*

CHAPTER TWENTY-THREE

Sierra burst through the front door in a panic, sending one of her brown bags of groceries scattering across the floor as she threw them to the side. The loud shrieks and screams she'd heard from outside had sent her heart into her throat. Fearing the worst, she had charged to the rescue, but now stood still as a statue as she processed the scene in her living room.

There was her best friend and her soon-to-be-girlfriend, or so she hoped, jumping and screaming in a heated competition. Confused as to how this had occurred, but relieved it hadn't been something serious, she picked up her mess and put away the perishables.

Even with the ruckus she had caused, Kara and Ronni hadn't noticed her return, allowing her to watch from afar. Much to her surprise, Kara was winning, and Ronni clearly wasn't happy. Their spirited verbal exchanges had Sierra chuckling as she cracked open a bottle of Knobby Tire Ale and waited for the battle to end.

"Last stage, Doc! Gonna need more than that big brain of yours to beat me," Ronni gloated despite Kara being in the lead. But it was close.

Kara kept her eyes glued to the screen and smirked as she said, "Bring it, chump change."

The nickname caught Ronni by surprise, giving Kara a jump on the final shootout. Several minutes later, a winner was crowned.

"Noooo! How is that possible?" Ronni fell to her knees in defeat. Her head dropped and her chin fell to her chest.

Behind Ronni's crumbled form, Kara threw a victorious fist pump into the air as a wide, pearly-white grin split her face. She bent over and gave her a pat on the back and said, "I'm a geek. Never underestimate our powers." Kara laughed as she stood, but fell silent when her sight landed on Sierra standing quietly in the corner.

Kara's eyes lit up and she skipped across the room. "Hey you." She pulled Sierra in and placed a chaste kiss on her lips.

"Hey back." Sierra grinned. Her arms circled Kara's waist, holding her close as she savored the moment. The free and easy smile on Kara's lips. The way those green eyes looked deep into her soul. The heat of Kara's body as it molded into her own. The feeling of intimacy, as if they were the only two people in the world.

For a second, they were. Nothing and no one else mattered. Not the garbage truck whirring outside. Not the ringing of a phone. Not even her best friend twenty feet away trying to comprehend her defeat. It was brief, but amazing, filling Sierra with warm fuzzies—something, she noted, she wouldn't mind enjoying on a daily basis.

Ronni got to her feet and grabbed her phone—the distraction reminding Sierra that they, in fact, were not alone. Too bad, because she could have stood there all day. With the mood broken, curiosity got the better of her. She poked her chin in Ronni's direction and asked Kara, "What did you do to my best friend?"

Peeling her eyes from Sierra, Kara craned her neck over her shoulder at Ronni. "Just some bonding time," she said with a half-shrug. Her grin grew ten-fold when Sierra placed a soft kiss on her cheek.

"You're just full of surprises," Sierra whispered low and husky into Kara's ear. A flurry of satisfaction swelled within when Kara shivered in her arms and buried her face in the crook of her neck.

"I was hustled," Ronni huffed. Her piercing blue eyes narrowed. Instead of basking in the power of her intimidation, she received a laugh in return, which only increased her grumpiness.

Kara's hand fell to her chest in feigned innocence. "What? You didn't know that everything in life could be solved with mathematical equations?"

A foreign feeling swelled in Sierra's chest as she puffed with pride. "See Ron? Like I said, quite surprising." She pulled Kara in and roughly peppered her neck with soft kisses that had her squirming in delight.

"Yuck to the power of ten." Ronni made a gagging sound as she plodded toward the door. She swiped her keys from the counter and then turned around. "I'm going to get your beer and we can settle up the rest after."

As Kara nodded, Sierra wondered what else the bet had entailed.

"You two got fifteen minutes to get all that sucking face out of your system. I want all G rated when I get back. Got it?" She glared as she pointed, first at Kara, and then at Sierra. With a shake of her head, she was off, leaving the couple alone.

"Okay, mom's gone." Sierra waggled her brows. "We can make out on the sofa until she gets back." Sierra dragged Kara toward the couch and fell back, bringing Kara down on top of her with a surprised yelp.

Boisterous laughter ensued, until they locked eyes. Then Sierra got lost—lost in the sea of green and the feel of warm lips and soft skin that created a high no ride could match. If kissing Kara felt this unbelievable, how would it feel when she finally got to experience all of her?

Kara's index finger traced the outline of Sierra's face, then trailed along her neck, down to her collarbone, and across her sternum ever so slowly as her lips ghosted over Sierra's. Kara smiled into their kiss as the body beneath her shuddered in pleasure. "Mmm, I like this," she mumbled against Sierra's lips.

Sierra wholeheartedly agreed, but there was something more she was dying to explore. Her fingers deftly slipped under the edge of Kara's shirt, teasing smooth skin that heated under her touch. Kara's breath caught, her lips frozen as a moan escaped. "And I very much like this," Sierra said. A seductive grin began to curl at the corners of her mouth, but was denied by a determined tongue demanding entry.

Her ability to rouse Kara's libido was an ego boost to say the least, but nothing she would ever flaunt. Sierra enjoyed her power, but wasn't blind to the fact that Kara had just as much influence over her. The slightest touch had her willing to do anything Kara asked.

The silence of the room gave way to soft whimpers and moans as teeth clashed and tongues dueled until desire gave way to a need for oxygen, though it did nothing to dampen the roaming hands that had worked their way up to massage firm breasts. No, that disruption came in the form of a knock on the door that signaled their time was up.

"I'm going to count to three and then I'm coming in," Ronni yelled through the door.

A groan of disappointment emanated from both women as their activities slowed to a halt.

"Damn, time flies when you're making out with the sexiest doctor on the planet," Sierra complained between heavy breaths.

"One."

"Or the sexiest downhiller on the planet," Kara returned the compliment. A lopsided smile appeared and she pressed her forehead to Sierra's. "Mom's home, so I guess we better behave...for now."

In that moment of silence, Sierra took the opportunity to memorize the finer details of Kara's face. The light splatter of freckles across her cheek bones. The tiny mole that sat above her left upper lip. The fine lines around her eyes that crinkled when she smiled. A cute little button nose. No makeup. Only real, honest beauty.

Sierra slowly inhaled the sweet coconut scent that always accompanied Kara's presence. Her eyes fluttered shut as she grumbled, "I guess."

"Two."

A laugh rolled through Kara's body. The vibration reached Sierra's core, making it that much harder to relinquish their positions. She didn't want to let go, so she stalled. Sierra opened her eyes and met Kara's, whose greens were darker than usual, but every bit as soothing. "Did I mention how happy I am to see you?"

"No. I don't believe you did." Kara's lips pushed out into an adorable pout that had Sierra grinning from ear to ear.

"My apologies." Sierra tipped her chin up to peck Kara on the lips. "I'm so happy to see you." That was the truth. She had been thinking of Kara all day, but didn't want to come on too strong, especially since it had been a work day. If she knew anything about the woman in her arms, it was how serious she was about her work.

"I'm happy to see you too."

Those six little words sent Sierra's stomach into a wonderful cascade of flips and flops—the same exhilarating feeling that came with dropping off a ledge and nailing the perfect landing.

"Okay, ladies..."

"That was an extremely generous three count." After one last, quick kiss, Kara unraveled her limbs from Sierra's.

"Yeah, I'll have to thank her later."

Not wanting to bear Ronni's ridicule for disobeying, they were quick to part and situate themselves on the sofa.

"Three!"

By the time the front door creaked open, Sierra and Kara were sitting innocently side by side, each with their hands folded in their own laps like good little children. If it hadn't been for the mussed hair, swollen lips, and disheveled shirts, no one would have ever known what they'd been up to only seconds ago.

Ronni craned her head inside with a hand over her eyes. "I hope you guys are decent. I'm uncovering my eyes now."

"Get in here, you goob," Sierra said with a laugh.

Ronni shut the door behind her. There was a six pack in one hand and a box of Cliff Bars in the other. "Good to know you guys can follow directions." She strode with confidence across the room, stopping in front of Kara and setting her beer on the table. She met Kara's amused grin with a thin smile. "I'm sorry about my behavior the other day. I promise to lay off and let you two navigate your lover's hell on your own," she stated dryly, then scrunched up her face, turned on a dime, and walked to the fridge, tossing the box onto the island on the way past. "But I won't forget you hustled me," she called out with her head in the fridge.

"Noted," Kara said, unable to stop smiling. She reached down, pulled out two of the chilled beers and handed one to Sierra.

It took a moment, but Sierra's brain finally registered the meaning of the apology and a slow smirk worked its way up. If there was anything Ronni hated more than losing, it was apologizing, and Kara had nailed both. Leaning into Kara's ear, Sierra whispered, "You really must've hustled her."

Kara tipped her head to meet Sierra's eyes. A look of apprehension crossed her face, seemingly uncertain of the intent behind the words.

"She never apologizes. She had to have thought she'd win if she bet an apology." It was a simple statement of fact, to which Kara just shrugged. "That's sexy as hell," Sierra's voice dropped an octave.

Kara's eyes fell to Sierra lips as she moistened her own, then replied just as seductively, "Also noted." She cleared her throat and looked back at Ronni, who was leaning on the countertop eating out of a nondescript container and staring at the two of them with rapt attention.

Sierra's arm wrapped around Kara's waist as Kara addressed their spectator. "Thank you, Ronni. I accept your apology. And I love the way you protect the people you care about. Can we call a truce?" She held out a beer as a peace offering.

Ronni set the container down, pulled a bottle opener from a nearby drawer, then made her way over. "I'm going to have to keep an eye on you. Watch out, Sierra, she's a sly one," Ronni said with narrowed eyes and a teasing smirk as she accepted the beer. She popped the top and then handed the bottle opener to Kara.

"Thank you." Kara reached down for a bottle of her own, popped it open, and then did the same to Sierra's before taking a large swig of her beer. "Ahh, the sweet taste of victory," she said after swallowing down the smooth, malty goodness with a toothy smile.

Ronni chuckled and kicked back in the recliner across the room. "Yuck it up. That's the first and last time you beat me."

"Tell you what, why don't you order a pizza, whatever you want, my treat?" Kara proposed.

If the brightening of Ronni's smile was any indication, the suggestion had proven popular. "You sure know the way to a girl's heart."

Sierra could only watch with wonder at how easily Kara had broken through her best friend's defenses, proving yet again that Dr. Kara Davies was unlike any other woman she had ever met.

CHAPTER TWENTY-FOUR

"Axel, I need a beer please," Sierra said as she flopped onto a bar stool. She had gotten to Taco'd before the evening crowd arrived as, once again, her plans with Kara had been postponed due to work. They had been dating for a month and a half now and in the beginning it was wonderful, but not long after it seemed as if Kara had begun to hide from her. And when they did get to spend time together, it felt like she was holding back—a contradiction to the boldness Kara had displayed earlier.

When asked directly, Kara would either brush it off as nothing or say that she wanted to go slow. Patience was not one of Sierra's strong suits, but dammit if she wasn't trying her best. All she wanted was a return of the easiness that had once existed between them.

The other thing eating away at Sierra was the undying carnal desire that had yet to be fulfilled. She wanted Kara in the *worst* way. There had been plenty of heavy make-out sessions—although even those had dwindled as of late—which did nothing but add to her frustration. Each time they had reached the cusp of crossing the line, Kara pulled back. It was torturous and exhausting and Sierra truly thought she might spontaneously combust if she was left hanging one more time.

Sierra could only figure it had to do with Kara wanting to protect herself, but the three-sixty from the heavy flirting and make outs of their first few weeks left her fearing it might be something else. Had she not been good enough?

"All alone again?"

Sierra bristled at the sound of Harley's voice. It was the second time she'd run into her after Kara had "rescheduled" one of their dates. Though they did frequent the same places around town, it almost felt as though Harley was stalking her—which made no sense after the way they had left things.

"Yeah, she has a big project at work to finish," Sierra replied, trying not to sound as dejected as she felt.

"Funny how the two of you were inseparable when it was all about the research, but now that you signed that contract, it's all 'Sierra, table for one.'"

"What the hell is that supposed to mean?"

"Nothing." Harley gave a shrug and cozied up beside her. "Just an observation. All I'm saying is no one offers help for free, especially where professional athletes are concerned."

"So...what, Harley? She only wanted me for money, for advertising? You don't think it's possible for someone like her to be interested in me for me?" The question disgusted her and she shook her head vehemently in disbelief, even though she had been plagued with her own doubts mere seconds ago.

"Well, you are hot, so there's that..." The dangerous look in Sierra's eyes gave Harley pause, but she raised a finger to emphasize another point and continued, "But what I meant was, you're from different worlds. What could you two possibly have in common? She's all business and you're all party."

This conversation was getting better and better. "Oh, so now I can't be taken seriously, because...what? I want success on my own terms? So what if I like to have some fun. I can be professional. I can be serious. Like right now, I'm seriously tired of your shit!"

"Dammit! Why are you always like this?" Harley's hands flew up, her frustration evident.

"Like what, Harley?" There was bite in Sierra's words as she stared her former lover down. She *really* wanted to hear the answer to this question.

Harley softened slightly, her head shaking side to side as a broken laugh tumbled out. "Like you. You never listen to reason. I've seen you two together. You're vibrant. You love excitement. She's stiff. Her idea of a fun night is reading a textbook. If you think you can change to keep her happy, it'll ruin you."

Sierra relaxed her stance. She didn't believe that one bit. Yes, they were different, but she had seen the other side of Kara and she wouldn't change a thing. In fact, she rather enjoyed being the only one privy to Kara's other side. Well, Ronni had also gotten a glimpse, but not the passionate side. Besides, Kara's stability and strict regimen had already been a good influence on her.

"You don't know anything about her or what she's like. And you don't know much about me. You and I," Sierra motioned between the two of them, "we fucked, Harley. That was it. We didn't do much talking."

"Whose fault was that? I wanted to get to know you. I wanted more, but all you wanted was sex. Why are you trying for more with her? Because she can help your career?"

Sierra's right hand balled into a fist. Harley had crossed a line. "You better watch yourself, Harley. And maybe if you weren't always busy trying to tell me what to do, things would've been different. So, thank you for trying to look out for me, but I don't want or need your help."

"Yeah sure, Sierra. That's why you always come running back to me when things go bad."

"Not anymore." Sierra meant it too. That cycle was over and if Harley wasn't careful, their friendship would be over as well. "If you ever want me to call you my friend again, then I suggest you leave now."

Harley did as she was asked without argument, leaving Sierra alone to her thoughts. There were so many thoughts. And feelings. And questions. Where was her beer? She needed one...or ten, if she was going to sort it all out.

Conveniently arriving with a frosty beer, the old barkeep offered up a soft smile as he slid the mug in front of Sierra. "Here you go, one chocolate stout." Axel studied the perplexed look on her face. "Everything all right?"

She shook her head and chugged half of her beer. What could she say? She had no idea what was wrong. She did know Harley had raised a few points that had wedged themselves in her craw and were now rubbing her raw like an old worn out pair of riding shorts, but despite Harley's perception of Kara's intentions, Sierra had never felt pressured or manipulated. In fact, Kara had even offered to remove herself from working with Sierra after their misunderstanding.

She honestly didn't think the contract was part of the problem. Still, it was enough to feed her insecurities.

She had plenty of those when it came to relationships. Maybe Kara was still hung up on Jamie or she had already met someone new. That was doubtful though, the woman hardly ever left work. Was Kara already tired of her? What else could it be?

Her brows scrunched and her forehead creased as her eyes squinted, as if the forced expression would help her figure out what had gone wrong so soon into their new relationship. Folding her arms and resting them on top of the bar, her head tipped to the side and her mouth pulled to the right in contemplation. "Axel, you've been married forever. Are relationships hard? What I mean is...is it supposed to be hard if it's the one you're meant to be with?" The question fell out without much thought, but as she pondered what she had asked, she was actually impressed. It had been a good question.

"Ah, I see." He patted her on the arm and tossed the towel over his shoulder. "All relationships are hard at some point. Even the best ones sometimes require a little give and take. The most important thing is communication."

Finishing off her first beer quickly, Sierra's brow rose in question. "I thought love was the most important thing?"

Axel laughed and passed her a second round. "Indeed, love is important, but not all love can weather the storm. You must be able to talk to one another honestly. That means communicating and understanding each person's needs, wants, and desires. Not just in life, but in regards to the relationship."

"Hmm." She nodded in understanding. "That makes sense. Thanks." There was so much to this relationship stuff. Maybe she needed some books, or better yet, a how-to video.

"Glad to be of help. For what it's worth, Sierra, you and Kara do have a connection. I hope it works out for you both."

Hearing the sincerity in his words and finding a ray of light in his advice, her doom and gloom faded. She would have to have a sit down with Kara to talk it all out. They'd both had issues in the past and they were both strong, independent, ambitious women who were hesitant to put themselves out there, but Sierra vowed to keep Kara from settling into that old familiar pattern with her. For that matter, she was determined to break her own patterns as well.

Time to break the cycle.

***

Sifting through the neatly stacked pages on her desk, Kara's hand stilled when it found its intended mark. Her eyes skimmed the black typeset and a smile took shape. With two weeks left in the research trials, all her hard work was coming to fruition and one of her life goals was on the precipice of realization. Kara held in her hand undeniable proof that the work chiropractors performed did in fact result in quantifiable improvement in athletic performance.

There had been a few other small focus groups that had produced comparable results, but those were often pandered by other medical professionals as being slanted due to their number of subjects or the company sponsoring the trial. That wouldn't be the case this time. She had been sure to secure an impartial sponsor in Traxx Labs and had not only used extremely controlled samples, but had chosen from a wide range of participants from various sports. When all was said and done, Kara planned to submit a paper for publication to the *Journal of Manipulative and Physiological Techniques*. If accepted, she would earn the opportunity to tout the benefits of chiropractic to other medical professionals through speaking engagements. She couldn't be any more excited about the possibilities ahead.

The ringing of her office phone broke the silence of the room, but not her focus. Kara's eyes continued to skim the page undeterred as she answered the phone with perfect professionalism, "Hello, this is Doctor Davies."

"Whatcha doin', Kara?"

It wasn't as much a question as it was an accusation. Kara had been on the receiving end of Nicole's little talks enough times to know the difference, only this time, she didn't know what she'd done to warrant a call. Kara's brows knitted and she set the page down, slightly annoyed by the interruption. "What do you mean, Nicole?" she asked with a touch of irritation.

"You know what I mean."

Actually, she didn't. Kara had a one-track mind and currently that track was on proving spinal manipulation could improve performance. "I've been busy comparing results from the experiment." A smile broke out as she glanced back down at the page on her desk. "I think I have enough to submit to J.M.P.T."

"That's great to hear," Nicole replied, though her voice lacked any signs of enthusiasm. "I'd love another chiropractic paper in the journal, but what you need to be busy with is the warm body that's head over heels for you and afraid she's done something to scare you off."

Kara's eyes snapped up at the mention of Sierra. "What do you mean? Sierra and I are fine. I just have a lot on my plate right now."

"Oh Kara," Nicole blew out a tired sigh. "Do I need a sledgehammer to drive this point home yet again?" When silence followed her question, she continued, "She's not Jamie. She's not Rachel. She's definitely not Bianca. You don't need to hide. You feel it with Sierra. You said so yourself. So, why are you trying to sabotage *this* relationship?"

Now that the light had been shed on the reason for Nicole's call, Kara still failed to see the problem. "I don't know what you mean. This is who I am. Sierra knows that and so do you. And it's not like we haven't seen one another. She was here Monday for her session."

"Seriously, Kara?"

Taking offense to the remark, Kara fired back, "Why? Did she say something? If she has a problem, she should speak to me instead." She would be pissed if Sierra had complained to her best friend.

"Not directly, no, but I could tell when we spoke the other day that something was off. Sierra is usually a bundle of energy when we talk racing. If you're reverting to your old patterns, which I suspect is the case, then she hasn't been able to speak to you, because you haven't been available for days. Tell me if I'm wrong, Kara."

Looking at the calendar, Kara frowned and shook her head. She couldn't believe that it had been nearly a week since she and Sierra had done anything more than exchange texts, besides their one business-related research session. She exhaled and ran her fingers through her hair, accepting defeat. "Noted. I'll talk to her tomorrow. Was there something else you needed?"

"You'll talk to her tonight."

"Nic-"

"I'm serious, Kara. You'll hate yourself if you screw this one up and I will remind you of it for the rest of your life."

"Fine," she relented with a huff, exhausted from the conversation. Nicole was right though, as usual. She needed to see Sierra and make up for the cancelled dates and disappearing act.

"And for goodness sake, Kara, eat something. You probably haven't eaten all day."

"All right, mom. Jeeze. Anything else?"

"Not really. We had nine new patients this week and I have some meetings set up from Sierra's wish list."

"Nice. You're a rock star, Nic."

"Mhm. I know. Maybe I'll make a weekend trip over for a visit. We haven't had a girl's night in a long time and I'd love to spend some time with you guys."

"That would be nice. And Nicole? Thank you for always looking out for me."

"That's what best friends do. Besides, you're more like my sister than my sister by blood."

"That's why I love you."

"Have a nice evening with Sierra. I expect a full report, by the way. Us married folks have to live vicariously through our single friends."

"Oh boy, I don't know about that." Kara leaned back and laughed. "Have a goodnight. Oh, and tell John I said hello."

"Will do. Goodnight, Kara."

Kara reached forward to hang up the phone and then leaned back in her chair, her eyes finding great interest in the patterns of the white textured ceiling. Had she alienated Sierra? That hadn't been her intention, although it had been one of her fears from the start. Work was her passion, so she wouldn't usually think twice about burying herself beneath a mountain of data, but it had become a convenient crutch and avoidance tactic when her fears and insecurities about relationships made her want to run. But wasn't Sierra her passion too? Didn't she deserve more? She suddenly felt extremely guilty for her treatment of Sierra. And it totally sucked.

With her other girlfriends, she had had an excuse— she simply lacked interest. Work was far more stimulating than spending time with them—with most people actually. That wasn't the case with Sierra, however, but she had been struggling with the whole "being open and spontaneous" since the first days of their relationship. Add in the fear that Sierra would become bored with the "real" Kara and you had one nervous doctor who had unconsciously slipped into the familiar safe space of her office. Putting herself out there was scary—especially when it had never been on her to-do list.

Now cognizant of the fourteen-hour days she had been putting in, Kara's energy waned. The emotionally exhausting conversation with Nicole had only added to her weariness. It was time to call it a night and do as she'd promised. She reached into her coat pocket and pulled out her cell phone. A missed text from Sierra screamed a reminder of how she'd forgotten to respond to the message earlier this morning regarding dinner tonight.

God, I'm a shitty girlfriend.

A deep breath released as she dragged her palms down her face and massaged her temples. Determined to set things right, she quickly typed out an apology followed by an invite to have dinner at her apartment with Chinese takeout and a movie. Barely a minute had passed before she received an enthusiastic reply. A smile appeared without thought. The butterflies that had been lying dormant since their last date made their presence known with a flutter that brought her a renewed surge of energy.

Wonderful thoughts of Sierra previously repressed by the dangling carrot of research, forced their way to the forefront. Kara had missed her more than she'd realized. She jumped to her feet and quickly packed her things, resisting the temptation to bring any files home with her. Tonight, Sierra would be her sole focus. She was the one person who could excite her as much as work. Added proof she needed to pay more attention to her girlfriend if she had any hope of making their relationship last. Kara couldn't fathom why Sierra still wanted to be with her after how she had treated her, but tonight, she planned to show her how much she really wanted to make their relationship work.

CHAPTER TWENTY-FIVE

Two knocks sent Kara rushing to the door. The little time she and Sierra had spent together recently had her feeling as jittery as if this was their first date. Her hand paused mid-reach for the doorknob. Second guessing herself, she took a quick step to the foyer mirror and checked her hair. Shaky hands smoothed down the front of her red button down and continued to her tan shorts.

Content with her appearance, she opened the door to an uncharacteristically shy-looking Sierra with her dark hair brushed behind her ear, dressed casually in long black shorts and a gold V-neck tee that made her eyes pop. She held a bouquet of yellow lilies and baby's breath—a gesture that melted Kara's insides. How appropriate that Sierra would avoid something as customary as roses. Everything about her was unique and unabashedly on her own terms.

"Hello, Sierra."

"Hi," Sierra returned, her nervousness giving way to a beaming smile. She held Kara's gaze for a long moment, then indulged in a quick trip down the length of her body before meeting her eyes once again. Sierra handed over the flowers and leaned in, placing a kiss on Kara's cheek. "You look great, as always," she whispered.

Was it the heat from Sierra's gaze or her proximity that had caused Kara's skin to redden and her breath to catch? She couldn't be sure, but a second later, when Sierra's shoulder "accidentally" brushed her breasts upon entering her home, a pleasurable tingle zipped down her spine and settled between her thighs. Her body's response chased away her fears, as was common in Sierra's presence, leaving her chastising herself for her stupidity in the handling of their relationship.

Sierra had had a such strong effect on her from day one. No one had ever looked at her like Sierra did— like she was the only thing that mattered in the world. Nor had anyone ever made her feel the way Sierra made her feel—excited and nervous, alive and afraid—she was fearless and terrified all at the same time.

Why the hell am I not spending every waking second with this woman?

It had been hard for Kara to comprehend how one woman could make her feel so wonderful yet so frightened, but now she knew why. Sierra was that one force of nature that could unequivocally compete with her other passions—a concept that left her fearing she would lose herself, one way or the other. Silly? Probably. But as Nicole so often reminded her, she could be sharp as a tack in academics, but dim as a foggy new moon night in regards to most anything else.

Kara caught herself staring and broke free of her stupor. Still standing in her open doorway, she shook her head, clearing her mind to focus on a quiet dinner with Sierra. Closing the door, she padded toward the kitchen where Sierra had already seated herself at the island and was waiting patiently—a half-smirk tiptoeing along her lips, seemingly proud of herself for eliciting such a reaction.

She should be proud. She certainly hit her mark.

Unable to do anything but smile, Kara's eyes locked with Sierra's and held as she rounded the island. No words were exchanged and Kara's gaze only deviated for the brief amount of time it took her to pour two glasses of NV Taltarni Brut Rosé Taché—her favorite wine to pair with Chinese food. Returning to the gaze of two alluring golden eyes that were locked on her with laser-like focus, Kara handed over a glass and said, "It's good to see you again."

"You too. I've missed you."

"I've missed you too."

"Good to hear."

Though Sierra's smile was sincere, Kara hadn't missed the twinge of pain in her reply. She had a lot of ground to make up. The moment was right to break into apology, but she didn't want to ruin dinner. Besides, she was enjoying the intense eye contact they were currently engaged in. Deciding to wait, she motioned toward the dining room table and asked, "You hungry?"

"Starving," was Sierra's quick reply, her eyes darkening.

Kara knew all too well she hadn't meant food and her body reacted in kind. A deep ache settled low in her belly as her heart rate rocketed. Her eyes were pulled to Sierra's mouth as she licked away the remnants from her first sip of wine, nearly drawing a groan out of Kara. The burning need to taste those lips again had her head spinning and it wasn't from the alcohol.

Continuing her admiration southward, she lingered on the swell of Sierra's breasts prominently displayed by the V-neck tee and the way she had knowingly pressed against the edge of the island. Clearing her throat and squeezing her thighs, Kara's voice cracked as she said, "Guess we should eat then."

Smirking again, Sierra stood up and walked slowly to the table, allowing Kara time to appreciate the way the long, form-fitting black shorts hugged Sierra's muscular thighs and toned backside. It had been four months since Kara had last had sex—a stat that usually meant nothing since work was all consuming. But right now...good lord, right now Sierra was like a cool glass of water in the middle of the desert, taunting her parched body. Kara swallowed hard and took a larger than normal gulp of wine.

Could I skip the apology and take her right here?

No. She shook her head and took a deep breath. She had to do this right. Their first time would not be out of desperate need. First, she had to make up for being such an ass. Properly.

Taking the seat across from Sierra, Kara smiled and opened the three containers. She took a serving of vegetable fried rice as Sierra helped herself to Chicken Lo Mein. Then they switched. Meaningful glances were shared over a comfortable silence and when all the food had been dished out, smiles were exchanged as they piled the first bites into their mouths.

The usual small talk ensued—work, riding, Ronni's antics, and Sierra's wish list—all with unexpected ease, which Kara noted and appreciated. As they neared the end of their meal, the time for the big talk had arrived.

Kara set her chop sticks down, wiped her mouth, and waited until Sierra met her eyes before beginning. "I'm sorry for being so absent these past few weeks."

"Why did you feel the need to do that?"

Taking a deep breath, she dipped her head in shame. "It's no lie that I'm swamped right now, but the truth of it is...I got scared."

"Scared of what?" Sierra asked without judgement. Her expression supportive, almost sympathetic.

"I..." Kara looked to the ceiling for answers. Finding none, she settled her gaze back on Sierra, the one place where her truth always seemed to make itself known. She spoke from the heart, "I don't know how to do this...relationships. What I know how to do is analyze and measure and calculate. I know how to piece together the puzzle of a patient's complaint and come up with a diagnosis and plan of care."

She rubbed her temples and continued, "Relaxed, spontaneous, concerned for another's opinions and feelings about my actions, escapes me. Jamie tried to change my habits, to drag me away from the office and research. I won't do that. I can't do that—not to the degree she wanted at least. She even texted me yesterday to see if I had alienated you yet, saying no one would ever be able to compete with my love of work. I had dismissed her as being jealous. I truly believed I was doing better, that I was making an effort, but after speaking with Nicole today, I realized I had done exactly what Jamie had accused me of. All I think about is work. Call it habit, self-preservation, avoidance...whatever. The result is the same."

Sierra's brow furrowed and she looked away as she asked, "Was I just work for you? Was it all about a contract?"

"What? No! Of course not!" Kara was shocked at the question and moved to quickly dispel any doubts. "I'm not rich, but I am financially comfortable. So is Nicole. Yes, the clinic does benefit from using your name and endorsement. We want to grow our business, spread the word about chiropractic, and help more people live a healthy lifestyle. If it means we can help you too, then we are extremely happy about it. We both think you have a bright future and that the right partnership would help all of us, but if you feel I've manipulated you in any way, then say the word and I'll tell Nicole to shred the contract."

"No," Sierra was quick to reply. "No," she reiterated, shaking her head for emphasis. "It was a stupid question. I...never mind." Her eyes cast down in shame, but she regrouped to address the problem at hand. "Look...I'm not asking you to change or to stop work. That big old brain of yours is one of my favorite things about you. All I ask is that you make some time for us and be open with me. This is new to me too. Sometimes I feel like you're holding back and I don't know why. That scares the shit out of me."

A brief pause followed where Sierra seemed to collect her thoughts, then she smiled brightly and added,

"I know we haven't known one another long, but I love that you can ramble on with fancy words one moment and then shock me in leather on a Ducati the next. I look forward to learning about all the different parts of Kara Davies, because no one makes me feel the way you do."

The heartfelt words hit Kara right in the chest, causing her eyes to sting. She never thought she'd hear such adoration directed at her and it made her want to do everything in her power to give them a real shot.

"Sierra, I promise I will try. You are the only person who has ever made me want to try. It may not seem like it, but I've been more open with you than anyone else. It's new to me, okay? Please be patient. I'm afraid to lose myself to these feelings, but I don't want to lose you either. I feel different when I'm with you and that scares me."

"See? Was that so hard to express?" Sierra asked, chuckling lightly as she took Kara's hand and pulled it to her lips for a light kiss.

"A little," she said with a half-hearted laugh. "I guess sometimes my mind takes a while to catch up with my heart. It's going take some practice, but I *am* working on it." Kara's smile returned and she reached her free hand across the table and placed it atop Sierra's.

Looking down at their joined hands, the mood lightened and Sierra glanced back up through her lashes as she said, "That's all I ask."

Feeling the weight of a thousand elephants step off her chest, Kara took her first full breath in what felt like days. "Let's finish this up and we can relax on the couch. I'll even let you pick the movie."

"Perfect." Sierra got up and set her dishes in the sink before heading to the pile of DVD's. She sorted through and when she settled on one, she popped it into the player, set her flip flops aside, and claimed a spot on the couch.

Opening a new bottle of wine, Kara took notice of the movie Sierra had chosen and smiled wide. "When Harry Met Sally. Nice choice. One of my favorites." With two glasses in hand, she circled the coffee table and sat them down.

"Mine too."

Once Kara was within reach, Sierra grabbed her wrist and pulled her down. Giggling washed out the opening scene of the movie as they maneuvered to let Kara lay down, ending up with her back flush against Sierra's front. A toned arm draped loosely over Kara's hip and settled on her stomach, drawing light circles that awakened the ache between her thighs.

Pulling Sierra's left hand up to her lips, Kara lightly kissed the palm and then brushed her nose across the soft skin along the inside of the wrist, inhaling a light mandarin scent before leaving a tender kiss. The delighted sigh she received in response ignited something inside, driving her wild, daring her to take what she so badly wanted.

So she did.

Bringing Sierra's index finger into her mouth, she sucked it softly before moving to the next, and then the one after that, until she had gotten her fill. Loving the soft whimpers and moans she was drawing from the woman who was pressing increasingly tighter against her back, she dragged Sierra's hand down to her right breast and squeezed. Kara's eyes rolled back, awash in the sensation of nimble fingers working their magic as they moved on their own accord. She had denied herself long enough. Exhausted from fighting her desires, tonight she would give herself over entirely and let the chips fall where they may.

A combined gasp accompanied the slow rocking of Sierra's hips against Kara's backside, silently working them both into a frenzy. Releasing Sierra's hand, Kara shifted her body so they were face to face. She cupped Sierra's cheek while a finger gently traced her own jawline in return. Golden irises gave way to black and the heat between them rose to a slow boil through a series of deep, slow kisses, each one spurring their need to feel the other's flesh. Eager hands roamed, grasping blindly for any free edge of clothing to slip under in search of skin.

When Sierra's hands finally found the hot pool of desire at the apex of Kara's thighs, she groaned and took Kara's bottom lip between her teeth. Releasing her lip, she whispered, "I've been dying to touch you."

"I've been dying for you to touch me."

"You're so wet. Can I-"

"Yes," Kara blurted out, unwilling to wait for the rest of the question. She ground her hips onto Sierra's fingers and released a heavenly groan. "God, you feel so good. Can we get out of these clothes?" She was panting heavily now and feeling no shame. All she wanted was to feel Sierra's naked body against her own and judging by the look in the Sierra's eyes, the feeling was more than mutual.

"Please."

They quickly sat up, yanking and pulling at one another's garments, both of them past the point of enjoying a slow reveal. Sierra's V-neck flew across the room. Kara's shirt lost a button. Bras were gone in a flash. Shorts and panties unceremoniously dropped to the floor. The flurry of arms and legs stopped when the last of the clothing had been dispersed.

"So beautiful," Sierra whispered full of awe as her eyes raked down Kara's long, lean body. Creamy white skin with a light dusting of freckles lay bare for her to explore. She laid back, bringing Kara on top of her, their eyes locked as they reveled in the feel of finally having skin on skin.

Kara settled one thigh between Sierra's muscled legs, pressing hard against her soaked core. A relieved groan fell from her lips when Sierra afforded her the same pleasure. A simultaneous slow grind began, each matching the other's increasing pace. The friction served as a delicious tease, yet provided the pressure needed to achieve her goal.

What she desperately wanted were those long, slender fingers, but that would have to wait. She was already too far gone. There would be time to map one another's bodies later. Right now, Kara needed a release and she would bet big money from the way Sierra was moaning and thrusting into her that she had the exact same idea.

Nipping and sucking her way up Sierra's neck to her ear, Kara was rewarded with a soft whimper when she took the supple lobe between her teeth. She noted the response and continued on until their mouths met again. Gone were the slow, deep kisses. Sierra took control, her tongue searching and finding a willing partner in a heated duel. Mouths were devoured. Their rhythms synced. Hips and tongues thrusted in unison—both women gasping and moaning until they came together in a symphony of passion.

Safe in one another's embrace, they came down from their high together. Kara was elated, relieved, energized. Sierra's touch, the feel of her body against her own—it had been everything she had dreamed of and then some—but rather than quenching her thirst for Sierra, her body only begged for more.

The bottle of pent up sexual energy had been uncorked and she was going to drain it dry. Kara wasted no time in following through with her vow to stop denying herself as she rolled Sierra over and commenced round two.

CHAPTER TWENTY-SIX

Letting go was exhausting. Exhausting, but liberating. Last night, Kara Davies had let go of everything she'd been fighting against and this morning she felt lighter. And sore. Sore in ways she had never been sore before, but still lighter, freer, and plain old fucking relaxed.

As she stretched out her lithe body, she struggled to recall the last time she had truly relaxed. She was always working, thinking, or thinking about working. At home alone, in a relationship, and even in social settings, her mind was on other things and not at all invested in the act of socializing itself. No wonder her girlfriends had always left her.

Rolling her eyes in admonishment, she noted Nicole had been right yet again. On the other hand, none of the other women had been Sierra. She still needed to work on thinking less and following her heart more. Sierra was worth it since she'd broken through the walls Kara had painstakingly built up.

Kara reached her arm back expecting to find her lover, but instead found nothing but sheets. *When did we make it to the bedroom?*

The question was quickly tossed aside in favor of panic. Had Sierra left without saying goodbye? She wouldn't. Would she?

Her chest tightened. Thoughts of her foolishness set in. How could she have let herself become a one night stand?

Suddenly, a crash followed by a hushed curse came from just outside her room. She breathed a sigh of relief and then scolded herself for thinking such horrible things. Slipping out of bed, she stretched and then threw on a tank and sleep shorts before peeking out the bedroom door.

The sight of Sierra in only her tee shirt fumbling through her kitchen was almost comical. The shirt barely reached below her ass, revealing those shapely, muscled legs that had Kara biting her lip. Unable to resist touching her any longer, Kara padded up silently and wrapped her arms loosely around Sierra's waist from behind.

"Jeeze, Kara! You almost made me drop the mug." She took a deep breath and laughed.

The sound was music to Kara's ears. Sierra was even more beautiful in the morning and Kara couldn't help but run her hands up and down her toned body. The touch left a trail of goosebumps and sent a shiver through Sierra, bringing a wicked grin to Kara's lips. She buried her nose in Sierra's mussed hair and inhaled her scent— sweet mandarin musk and sex. They should bottle that. It was sexy as hell and already had Kara's arousal making a return visit. Last night had opened the flood gates and now she couldn't get enough of Sierra.

"Hey pretty lady, why are you going through my drawers?" Kara inquired, her voice raspy and low.

Turning her body within the circle of locked arms, Sierra flashed a smile that hinted at mischief right before she placed a chaste kiss on Kara's lips.

"I thought you liked me in your drawers?" One brow rose and she laughed as her fingers teased the warm skin under the band of Kara's shorts.

"I wasn't complaining," Kara replied with a smirk. Her body ready for more, responded to the touch with a subtle, uncontrollable push of her hips.

Sierra's eyes darkened. The race to full-on arousal was well underway. "I was trying to be the good girlfriend and make you breakfast before you got up, but you caught me." Her fingers moved slowly down the valley between Kara's thighs until they reached their target, sifting through the soft curls they found there.

"Fuck breakfast," Kara said with a mix between a growl and a laugh. Her eyes immediately fell to Sierra's chest, whose shirt clung beautifully over two perfect, full breasts that seemed to appreciate her admiration as they rose to attention. And boy did she love to admire them.

"Doctor! Language!" Sierra laughed at the surprising outburst of profanity, but it quickly transformed into a pleasure filled moan when Kara's hands slipped under her shirt and took her right breast into her palm, massaging it gently. "I thought...mmm...god..." Words went out the window when a hot mouth covered her sensitive nipple through the soft cotton of her shirt, bringing it to a hardened peak.

"I thought breakfast was the most important meal of the day?" Sierra whispered breathily, rushing to get the words out, but anxious to hear how Kara would respond.

"I didn't say I wasn't going to eat anything at all," was Kara's tongue in cheek answer. "However, what I want to eat doesn't require the stove to heat it up."

Last night, Kara had let down her guard and it was all Sierra had wanted. It had truly been an evening to remember. Hopefully, it was the first of many times to come, because this morning Sierra was seeing an entirely different Kara Davies— one reminiscent of the Ducati reveal—which had not only surprised her, but made her aroused beyond belief. Kara was definitely *not* vanilla and Sierra wondered how far she could push their little game.

She yanked Kara's tank up over her head and
openly admired her lover's form. Unable to resist the urge
to touch, her hands lightly traversed Kara's sides and
along the swell of her breasts, finally settling on her hips.
"The doctor does know best." A seductive grin took
shape. "What do you recommend?"

"I should take you two times in the morning and
two times before bed," Kara husked, lunging forward to
drag open mouth kisses across Sierra's collarbone while
cupping the bare buttocks that had taunted her from the
start. Snaking a hand between Sierra's thighs, Kara
indulged in the slick heat that awaited her. She pulled
back with a smile and glanced down, then back up to
meet Sierra's hooded eyes.

"You're burning up. I recommend you spend the
day in bed," she said, her voice dripping of sex. Her
lustful gaze belied her intentions, causing Sierra's heart
to pound, echoing into her ears and pulsing into her
throat.

"It's that bad, huh?" Sierra was quickly falling
under the influence of Kara's touch, but willed herself to
stay sober. Wanting to partake in some fun of her own,
her hand slid back under the waistband of Kara's shorts.
What greeted her pleased her to no end. She wasn't the
only one hot and ready.

There were no words, only a simple nod before
Kara hastily disposed of the one piece of fabric standing

between her and Sierra's naked body. A woman on a mission, Kara went directly to the object of her desire, lavishing both of Sierra's breasts with her full attention.

She really is a boob girl, was Sierra's last thought before her knees buckled from the jolt of a hot, wet suck on her nipple.

"Don't you have other patients to attend to today, Doctor?" she asked between heavy breaths, keeping up their charade.

"Your condition requires my undivided attention." Kara used her body to press Sierra against the counter and steadied her with the most arousing prop of all time— a thigh between her legs.

A guttural groan fell out and Sierra ground her hips against the firm resistance. She could get used to this Kara, the one that took what she wanted—not that she hadn't enjoyed any of the other "Karas" she'd had the chance to experience. Sierra was quickly finding she loved being owned by this woman—something she couldn't say about any of her previous lovers.

The feel of Kara's hands all over her body, the heat of Kara's mouth against her skin, the knowledge that this was the only woman who could make her feel *so fucking good*, spurred her desire to new heights. Her hips worked feverishly to relieve the delicious ache pooling low in her belly, heating her skin, and tingling her toes.

"I think your condition is critical. There's no time to get to the bedroom." With a wildfire of desire burning in her eyes, Kara helped Sierra up onto the countertop and pushed her legs open wide. She held Sierra's gaze as her tongue slowly swept up the length of her dripping folds.

"Oh god!" Sierra screamed, both from the pleasure of Kara's attention and the sheer intensity in her gaze. A second taste sent Sierra's eyes rolling as her body fell back against the cabinets. "So good. More please," she gasped out in pleasure.

Request granted. Two fingers plunged deep inside while a dexterous tongue continued to ravish her, driving Sierra closer and closer to the sweet oblivion she so desperately craved.

Prying her eyes open again, Sierra nearly came at the sight of Kara touching herself. "Holy..." Her words fell away with the soft vibration of Kara moaning against her hypersensitive center. A new need rose from within and she wasn't shy about making it known. "Come with me, Kara."

Sierra was close. So close. She refused to be weak this time, forcing her eyes to remain open and locked on her girlfriend, who was stroking herself in time with the rhythm of her tongue and fingers. The paced quickened, thrusts deepened, resulting in a crescendo of passionate cries as their bodies convulsed in the most wonderful of ways.

Sierra collapsed onto Kara's shoulders. Air was hard to come by, but she managed to rasp out, "That was just what the doctor ordered."

***

Sierra rolled onto her side and propped her head in her hand, resting her elbow against the mattress. She studied Kara carefully, watching as her girlfriend slid on a pair of worn out jeans and a blue tee shirt with the picture of a spine on the front. When Kara bent over to tie her shoes, Sierra pulled her bottom lip between her teeth. *That's a heavenly sight, but so much better naked.*

"Why are you getting dressed? I thought we were staying in today?"

"We are. I'm going to run to the store. I haven't shopped in a while and after our marathon, we need to rehydrate and refuel. I'll buy plenty of proteins and electrolytes so we'll be ready for anything," Kara spouted. A slight blush crept onto her cheeks when she realized how she sounded.

Sierra noticed and rolled out of bed with a smile. She approached and slowly enveloped her into a warm embrace.

"Any special requests?" Kara asked. As a wickedly seductive laugh rolled out of Sierra and she quickly added, "From the store, I mean."

"Bummer." Sierra stumbled backward from the force of a playful shove. With a chuckle, she asked, "How about some whipped cream?" She added the wiggling of her brows for effect.

Kara rolled her eyes and grinned as Sierra kissed her cheek. "Maybe," she replied as if it were not an option, but the gleam in her eyes gave her away. "I'll be back shortly. You make yourself at home."

A grumble accompanied Kara's release as she headed for the door.

"You're not going to work, right?"

"Not work, but they do need my signature on something."

Kara's admission was met with the unmistakable look of disapproval.

She trotted back, tugged Sierra flush against her, and hit her with a long, lingering kiss. Pulling back breathless and flustered, she said, "I promise I won't be long and we can pick back up when I return."

"Fine." Sierra used her best pout. "But hurry back. You got me all hot and bothered now and you shouldn't leave hot things unattended for long."

"I won't. I promise."

After one last, far more innocent kiss, Kara walked out the door, leaving Sierra to her own devices.

Wrapped in Kara's light green terry cloth robe, she resigned herself to the sofa with coffee and television to keep herself entertained.

"Crap."

She was supposed to have lunch with Ronni at one. It was noon now and there was no way she was leaving Kara's apartment—Not after the night and morning they had shared and the possibilities that lay ahead. Plus, she needed a nap.

She grabbed her cell from the table and tapped the screen, quickly getting a ring tone. She couldn't wait to tell Ronni about last night. A toothy smile split her face as the excitement of her big reveal built.

"Go for The Ron. What up?"

"I'm not going to be able to make it to lunch today."

"Can I assume everything went well? Did she crack open the door to her heart?"

"Better than that. She blew the doors off that bitch." Sierra laughed heartily. "God, Ron. She is amazing and still so unbelievably surprising in-"

"La la la la. That's enough. I don't need to know the mating ritual of nerds. So, why are you on the phone with me then? Shouldn't you still be...ya know?"

"She ran to the store, something about refueling...anyway, let me just say that you can never call her vanilla again." Sierra snickered.

S. W. Andersen

"TMI! You stay put like a good little girl, Sierra, till mama gets home. You are so whipped." Ronni snorted with laughter. "Anywho...I'm going to ask Blake to join me then, since you're bailing."

"Ohhh, Blake. When are you guys finally going to quit playing games and get on with it? I know you're into each another. It's almost exhausting at this point." That was a fact. The way they were always hanging all over one another, but repeatedly denied interest, was really getting old.

"Shut it! I'm not the one who's whipped already. Where's my 'nobody's the boss of me' best friend?"

An evil grin appeared. Sierra knew exactly what would end the teasing. "Hey. I don't have a problem with whips, but I'm not sure it's Kara's thing."

"Ewww gross, Sierra. That's an image I don't need in my head. I'm hanging up now. Enjoy your lady."

"You know I will. And have a good day with Blake. Catch ya later."

"Okey dokey smokey...and Sierra?"

"Yeah, Ron?"

"I'm happy for you guys."

"I know. Thank you for the tough love."

"It's what I do. Now go. It's getting too heavy in here."

"Love ya." Sierra blew a kiss into the phone before ending the call. She laid back and thought about their

288

conversation. Her smile stretched wider. Putting herself out there had been terrifying, but rewarding—more than she had ever dreamed. Now she hoped Ronni would practice what she had preached by taking a leap of her own.

CHAPTER TWENTY-SEVEN

Eager to get back home, Kara signed what was needed at the lab and then hurried off to the store. When was the last time she had ditched work to spend time with someone? Oh yeah, her first date with Sierra. Would that be a recurring theme? No. Definitely not. She wasn't that kind of woman. But for today, knowing Sierra was waiting for her, wanting her, possibly naked...it was all consuming. Her mind was on some kind of primal autopilot and her body screamed to get the whipped cream and get home already.

Wasting no more time, she hurried through the store grabbing a few needed items, including the now mandatory whipped cream. The fun, but nutritionally-void food product, had supplanted vital sustenance on Kara's list and the ache between her legs wholeheartedly approved.

In and out of the store in record time, Kara quickly loaded the bags into her Jeep and jumped into the driver's seat. In the rear-view mirror, the top of the whipped cream peeking out of the bag caught her eye. Her heart raced and her core throbbed. "Good Lord! What's she done to me? I'm getting horny over a can of whipped cream." She smiled at the unexpectedly welcomed change in her behavior as she started her car and sped toward home.

Arriving home to silence, Sierra was nowhere to be seen. After putting the groceries up, Kara padded to the bedroom and peeked inside. There lay Sierra, sound asleep on her right side. The light blue sheet ended at her hip, leaving her naked upper body exposed for Kara's viewing pleasure.

A soft smile graced her lips. Sierra looked even better in her bed in the light of day. It was a sight she could get used to. The whipped cream forgotten, Kara slipped out of her clothes and slid under the covers to snuggle against the warm body of her lover. Sierra reflexively folded back into her, making Kara sigh in delight. She draped her arm over Sierra's hip and pulled them closer, their bodies forming a perfect spoon.

Kara hadn't realized how much she could enjoy being physically close to someone until she had met Sierra. Now, she couldn't get close enough. Having finally cleared some of her emotional cobwebs, she could finally let herself accept that she wanted to share herself with someone else in mind, body, and soul—as long as that someone was Sierra Cody. As scary as it was, she was ready and willing to fight her habits, fears, and insecurities to give their relationship an honest chance.

Willing her mind to shut down completely, Kara drifted off to sleep, feeling more at peace than she ever had before.

✳✳✳

When morning arrived, Kara was surprised to find she and Sierra worked well in tandem. Never once had they gotten in one another's way as they showered, dressed, and made breakfast. Even more surprising, was how she had been able to resist pulling Sierra into the shower for a quickie. She had never considered herself a slave to sexual desires, but when it came to Sierra, everything she thought she knew about herself had been tossed away like week-old milk.

Kara smiled as she washed the dishes. She had believed herself to be a creature of habit, but with Sierra, she was enjoying the discovery of a whole new self. Well, maybe not a "new" self. More like one that had gone into hibernation. But still...spontaneity had been absent since her accident and Kara hadn't felt so alive in a very long time. While she had plenty of work to do at the lab, she was already counting the hours until she could see Sierra again.

Ten. It was ten hours until she could see Sierra again.

"I'm going to take Ronni out for lunch to make up for skipping yesterday," Sierra said as she openly appraised Kara's backside from her kitchen chair.

"That sounds nice. I'd say I'm sorry I ruined your plans, but I'd be lying." Kara glanced over her shoulder, saw the look Sierra was giving her, and smirked.

"You'll get no complaints from me. I enjoyed spending the day with you." Sierra stood and closed the distance. Her arms wrapped around Kara from behind and she peppered Kara's neck with kisses, earning her a hum of enjoyment. "You are delicious," she whispered, her warm breath tickling Kara's ear.

Kara turned and draped her arms around Sierra's neck. Her gaze darted between Sierra's twinkling eyes and enticingly parted lips. "And you, are devastatingly gorgeous."

"Are you sure you have to work today? We could do a repeat of yesterday or even venture outside," Sierra finished, sounding hopeful.

Kara's sense of responsibility was saying one thing, but her body was nudging her in the opposite direction. Sierra was tempting. So agonizingly tempting. Kara was certain she could hole up in a room with her for days and never tire, but there were deadlines to meet and patients to be seen. Life was calling and Kara never failed to answer. Although, truth be told, today was the closest she had ever come to saying, "Fuck responsibility."

It was very evident that she would need to find a balance between work and Sierra.

Disappointment rolled out in the form of a groan as she declined the offer. The light dimmed as Sierra's expression fell at the realization that their twenty-four hour love bubble had finally burst. As adorable as Sierra's pout was, Kara much preferred the sparkle of happiness in her eyes, so she set forth to make it reappear as fast as possible. "But I'm all yours again at six."

A wide grin appeared and then there it was, shining like stars in the Oregon sky on a dark night, the brilliant twinkle in a pair of golden eyes that sent Kara's heart aflutter. Seeing Sierra happy made her warm all over and knowing she was the cause of that joy was priceless.

"Okay. I will see you soon, Doctor."

"Yes, you will."

With one last parting kiss, they went their separate ways.

***

Sierra quietly slipped through the front door of her home and tiptoed through the living room to the kitchen. The clock read 9:15 and, as a rule, Ronni would be asleep until at least ten. The only exceptions being race days and travel days. And apparently, today.

Sierra looked up as Ronni's door creaked open. A witty remark popped into her head—because nothing was as much fun as aggravating her best friend first thing in the morning. In the old saying "poking the bear," the bear had nothing on Ronni. As soon as her mouth opened, the words backed up in her throat like a five-car pileup. She coughed them free and smiled wide.

This was going to be good.

"Morning, Blake."

"Uh...hey, Sierra." He folded his arms in a failed attempt at covering his naked, chiseled torso.

A ruckus from Ronni's bedroom was followed by mumbled curses. Ronni poked her head out, her hair a jumbled mess and a sheet covering her chest. She scowled and grumbled, "Blake, get your fine ass back in here and put some clothes on. Those abs are for my eyes only."

Sierra broke into a boisterous laugh. "I thought best friends shared everything?"

"Don't even go there. I doubt you'd want to share Kara...ya know...if I was into that sort of thing."

No. Sierra wouldn't want to share, but she had no concerns about that and laughed even harder at Ronni's attempt to stifle her. Oh, how the tables had turned. Now she would be the one doing the teasing over a crush.

A blushing Blake hurried back into the bedroom and Ronni quickly shut the door behind them. The wall between them muffled the voices, but Ronni was clearly chastising Blake for having been caught, which only prolonged Sierra's enjoyment. She didn't know why Ronni kept denying her interest in Blake, but she was glad they had finally broached the subject. And apparently, they had done it in a big way.

Sierra prepared a pot of coffee. As she poured herself a cup, Ronni reappeared. Her hair was still a mess, but at least she was dressed, wearing a pair of red and white polar bear boxers and a blue tank top. She plopped unceremoniously onto a stool across from Sierra and leaned her elbows on the island.

"Helloooo there," Sierra sang, enjoying the flustered look on Ronni's face.

"Hi," was her curt reply. "Why in the world are you home this early? You usually sleep late after sex, much less a twenty-four hour sex-a-thon."

"Kara had to work, so I got up with her. I must say, if these are the things I miss by sleeping in, I may have to start getting up earlier."

Ronni narrowed her eyes and scrunched her face. "Ha, ha. Damn Doc McHottie and her early bird hours." She accepted a hot cup of coffee from Sierra without meeting her eyes. "If you must know, this is the first time we've hooked up, so you haven't been missing anything."

Leaning forward, she whispered, "Except those abs. Did you see those abs?"

Sierra chuckled and nodded. Blake had been gifted with a perfect six-pack, although she preferred Kara's toned midsection.

Ronni's eyes closed as she hummed in delight. "Oh. My. Gawd!"

"They are impressive." Sierra set her cup down and stepped around the island to wrap Ronni up into a tight hug. "I'm happy for you guys. It's about time."

"Thank you. And I know, right?" When Sierra released her hold and stepped back, Ronni took a sip of coffee and stared at her over the brim of her cup. "So, I guess you guys are doing well?"

"Yeah. And it looks like you and I hit the jackpot." She raised the mug in a toast.

Ronni tipped hers in return and winked. "Totally."

"Ahem."

Sierra and Ronni broke their moment to find a fully clothed Blake with his hair perfectly swept to the side, as usual. He ran his hands down his thighs and then slipped them into his jean pockets, unsure of how to proceed.

"Relax, Blake," Sierra said, hoping to calm his nerves. "I'm happy for you guys, but I couldn't resist a little teasing."

"It's cool," he said, but he was obviously not feeling very cool at all. He made a slow approach that ended with a kiss on Ronni's cheek. "I should get going. I'll see you tonight?"

"Yes, you will," Ronni answered. Her cheeks reddened under his open appraisal.

"See you later, Sierra."

"Bye, Blake."

As he headed for the door, Ronni tore her eyes away and turned to Sierra. She mouthed, "Look at that ass," and rolled her eyes as if she had just taken a bite of the most delicious thing in the world.

Sierra glanced down and wiggled her brows in jest.

Blake turned quickly, hitting them with a suspicious stare. Sierra wore an innocent smile upon her lips, which Ronni matched. He glanced between them, then narrowed his eyes. "You two behave."

"No worries, I'm going to take her to lunch," Sierra said and then winked at Ronni. "Can't get into too much trouble with that, can we?"

Blake turned in the doorway and laughed. "Please. I've known you two long enough. You can always get into trouble." He shut the door behind him, leaving the grinning duo alone.

Ronni finished off her cup of coffee. "How about brunch instead? I could go for some pancakes."

"Sure, whatever you want." Sierra replied. "I bet after all that physical activity you could use some carbs and proteins to replenish."

"What the-?" Ronni feigned disgust, but the corner of her lip quirked into a smirk. "Has the Doc brainwashed you? What kind of language is that? Really, Sierra. I'm afraid of what might happen if you two keep going out."

Laughing, Sierra gave Ronni a playful shove in the shoulder. "Get used to it. I plan on her being around for a long time. She's the one, Ron." The statement was meant as a joke, but after saying the words out loud, something inside Sierra clicked and she fell silent.

Ronni stared at her with one brow arched. Sierra wasn't sure if it was a look of surprise or confirmation. Had Ronni already known Kara was her match or was she just as surprised to hear her speak the words? Ronni always seemed to know things long before she did, but if she was being honest, Sierra had known the moment she'd met Kara that she would be the one who would change her life forever.

***

"Good morning," Kara greeted Christie, but was lost in thoughts of Sierra. *Maybe it's time for a vacation. I can't remember the last time I took one. Maybe somewhere warm and sandy. I bet Sierra would look amazing in a bikini.*

"Good morning, Doctor Davies."

The unusually upbeat tone drew Kara's attention. Christie was smiling at her. She never smiled at her. Confused as to the change in demeanor, Kara glanced around before she settled her gaze back on the cheery receptionist. "What? What's going on?"

"Nothing."

Not satisfied with the answer, Kara narrowed her eyes. Christie grimaced at the stare and held up her hands. "Nothing. It's just..."

"Just what?"

"It's just that you never smile when you come in and today, well...you're beaming. That's all. Sorry. It's nice to see you in a good mood, that's all."

Softening her expression, Kara shifted from agitation to embarrassment. "Oh." Her eyes fell away, drifting to her feet as she offered an apology. "I'm sorry. I never realized." She looked up again and smiled. "Thank you. I hope you have a good day."

"Thank you. Same to you, Doctor Davies."

Kara hurried down the corridor, ashamed of her behavior. How long had she been walking around with whatever look it was that made everyone assume she was unhappy? Sure, she was in a fantastic mood right now, but she hadn't been in a foul mood before. She loved her work and took it seriously. Maybe too seriously for others to comprehend. Yes, her mind was constantly occupied with one of the ten irons she kept in the fire, but she had never considered herself unhappy.

Though, if she were being truthful, she hadn't been happy with her personal life in a long time. But professionally? Yes. So much so, that she had forced work to spill into her personal life until it encompassed everything. Besides Nicole, Kara had no friends, didn't socialize, and rarely engaged in any of her old hobbies. None of that had bothered her until now.

Meeting Sierra stirred something deeper. Color now invaded a life that had consisted of muted grays. She needed more, wanted more. She missed riding her motorcycle and hiking and going out for a beer. Life was passing her by and for what? There was plenty of time for work and play. All she had to do was let go and she had one very special woman to thank for showing her the light.

CHAPTER TWENTY-EIGHT

Fall had given way to winter and snow now covered the trails. Though spring wasn't far off, this season's heavier than usual precipitation meant the mountain wouldn't be rideable until late May. Sierra had saved up to make a few trips south where she and Ronni could get some riding in, but until then, she was taking some cues from her girlfriend.

Sierra stood atop the snow-covered summit of Mt. Hood with her snowboard in hand and stared at the horizon. So much had changed since this time last year. Kara's strict daily regimen had rubbed off on her. Her once random and half-assed off-season workouts had been transformed into a dedicated routine of healthy eating combined with high intensity and endurance exercise in a way best suited for her sport. With Kara's research project completed, the doctor had found a whole new experiment in Sierra's fitness sessions. She was constantly on the phone and internet to find the most cutting-edge techniques to help Sierra reach her goal.

At first, Sierra thought it was weird that Kara had taken such a vested interest in her off-season training routine. That deep insecurity that Kara was only concerned with her success because she had a financial stake had risen its ugly head again. Sierra was a stubborn soul anyway and her insistence on doing things her own way had led to several walk-offs. Kara never followed. She never pushed. She let Sierra know that success was all on her own shoulders, but she was there to help if Sierra wanted. Then Kara would do the workouts herself and go about her day, leaving Sierra to her own devices.

If Kara had been hurt or angered by the rejections, she never let on. She never once commented on Sierra's refusal to do the routine. She would give her a kiss, say she was proud to be a part of "Team Cody," and then be on her way. That bugged the crap out of Sierra. She had let it fester for two weeks before she realized Kara enjoyed the challenge all on her own. Whether Kara was mad at her or not, didn't seem to matter. She may have started the program for Sierra, but Kara liked to push herself and the limits of her own body. A few times, she had even brought equipment to perform a before and after analysis on herself. Every day she worked her way through the exercises that were intended to increase Sierra's stamina and control, upping the ante each time she learned something new. The doctor dove head first into everything with a passion and that was something Sierra envied.

Watching Kara's hardcore pursuit of perfection in herself renewed Sierra's own quest for excellence. Her eyes opened to the fact that her resistance to accepting help would only keep her from reaching her goal. Kara was just like Ronni. She wanted to give Sierra access to everything she needed to be the best. It was up to her to take advantage of the tools at her disposal. So, at long last, she did.

On a Wednesday morning, Sierra surprised Kara by meeting her at the gym and agonizing through the first of many brutal workouts. That had led to Kara negotiating with Volden to rent the virtual lab to riders during the off season as a means of staying in shape. Sierra had logged many long sessions and had even taken Ronni up on her offer to analyze her Go Pro race footage. Having taken a page from her girlfriend, Sierra began her own attack on perfection. She had to admit she was feeling really good— not only physically, but mentally—and she had never been happier.

With the new season still several months away, the thing bringing her the most joy right now was Kara's competitiveness. Her girlfriend may not have been a mountain biker, but she challenged the hell out of Sierra, both intellectually and in the gym. That meant Sierra would often have to bring Kara back up for air. The woman had a knack for drowning herself in research and forgetting about real life, but she loved her more for it and made it her mission to get her out of the house as much as possible. Like this weekend.

She turned as Kara stepped out of the little chateau and zipped up her jacket. Her nose was red and she looked so adorable in her wool monkey ski beanie. Sierra never imagined a woman as serious as Kara would even own such a thing, yet it fit her so well. Little by little, Kara had opened up and Sierra couldn't get enough of her dry wit or silly clothes that would pop up at the most unexpected times.

A newfound passion for competing may have pounded through her veins and chomped at the bit for release, but Sierra was also content enjoying these little moments with the woman who had changed everything for her. She would continue to work hard, but this weekend was a time to play hard. Having learned that Kara shared a love of snowboarding, Sierra couldn't resist a long weekend together on the slopes. It had taken a day for Kara to get her legs back under her, but she had impressed Sierra with her skill.

Kara came to a stop, blocking Sierra's view of the landscape. Her smile had disappeared, leaving the furrowed brow of concern in its place. "Hey, you okay?"

"Yeah," Sierra said as she snapped out of her daze, her gaze moving from the beauty of nature to the beauty whose arms had just wrapped around her waist. "I'm fine. Why?" Sierra followed Kara's lead and wrapped her up just as tight.

"You looked so serious. I was worried something had happened while I was gone."

"No. Just thinking."

"Ah. I should have recognized your 'deep thought' face."

Sierra laughed and asked, "I wonder if it looks as weird as your 'analyzing data' face."

Kara's attempt to pinch Sierra's side was all for naught. The ski jacket made the feat impossible, so she gave her a playful shove instead. "I don't make weird faces."

"Of course not. All of your faces are beautiful."

"That's more like it." Kara smiled. She turned toward the blue trail that would take them to the bottom. She had insisted they stay on intermediate trails to lessen the chances Sierra would get injured. "First one down gets to do whatever they want tonight."

Atop the tallest mountain in Oregon, Kara had thrown down an unexpected gauntlet. Sierra never backed down from a challenge, but she had her doubts about the prize. "Anything?" she asked, her mouth tight. She was skeptical about there being no limitations.

Kara planted a firm kiss on her lips. As she tried to pull away, Sierra held her close and kissed her again, hard and fast. Sierra eyed her curiously as she asked, "Are you messing with me?"

Leaning into Sierra's ear, Kara gently took the tender lobe between her teeth, drawing a gasp and a shiver as her reward. "I don't mess around when it comes to bets," she said in her sexiest voice. "And I always pay up. So, when I say anything, I mean ab-so-lute-ly any-thing, lover." She spoke the last words slowly, letting them sink in.

Goosebumps crashed like a wave and rolled across Sierra's skin as the meaning registered in her brain.

With a devilish grin, Kara strapped in and prepared for battle. "If you're thinking what I'm sure you're thinking, you better win, because if I do, we're watching animated movies and having hot cocoa. I haven't done that in ages." The blank expression on Sierra's face had her snickering.

Sierra was not amused. She hated to be teased almost as much as she hated to lose. Kara's cockiness was grating, yet it was every bit the turn on. She had every intention of having her way with her girlfriend after she won the race.

"Get ready, because you're going down. And I mean that literally." Sierra smirked back.

The gleam in Kara's eye said she was ready for a fight. Bragging rights were on the line and there were a few new things she had hoped to talk her girlfriend into trying, so now was the time.

"Grab that guy over there and have him start our race," Kara suggested.

"Why?"

"So neither of us can cheat."

"Good idea. I know how you are." Sierra winked when Kara blew her a raspberry.

The gentleman was happy to oblige. Once they were both set, he gave the order and they were off like rockets. Halfway down, they were nearly neck and neck, carving the slopes with expert finesse. The end was quickly approaching. One lone jump lingered to the left, which they both made a beeline to hit. Kara choose a lower angle, giving her a slight edge over Sierra, who had elected to go for big air. Sierra fumed at her decision as she stared at the back of her girlfriend. She lowered her stance, willing herself to go faster, but it wasn't enough. Kara had edged her out for the win.

Pumping her fist into the air in victory, a breathless Kara yelled, "Yessss! Hot cocoa and movies!" She bent down and freed her feet of the snowboard so she could do a little jig.

Sierra struggled to catch her breath, still mad at herself for blowing it, but secretly in awe of her girlfriend's skills. "You're not serious, are you?" She released her bindings and stepped away from her board.

Still celebrating, Kara kissed Sierra's wind-burned cheek and said, "Honey, it's my night. I get to do whatever I want."

"Guess I'll just hope one of the things you'll want to do is me," she teased. "Your loss though. You have no idea what I had planned if I had won."

"Next time, bring your A game and maybe you'll get the chance to show me," was Kara's retort.

"Someone's cocky." Sierra smiled.

"Nah, I'm just that good and you love it."

Kara's beaming smile turned Sierra to goo. The feel of her girlfriend's arms draped around her neck was better than winning an Olympic medal. In Kara's arms, she felt weak and strong at the same time. She could be a puddle of goo, but conquer the world in the same breath. "Yeah, I do." Sierra smiled and met Kara's eyes. "And I love you, Kara."

"You do?" Kara pulled back, a nervous smile twitched at her lips.

"I am in love with you, Kara Davies. The doctor, the adrenaline junkie, the gamer, the sex goddess, and all the other parts I have yet to experience. I love them all." Sierra was surprised at how easily she had said those words. She had never said them before, but right now with Kara, they had never felt more right.

"Sierra," Kara began, her voice cracking slightly with emotion. "I am so in love with you. Completely and irrationally in love with you."

Their lips met softly, slowly moving together as their tongues touched and teased. A moan rumbled from Kara, deep and low, spurring Sierra to deepen the kiss. Her body arched uncontrollably, searching out more contact, but was denied the pleasure by the impenetrable wall of bulky winter gear. Sierra grumbled her annoyance, to which Kara sucked Sierra's bottom lip between her teeth, ending with a light tug that ignited a new flame of desire in them both.

"I think you may have earned a little something besides movies and cocoa tonight," Kara rasped.

"God, I hope so," Sierra said with a sigh. "At least we can watch the movies naked, right? Unless you have some grownup onesies hidden somewhere?" A daring glare followed.

"No, I don't have any onesies. At least, not here." Kara laughed. "But I am so ready to get you naked."

"I was curious about what kind of onesies you had, until you agreed with getting naked."

"You have a one-track mind, Sierra Cody."

"Only for you, Doctor Davies. Only for you."

"Suck up."

"Is it working?"

"Always." A sexy grin made its way to the surface as Kara grabbed her board and walked away. "Let's go warm one another up."

Sierra smiled wide, scooped up her board, and trotted after her. "Whatever you say, Doctor."

***

"Now this is what I'm talking about. Snow on the ground, a roaring fire, some wine, and a sexy woman. It doesn't get much better than this. Using Airbnb was a great idea." Sierra flashed her million-dollar smile. She swept her damp hair from her neckline and pulled her robe tight. When she kicked her feet up on the coffee table, a grimace shoved her smile aside. Her aching muscles were not at all happy with the move. "Ouch! All that snowboarding is catching up with me. It's been a while since I've done it."

Kara toweled off her hair, then wrapped herself tightly in her own robe. She stepped out of the bathroom and smiled as she took in the sight of the woman she loved reclined on the couch staring at the fire. Kara had uttered those three little words before, twice actually, but never had they come from the heart. The previous "I love you's" had felt like something she had to do, like a formality for someone with whom she had spent significant intimate time. Maybe she had had some love *for* them, like Jamie. She had cared greatly for Jamie, but with Sierra, the difference was unmistakable and monumental. Kara was truly and deeply *in* love with this woman. For the first time in her thirty years, she couldn't imagine life without someone. And that someone was Sierra.

As if knowing Kara's thoughts centered on her, Sierra craned her neck and met her eyes, yanking her from her moment of deep reflection. Kara vaguely remembered the last thing her girlfriend had said and responded, "I love the mountains. They make me feel so alive."

"Definitely. They're beautiful. Almost as beautiful as my girl."

Kara took a seat beside Sierra, watching her girlfriend's joyful smile turn wickedly teasing as she licked her lips and visually devoured her body. She loved being on the receiving end of that look. No one had ever made her feel as beautiful and desired as Sierra. "Oh yeah?"

With a glint in her eye, Sierra answered definitively, "Yeah." Her fingers toyed with the collar of Kara's robe, dipping inside to tease the soft skin hidden underneath.

"You're such a sweet talker." Kara leaned in and placed a soft kiss to Sierra's lips. She went to stand, wanting to finish her after-shower routine, but was stopped by Sierra's hand on her own.

"Hey, um...I want to tell you something."

Sierra took a turn toward serious, sending a bolt of fear straight to Kara's heart. "Okay." She sat dead still. Dread had chased away all the happiness that had resided within her just seconds ago. Something inside screamed that whatever Sierra said next would change everything. Was it a confession? Had she slept with Harley again? Would it be a need for space? One of those "I love you, but" confessions? Though she radiated confidence for Sierra's benefit, her internal world was under the upheaval of a cataclysmic earthquake.

Sierra reached up and cupped Kara's face with the most tender of touches, her thumb tracing idly back and forth across her cheek. Her eyes glossed over as she said, "I'm sorry for ever doubting your intentions. I'm sorry for letting other people get in my head. I'm sorry for being a stubborn ass when you only wanted to help me. I should've listened to my heart, but I was afraid you were too good to be true. I mean, why would someone like you want someone like me? Unless..."

Her words were cut short by Kara interjecting, "Unless I wanted something from you." She understood what Sierra was saying, but hearing it come from such a confident woman broke her heart. Understanding that Sierra's past relationships had been more sex than substance, Kara made a silent vow to never let her feel that way again. Sierra was deserving of true love. They both were—no matter how much they had denied needing or wanting it until now.

Sierra's hand fell away. Her eyes cast down in shame as a half-nod served as her acknowledgement. She chased the lump from her throat and continued, "But I want you to know that I do trust you with everything." A set of teary amber eyes rose to meet Kara's warm greens as she added, "Especially my heart. I hope you know that."

Kara took Sierra's hand in her own. "Thank you. That means a lot to me. I'd be lying if I said it hadn't bothered me, that your actions hadn't stung. But I'm glad it's out in the open. We're moving past it. I trust you too, with everything." She brought their joined hands to her heart and held them to her chest. The words were spoken in truth, despite fighting her own lingering fears. "If I didn't, we wouldn't be here now."

She kissed Sierra's lips gently. Her eyes opened as she pulled back a breath to memorize every detail of Sierra's outpouring of expressions during the emotionally intimate moment. As much as Kara had made it her mission to avoid drama and feelings, sitting here with Sierra, both of them vulnerable and open, had been exhilarating rather than exhausting. Finally revealing their truths had brought a closeness she had never experienced. Emotionally naked rather than physically naked had felt every bit as rewarding.

"Kara, I want you. I want us. And I know we're both bad at talking about our feelings, but I'm glad we did this. It feels good. I feel lighter." Sierra's lips curled up and her eyes sparkled.

As a long, slow breath left her lungs, Kara agreed. "Me too." There was a sense of relief at having finally let go, to have given herself to someone. Her smile climbed to the arches of her eyes as the woman that held her heart stared back with such deep affection.

"So, oh great victorious one..." Sierra pulled Kara onto her lap and looped her arms in a loose embrace. "It's your night. What do you want to do?"

"I'd like *you* to make us some dinner, naked of course, and then..." Her eyes drifted to the ceiling in deep thought, pausing for a moment before making her decision. "I want you to show me what we would've done if you had won."

Sierra practically threw Kara off her lap when she hopped to her feet. She ran to her suitcase and yanked out a bag. With a seductive wag of her brows, Sierra allowed her robe to slip down her shoulders and pool at her feet. The sway of her hips as she made her approach left Kara enthralled. She paid no attention to the bag in Sierra's hand or the fact that it had been placed by her side on Sierra's way to the kitchen.

"I know it's your night, but I think you should also have to be naked while you watch me cook." Sierra threw the words out casually without so much as a glance.

Entranced by the enticing view of her girlfriend bent over in the fridge, it took a few seconds for Sierra's request to register, but when it did, Kara happily obliged. She untied her robe and let the front fall open to expose her torso. The results of her intense workouts were proudly on display as the once flat muscles of her stomach now had a slight cut to them.

Kara finally noticed the generously-sized bag and looked inside. Her eyes grew wide and a smirk hit her lips. "Really?" She glanced up at Sierra, her heart rate rising rapidly as the possibilities flashed through her mind.

Sierra looked over her shoulder, flashed the smile that always made Kara all gooey inside, and winked.

Kara couldn't say she had never used toys in the bedroom, but it had been limited. She hadn't really deemed them necessary and truth be told, many of them were intimidating—not really the vibe she wanted in the bedroom. Apparently, Sierra didn't have that problem and had decided to bring a small selection for the weekend. The move managed, much to her surprise, to excite the hell out of her as that lovely familiar ache between her thighs made itself known and she began to grow restless.

She didn't feel the same insecurities about sexual experimentation with Sierra as she had with former lovers. The love they shared was the most likely reason and it gave Kara a sudden boost of confidence. She was curious by nature, which was why she loved experiments so much, and she was struck by the sudden need to do some exploration—for research, of course.

"Hey, Hon? Maybe we should just have energy bars for dinner."

CHAPTER TWENTY-NINE

Sierra stared at Ochoco Lake and let out a soothing breath. They had decided on a lazy Saturday to unwind, so she and Kara took a drive to take in the beautiful view and have lunch. If only she could relax.

The season opener was just two weeks away and Sierra was nervous. The feeling was foreign to her. Usually she was filled with confidence and anticipation. Those feelings still surged through her veins giving her a boost of energy, but this season would be filled with heavy expectations. Expectations she had set for herself. There could be no excuses this year.

She was more fit than ever, thanks to the consistent training, healthy diet, and mental preparation. Kara had offered her strength, stability, and encouragement, as well as keeping her body well-adjusted. Nicole had made good on her promises of securing several new sponsors, giving Sierra a chance to compete in a few World Cup races overseas, like Ronni.

Nicole had even gotten Leo, the mechanic she had requested, so her bike was fine-tuned like the instrument it was meant to be. She was one step closer to becoming a full-time pro like Ronni. Everyone had done their part. Now, it was all on her. If she did well, a full World Cup tour could be in her future with the big names like Atherton.

A squeeze of her thigh caused her to jump. The sympathetic smile directed at her said Kara knew exactly what she was feeling. Not wanting to ruin their afternoon, Sierra opted for some light conversation to occupy her busy mind.

"Dinner last night with Ronni and Blake was fun." Sierra recalled the raucous evening. When was a night out with her best friend not an event in itself?

"Yeah, it was," Kara agreed.

They chuckled as they recalled the memory of Blake begging to go dancing so he could be seen with "three fine ass hunnies." Blake was always so prim and proper that he had blushed redder than a firetruck the moment the words left his mouth, causing everyone to burst with laughter.

"They make a great pair too. Ronni is really bringing him out of his shell. He's funnier than I would've thought," Kara said.

"She's definitely rubbing off on him. Glad they finally got together. All that eye sex was exhausting."

"You and Ronni are good at breaking down walls." Kara tipped her head, catching Sierra's smile from the corner of her eye. "I'm thankful for that."

"Me too."

Their hands joined on the shared arms of their chairs, fingers interlacing without thought. Silence fell between them as they basked in the late morning sun and the distant voices of happy park goers. Sierra let her head fall back and her eyes slipped closed.

"You ready for the season opener?" Kara asked casually.

Taking a deep calming breath, she gave Kara's hand a light squeeze, but her eyes remained closed. "I think so. A little nervous, but I've never been in this good of shape in my life. You've played a huge part in that, so thank you."

"You did all the work."

"After I got my head out of my ass," Sierra said with a laugh. "But you inspired me to be better and all the after-hours cardio we've done, well..." Sierra's eyes opened as she dropped a sexy smirk and glanced over the top of her sunglasses.

Kara's cheeks tinged pink and it wasn't from the sun. She rolled her eyes and offered an amused grin. "Well then, I'm glad I could help."

Sierra loved the shyness of her geeky girlfriend, but knew how dead sexy she could be without even trying. She sat up and leaned across the chairs to place a kiss on Kara's cheek, then held her position, meeting her eyes. "But seriously, Kara. Using the virtual racing simulator all winter helped me keep my edge and I learned a few things about myself. Plus, you helped me learn the one thing I needed the most."

A crease of confusion dipped between her brows. "What was that?"

"Control. Control over my body, my actions, and my life. I feel so tuned in to everything now, and it's all because of you. My life changed for the better the day I met you."

"It was always inside of you, Sierra. You just had to trust yourself." Kara closed the few inches between them and delivered a chaste kiss, pulling back when Sierra tried for more.

Licking her lips as they parted, Sierra smiled at the taste. She could never get enough of Kara in any form. "I know that...now, but without you believing in me, guiding me, I'd still just be throwing myself down the side of a mountain on two wheels and hoping for the best. So, thank you, Kara. I mean it. And I need to thank Nicole for all the work she's done for me too."

Tears stung her eyes. Sierra was caught off guard at the unexpected rise of emotion. That had never happened before. Kara was turning her into a big softie. She stared at the most sincere, loving grin she had ever seen spreading across Kara's lips and suddenly, she felt lighter—like floating on a cloud of happy.

"You're welcome. You deserve it, Sierra. No one is handing anything to you. You're working hard for everything you have."

"I hope I can make you guys proud, you know, to repay you for everything."

"I don't know about Nicole, but I can think of a few ways you can repay me." Kara grinned and bit her lip.

"You better hope Nicole doesn't want the same type of repayment. If she does, I may need to repay you both at the same time. I'm a busy girl, you know." Sierra waggled her brows and smiled wide at Kara's dropped jaw.

"Oh my god!" Kara shrieked as she slapped Sierra's arm, then broke out laughing. "I love her like a sister and I'd do anything for her, but I won't share you," she said as she continued to laugh.

Sierra laughed along with her, but didn't miss the possessive tone in Kara's words. For a woman who thrived on being independent, she didn't mind being owned by Kara one bit.

***

Per her usual preparation the week before a race, Sierra sorted through her race day song list, deleting songs that no longer pumped her up and adding new ones. When she reached the letter N, an old favorite popped up—Limp Bizkit's "Nookie." An uncontrollable laugh escaped. The song had been so appropriate for so long. For so many years she had done things for all the wrong reasons and now...now, there was so much more. Now, she had Kara. Their "nookie" was pretty epic, but that wasn't what life was all about anymore. Sierra no longer looked for her next hook up and didn't need sex as a coping mechanism. The adoration of the beautiful doctor who had more faith in her than she had in herself was all she needed.

With her girlfriend on her mind, Sierra deleted the song and then scrolled to the one that reminded her most of Kara. With a goofy, lovesick grin on her face, she hit play on Justin Timberlake's "Damn Girl." When the beat began, her hips moved in time with the rhythm and she sang along while packing her new race gear.

She was so lost in her jam, she hadn't noticed Ronni recording her from the doorway. The words flowed out at the top of her lungs and her body moved with great enthusiasm, causing Ronni to drop her phone when she doubled over in hysterics.

The thud drew Sierra's attention and humiliation painted her face a lovely shade of red when she saw her camera-wielding best friend. Horrified, she dove onto her bed and pulled a pillow over her head. "Oh my god! Oh my god! Ronni, turn it off." Her plea was muffled by the bedding.

With tears rolling down her face, Ronni pounced on the bed beside her. "Oh c'mon, Sierra. It's not even the most embarrassing thing I've ever caught you doing, sad to say. What's with the shy all of a sudden?"

A bright red face turned sideways. "How long were you standing there?"

"Just a few seconds. That was awesome, by the way. I will never, *ever* forget those moves. Do those work on Doc McHottie?" Ronni laughed so hard she nearly fell off the bed, saved only by the quick grasp of the comforter anchored by Sierra's body.

"Dammit, Ron! If you tell anyone..." Sierra would die if anyone ever saw that video.

"Don't worry about that, my good friend. This is my secret to hold over you until death, so remember never to mess with this chick." She laughed and then collapsed on top of Sierra, giving her an awkward hug. "You are so cute. Look at you all in love. You guys are great together. Lord knows if she can make you do that, then it must be the real deal, because that was...Ah-mazing!"

Sierra rolled over and punched Ronni lovingly in the shoulder. "It is a great song though." She felt the need to defend her choice.

"Yes, and you should leave J.T. to perform it. Although, Kara may like to see your version sometime."

"No!" Sierra screeched and reached for the phone, failing miserably.

Ronni snickered like a crazy woman and jumped off the bed. "If she doesn't run away, then it's definitely love. Catch ya later, Wylie," she said, then skipped out of the room.

"Arghhh!" Sierra rolled back face down on the bed, her mind instantly drifting back to Kara. Unable to focus on anything else, she decided to head over to the lab to get a few minutes alone with her girlfriend.

***

When she rounded the drab white hallway that led to Kara's office, she froze. She had hoped to surprise her girlfriend, but instead, she was the one on the receiving end. A good-looking man with dark hair and a strong jawline was fawning all over her girlfriend. Okay, so maybe he wasn't quite that obvious, but he was giving all the signs that he was into her. Kara, as usual, was lost in some type of geek trance, talking shop and oblivious to the signals he was throwing out. Sierra had never met anyone so consumed with their work.

Normally, she would take time to admire Kara in her lab coat and pressed pants, but she was too busy boring a hole through the handsome stranger with her death stare. His cocky attitude and smug grin rubbed

Sierra the wrong way and a flash of jealousy rose up. Her eyes narrowed and fists clenched. She wanted to walk up to the man, introduce herself, and pull Kara in for a searing kiss to demonstrate how extremely off limits she was to everyone else, but she knew that wouldn't sit well with Kara. No, she needed a more diplomatic approach and fast. The pair had turned and were headed her way.

She took a deep breath, regrouped, and pretended she had never noticed a damn thing as she walked right toward them like she hadn't a care in the world.

Kara's eyes popped wide at the sight of her, but her smile was unmistakable. "Sierra? Hi. I wasn't expecting you."

"Sorry for the unscheduled visit, Doctor Davies. I didn't know if you might have a few minutes to discuss something." Sierra glanced between them. Kara wouldn't have told the man about her personal life, so Sierra made sure to keep it strictly professional.

"Sure. One moment. Sierra, this is Doctor Thomas Moore. He's worked with NHL players and Olympians, and his work is known around the world in the field of sports psychology and neurology. Quite a genius," Kara gushed.

"Stop it, Doctor Davies. Your research is quite remarkable in itself. It's one of the main reasons I took this little opportunity to work at Volden. You're the genius here," he countered sweetly.

His predatory smile made Sierra's stomach turn, though she kept her expression free of judgement. Of course, Kara was phenomenal. She knew that in far more ways than he would ever have the pleasure of knowing. The thought allowed a subtle half-smirk to pull at her lips.

Uncomfortable with accolades, Kara blushed lightly and deflected to work, "Sierra was a participant in one of my projects and she's a rising star in professional women's mountain bike racing."

"That is fantastic." He turned to Sierra and extended his hand in greeting. "It's wonderful to meet you."

Sierra accepted the handshake, delivering a firm grip that was sure to hurt. Since breaking his hand would be unacceptable, she wanted to be sure she at least left a memorable impression.

A slight grimace shook his grin, but he didn't falter. "I'd be happy to give you a session sometime to go through your pre-race routine and maybe help you fine tune some visualization techniques." Upon release, he flexed his hand lightly, trying to hide his discomfort from the squeeze she had put on him.

He was subtle, but Sierra noticed and forced a sweet smile as she replied, "That's very generous of you. I'll consider it. Thank you."

He tipped his head in acknowledgement and straightened his jacket. "Well, Doctor Davies, I can see you have things to do. Are we still on for dinner?"

"Yes, of course. I'll meet you there."

"Fantastic. I can't wait. I have so much to I want to ask you." He flashed a toothy grin that may have dropped many a panty, but only made Sierra groan.

Once again, Kara was oblivious. She turned, all smiles, and waved Sierra to accompany her to her office.

"Where are you going with Doctor McSleazy pants over there?" Sierra was in no mood to hide her possessive tone or her frown.

"Nowhere. We're just going to have a sit down at Taco'd on Saturday and talk about our projects."

"Are you kidding me? Didn't you see the way he was drooling all over you?"

Kara quickly shut the office door behind them and turned to Sierra with a look of shock and irritation. "Sierra," she spoked in a hushed voice to avoid a disturbance. "What are you doing? I don't need to get approval to have dinner with a colleague."

Could Kara really be so dense? Had she really missed all the signs?

"I don't like him. He was eyeing you up and down while you were in geek out mode. He wants to get you into bed." She folded her arms tight across her chest and stared Kara down.

"Do you trust me?" Kara raised a brow. An unreadable mask now covered her emotions.

"What?" Caught off guard by the question, Sierra's hands fell to her hips and her mouth dropped open to answer, but she paused. Was Kara really asking her that, or was there a hidden agenda? Kara was not the problem here.

"Do you trust me? Simple question, Sierra," Kara pushed, her tone neither accusing nor harsh, as if she were asking apple or banana.

"Yes. Of course, I trust you, but..." Frustrated, Sierra threw her arms up in the air. She just wanted to protect her girlfriend. She wasn't trying to control her. And damn that monotone voice Kara got whenever these situations popped up, because Sierra couldn't read what was going on in that brilliant, over-analyzing mind of hers.

"But nothing. Yes or no," Kara jumped back in quickly, still no fluctuation in tone or expression, "It takes two to tango, Sierra, and I will not be doing the tango with anyone but you. Okay?"

There was no winning this argument, so she relented, "All right, but for the record, I don't trust that guy." Sierra pouted and leaned back against the wall.

"So noted." Kara finally cracked her stone expression with a sincere smile. In one swift step, she pinned Sierra's body against the wall with her own. "For the record," she spoke just above a whisper, "I love it when you're protective of me. It's very sexy."

Kara kissed Sierra hard and deep, leaving no doubt who held her heart. The electricity sent Sierra's pulse through the roof. Her mind fell blank. Her body emptied of all fight, becoming an empty shell that felt as if it could float away, yet her heart overflowed with love, anchoring her there in Kara's passionate embrace.

Kara was the one to slow their kiss, pulling away and pressing their foreheads together. Sierra peeked through one eye. Kara was so beautifully breathless. She was still amazed this was the same reserved woman she had met that day at the care center, the one with the expressionless demeanor and opposition to socializing.

Sierra dropped her head back against the wall. Kara nuzzled into her neck, stoking the flames of desire smoldering deep in her core. She wanted Kara and she wanted her now. Damn her girlfriend's professionalism, because a desktop rendezvous was on her bucket list. "Any chance you can get out of here early?"

"Mmm. You read my mind." Kara tipped her head up to reveal a sultry smile gracing her lips "Give me an hour and I'll meet you at the apartment."

A wickedly seductive smile made its way to Sierra's lips as Kara extracted herself. She may not have been able to punch that sleazy doctor, but that was fine.

Stealing her girlfriend away and making love to her all afternoon was a much better victory anyway.

CHAPTER THIRTY

Kara protested when Sierra rolled out of bed and began to dress. Saturday had arrived quickly and there were just a few days before Sierra would head out for her first race of the season.

After pulling on her riding shorts and sports bra, Sierra crawled back into bed and into the arms of her girlfriend. She went right for her favorite spot—where Kara's neck met her shoulder—and roughly bombarded the soft, freckled skin with kisses, causing Kara to laugh out loud. Sierra loved that sound. She pulled away, happiness radiating from every pore as she gazed into Kara's eyes and said, "I'm sorry I have to go. I have so much to do before Wednesday and I know if I wait any longer, I'll thoroughly exhaust myself in the most pleasurable way possible and never get anything done."

Kara smiled seductively and tightened her grip on Sierra's arms. "I would argue that you've been 'doing' plenty." She placed kisses along Sierra's jawline, not wanting her to leave, but impressed at the newfound dedication to detail she had found.

"Yes, I have been very productive in that area." A proud grin formed as Sierra admired her handiwork—a darkening blemish above Kara's right breast. "But I have to meet with Leo about some last-minute tweaks on my bike. I should only be a few hours and then I promise to come right back and get plenty more done." She wiggled her brows and pecked Kara's lips one more time before extracting herself from the strong arms of her girlfriend.

"He's a bit of an arrogant ass, isn't he?" Kara huffed as a statement more than a question. Her irritation was more from the loss of contact than anything else.

"Yes, but he's the best mechanic in the business. I still can't believe Nicole wrangled him away from Evie. Speaking of Nicole, is she coming next weekend?"

Watching Sierra dress, Kara was enamored with every well-defined muscle and each shapely curve. She frowned at the loss. "She said she was planning on it."

"Sweet. I'll be back soon, babe." Sierra turned back toward the bed and asked, "Want to do something tonight?"

"I have that meeting with Thomas at five."

Sierra rolled her eyes, not even remotely trying to hide her displeasure.

"I know what you're thinking, but I promise I'll be fine. I'm a big girl. Okay?"

"Not really. If he tries anything I want to know, because I *will* kick his ass." Grabbing her bag, Sierra strode back to the bed and kissed Kara again. The woman really was irresistible.

Kara smiled and looked up at Sierra with adoration as she pressed her hand to Sierra's cheek. "I love you. Be careful riding today."

"I will, but you be careful too. I love you." Sierra couldn't resist leaving Kara with one more lingering kiss before hitting the road. This would be a good test for her and she hoped she'd be able to keep her focus on riding and not her girlfriend out on a date with that sleaze ball.

***

Dr. Moore laughed harder than was necessary at Kara's cheesy science joke. As usual, she was oblivious to his behavior, as well as Axel's hovering in the background. He stepped up and interrupted their conversation, "Everything satisfactory? Do you need anything else?"

Thomas and Kara looked at one another and then shook their heads no.

"Thank you, Axel, but I think we're good right now," Kara said with a smile.

"All right. Give a holler if you need anything." He walked away, throwing one more glance over his shoulder before checking on his other patrons.

"Kara, you should consider joining me in London. There are so many great projects. You could do so much more with the billions at their disposal. Your brilliance deserves a larger outlet."

She cringed at the accolades, but smiled genuinely before declining the offer. "No thank you, Thomas. Things are going well for me here and I think I'm finally where I'm supposed to be."

The disappointment hit Thomas hard, but he had seen the glint in her eye at the enticing offer. He placed his hand over hers. "Think it over. I'll be here two more weeks. If you'd like to go over any of the details in private, I may be able to convince you to come with me."

Kara's breath caught and she looked down at their hands. She carefully slid hers free, trying to hide her shock and anger as she chastised herself for being so ignorant. Sierra had been right. *Dammit! Did I lead him on? I wasn't trying to. I would never...shit!*

"Thomas, I'm sorry if you got the idea that anything could happen between us, but our relationship will only ever be professional." She used the most sympathetic voice she could muster, despite being aggravated by his unwelcome advance.

His confident grin fell into a lopsided frown and his shoulders drooped. "I see. I thought we shared a little connection. Did I misread that?"

"I'm afraid so. First off, I only date women. And second, I'm in a committed relationship."

"Well now, that is a surprise. I guess I missed the lesbo thing. I had heard the great Doctor Davies did many things well, but relationships weren't one of them. Apparently, you can't believe everything you hear," he spewed callously, throwing his arm back over the top of the booth. Now that the chase was over, his true colors were coming through.

Kara cringed at the "lesbo" remark. For the first time in many years, her anger threatened to show its face, but she forced herself to maintain her calm. "Apparently not. I heard you were highly professional, not out chasing geeks in skirts, but then again, I'm sure it's a lot easier to get women who are just happy to be looked at by someone with twenty-twenty vision and a nice smile, right?"

The words had come out more harshly than intended, as evidenced by the look on Thomas's face, but his attitude had chaffed her the wrong way and she was not one of those girls who needed the attention to feel worthy. Even those girls deserved better than his arrogant ass.

"Good night, Dr. Moore."

Kara took her leave quickly, dropping her bill with Axel before racing out of the brewery. If she had listened to Sierra, they'd be curled up in front of the television enjoying a night of peace, but instead she'd now have to deal with the aftermath. Sierra was not going to be happy.

When Kara arrived home, Sierra was waiting on the sofa with an open bottle of wine and the latest issue of *BIKE* magazine. "So, how did your date go, Doctor?"

Sierra tried to play it off, but Kara could tell she was concerned, and a little buzzed. Some liquid courage would help this conversation go a lot smoother, or so she hoped. She slipped off her shoes and removed Sierra's glass from her grasp. Staring at her girlfriend from over the rim as she took a large gulp of the sweet red wine, Kara noted the worry in her eyes. As wrong as it may have been, she liked the feeling of having someone so concerned about her.

Kara returned the glass, bent down to place a soft kiss to Sierra's lips, and took a seat beside her. "First, it wasn't a date. I'm already taken. Second, you were right. He wanted more than talk."

Kara stole the glass for another sip as if nothing had happened, but Sierra bolted upright, fury blazing in her eyes. Kara pushed her back down into the sofa. "Relax. I handled it. I told him I already had the most beautiful, wonderful woman waiting at home for me and that I couldn't believe I had left her there for his pathetic attempt to use the experimentation of the change in mechanoreceptor, temperature, and nociception in tissues after injury as a pickup line."

Sierra laughed and relaxed back into the leather sofa. "That's like...the nerdiest turn down ever."

"Maybe." Kara's lip quirked up. "But it was a turndown nonetheless." Cupping Sierra's cheek with her hand, she ran her thumb slowly across her cheek bone and locked eyes with her girlfriend. "Sierra, no one stands a chance against you, you hear me?"

"Yes ma'am." A beaming smile lit Sierra's face as she pulled Kara into a tight embrace. "The same for you, Kara. There is no one for me but you."

CHAPTER THIRTY-ONE

"I believe in you, Sierra, but you have to trust yourself. You are the champion." Kara hoped she appeared as confident as she sounded.

Sierra was tense and fidgety, not at all what she needed for a solid performance on opening weekend. She had already finished poorly in qualifying by being overly cautious. Kara needed her to relax and trust all the hard work she had put in during the off-season. The woman standing in front of her looked more like a frightened little girl than the cocky woman she had met last year. So strong, yet so delicate. Kara had to remind herself that Sierra could be broken, despite seeming so invincible most of the time.

The thin cloth curtain did nothing to block the sound of the busy medical center, reminding Kara that there was work to be done, but staring into Sierra's eyes that revealed both love and fear, everything faded into the background. Nothing else mattered. Kara closed the distance and kissed her lightly.

"I feel like I've already won with you," Sierra whispered against Kara's lips.

"Cheesy," Kara mumbled back and grinned, then kissed her again.

"Maybe, but it's true." Sierra stepped back, making eye contact as she continued, "I love you, Kara. You give me strength. Thank you for having my back."

"I love you too." Snaking her arms around Sierra's back, Kara pulled her in close and spoke softly into her ear, "You know...it's not in the contract or anything, but there is the possibility of an extra bonus if you win."

Sierra's smile grew, crinkling the corners of her eyes. "Oh, yeah? What is it?"

"Nope. Eyes on the prize first. You're going to have to win to find out." Kara pulled back and smirked.

"Believe me, my eyes are definitely on the prize," she said, allowing her gaze to travel down to the exposed valley between Kara's breasts.

"You never stop, do you?" Her girlfriend had always been able to make her shiver with just a look.

"With you? Never."

"And it always affects me just the same."

"I know and I love it," Sierra stated with pride.

"I know you do, but I wish you wouldn't do it in front of others. I got a rep to protect." She was only half-joking. While Kara loved the attention, she did prefer to keep her personal life private. Thank goodness they were hidden behind the curtain.

"I think that rep has been shattered, Doctor Davies. Christie told me you smile at work now."

"That's a bummer." Kara scrunched her face, then shrugged. The time for Sierra to go had arrived and Kara sighed as she searched for the perfect words of wisdom to impart. "Sierra, forget about the qualifying round. Chalk it up to first race jitters. Now, you know what's out there and you're going to do great today. Win or lose, I know this will be your best race yet."

"Thanks." Sierra released a heavy breath and sunk deeper into Kara's embrace. "I wish you could be out there watching."

"I know, but I can see a lot more on the TV in here. I'll make sure I'm free to watch your run. Now go get 'em, tiger!" Kara unraveled their limbs and sent Sierra off with a smack on the ass.

"Whoa! That's not the way to get me to focus on the race." Sierra chuckled, then kissed her one more time before trotting away.

Kara could only watch as Sierra slipped out the front door, hoping she had done enough to soothe Sierra's nerves. No matter the outcome of today's race, she was sure this would be a great year for them, on the track and off.

***

Due to her poor qualifying effort, Sierra would be among the first to go, so she had to set a good pace. Then, all she could do was wait and hope it held up. As she sat alone in the starting gate atop the mountain, her sights locked on her line of choice. Her eyes drifted shut and she went through her pre-race routine, visualizing every inch of the track through to the finish, only this time, her vision ended with her sitting in the leader chair.

She set her bike against the start gate and readied her pedal leg. Muscles tensed in anticipation of the green light. Her heart beat the only sound until the first beep of the starter. Then there was silence.

All right, Sierra, you got this. Here. We. GO!

Rocketing out of the starting gate, Sierra exploded down the trail. The picture of focus, trusting her instincts, she no longer forced her path as she easily handled all obstacles. With her bike in perfect balance, it felt as if she were floating down the mountain. Trees, rocks, and fans passed by in a blur. Sierra was sure it the fastest she had ever ridden.

Crossing the finish line, she looked up to see her name in first position. There were many more riders to go, but her time had been solid. Skidding to a stop, she was all smiles as she leaned her arms on her handlebars, feeling her lungs and legs burn from her effort.

Ronni was the first to congratulate her, throwing down an enthusiastic fist bump for a kick ass job before heading up for her own run. "Damn. You were on fire! Got my work cut out for me, but I love a challenge. Loser buys tonight."

Still recovering from her run, Sierra laughed. It always amazed her how they had always been able to be so supportive, yet so competitive. Smirking with confidence she replied, "Yeah well, remember your wallet this time or I'm leaving you to do dishes tonight."

Ronni gave her a salute and then hopped in the back of the truck with Blake to head up to the start line.

Sierra set her bike aside and before she could take her spot in the Hot Seat, Nicole caught her with a congratulatory hug. "Sierra, you were phenomenal and there's someone else who wants to congratulate you." She handed Sierra her phone with Kara on the other end.

"You did so great, Hon! I'm so proud of you. I knew you'd kill it."

"Thanks. I wish you were out here, but I'm glad you got to see it. I want to take you both out for dinner this week." She nodded to Nicole. "As a thank you for everything this fall and to the start of a successful season."

"Sounds great. Okay, I gotta go, but I love you and remember, no matter what, that was an amazing run."

"Thank you. I love you too and I couldn't have done it without you." Sierra ended the call and handed the phone back to Nicole. She couldn't wait to see her girlfriend, but for now, she would soak up every moment, however long it might be, sitting in the leader's chair. Nicole handed her one of her sponsor's protein drinks and a hat, then she claimed her seat with pride.

No matter the outcome, Sierra decided that today was a top five moment in her life. She thought she had been doing well before, but life with Kara just showed her how much better it could be. Sierra had been disciplined and dedicated the entire off-season and it showed. She had never ridden with the control she had had today. Plus, she finally had a woman she loved and who loved her in return, great support around her, and a great opportunity with a new team. Even though a win would be sweet, she couldn't ask for a better day.

One by one the riders finished and Sierra remained in the chair. The closer they got to the end, the less she found herself able to breathe. She nearly passed out during Ronni's run as her best friend had been putting the squeeze on her times, but a slight slip in the gravel banking set them apart.

When the last rider crossed the line, it took a minute for Sierra to realize she had won. She stared at her name atop the leaderboard as it flashed the words "official results." Slowly, her breath returned and filled her lungs in a sharp gasp as if she had been under water too long. She jumped from the chair with her hands raised as she was swarmed by Ronni, Blake, Nicole, and Leo.

Overwhelmed by feelings like never before, her eyes teared up at the realization that she was on the brink of her dreams becoming a reality. If only Kara had been here to celebrate with her, it would have been perfect.

A pair of strong arms wrapped around her neck and pulled her into a kiss. Last year, she would have celebrated with the random kiss-stealer, but now, Kara was the only one she would be kissing. Shocked and appalled, Sierra yanked herself free, but before she could scold the offending woman, her face transformed from one of anger to shear surprise and affection. "Kara? What? How?"

"I knew you had it, so I hurried over to celebrate with you. I have someone covering the clinic for a little bit. There was no way I would miss this."

"I'm so glad you did. Now everything is perfect." Sierra smiled and pulled Kara close for a proper kiss, which didn't last as long as she had wanted. But then, no kiss with Kara ever lasted as long as she wanted. However, her winner's duties beckoned and she couldn't be too upset about that. Medal presentations, podium pictures, team and sponsor pictures all came and went in a flash, though she did enjoy the one with Nicole and Kara holding the clinic banner.

It wasn't her first win ever, but it was her proudest to date. Last year she seemed to be spiraling out of control. She had been getting more reckless on the course and not working out as often. Sierra had held onto her dream, but she had lost her focus—unless you called hooking up with random race groupies focus. She hadn't won in quite a while, despite ending up in the top five in points. She was on the verge of being another cliché, the "got talent but too lazy to use it" type. Sierra had been pissing all of her opportunities away, until she met Kara. So, this win was extra special and having Kara with her when it was announced, was even better.

Once the pomp and circumstance of the victory finally died down, Nicole asked Sierra, "Are you ready to take that trophy of yours home?"

"I sure am." Sierra scooped Kara up off her feet, causing her to yelp in surprise before laughing hysterically at Sierra's enthusiasm. Sierra planted a hard kiss on Kara's lips, not meaning to be so rough, but she just couldn't control the joy she was feeling any longer. She hadn't expected the doctor to leave the clinic, but knowing that Kara cared enough to make arrangements to celebrate with her meant more than she would ever know.

Smiling brilliantly, Kara draped her arms around Sierra's neck and stared into sparkling eyes. "You are silly, but you are mine and I love you."

"I love you too." Sierra kissed her again, softly this time, and she set Kara back on her feet. "Now let's get you back to the clinic. The quicker you get packed up, the quicker we can celebrate."

CHAPTER THIRTY-TWO

Sierra didn't seem to understand how distracting it could be to have her so close. When Kara was trying work, those sultry looks and "accidental" touches had a way of sending her blood pumping to areas other than her brain. After a bit of persuasion and a little bargaining, Kara had finally gotten Sierra to go to the pub with the rest of the crew while she finished closing the med center.

She set the last box aside to be loaded into the truck and let out a breath. A smile overtook her features. The weekend had been a success. She was excited for the possibilities the season held not just for Sierra, but for their sponsorship as well. She was nearly finished with her work at the lab and had many decisions to make. But those could wait. All she wanted to do right now was celebrate with her girlfriend.

After hitching a ride with one of the med staff, Kara entered the old Irish pub, McVay's, with one person on her mind. This time last year, Kara would have skipped the pub and gone back to work, but now her heart thumped wildly at the thought of "celebrating" later with her girlfriend. They had come such a long way and sometimes she still couldn't believe it was all real.

Kara stood at the front of the room and scanned the faces in the crowd. One by one she passed them by, but then her smile fell and her heart came to a screeching halt. Harley was all over Sierra. Her Sierra. Her girlfriend, Sierra. How could Sierra do that to her? And in public with their friends present?

The appalled look on Nicole and Ronni's face said it all. She couldn't look anymore. The image was already burning a hole through her brain. But just as Kara was about to rush from the room, Sierra shoved Harley back and slapped her hard across the face. The room fell silent as everyone stopped and stared at Sierra giving Harley a piece of her mind. The words were sharp and profane, but Kara couldn't focus on them.

There had always been a lingering fear in the back of her mind that Sierra would end up with her ex again. Kara wouldn't have been able to bear it happening, but her feelings for Sierra had been too strong to ignore. She had laid her heart out there in hopes it wouldn't be crushed and Sierra had just proven that her faith had not been ill-placed. Relief was an understatement. While Kara had believed her feelings for Sierra to be strong before, they were nothing compared to the heat coursing through her veins now.

As if Kara had stood out like a beacon in the night, Sierra's attention was immediately drawn to her. When their eyes met, Sierra's had a fire in them that made Kara quake with excitement. Sierra's demeanor changed in an instant. She pushed Harley aside with disgust and strode with steely determination toward Kara. She opened her mouth to speak, but was cut off by Kara's lips crashing onto hers. Sierra wrapped her up tight, lifting her slightly as the kiss escalated in a hurry, becoming deeper and needier as Kara's body melted into Sierra's passionate embrace.

Kara could have lost herself in the taste of Sierra for hours. She felt every ounce of emotion Sierra poured into their exchange, savoring it even after it had ended. The love she felt enveloped her like her favorite blanket on a cold night, bringing her a warmth and comfort like none other. When she finally awoke from her kiss-induced stupor, all eyes were on them and Kara reddened from head to toe with embarrassment. Sierra, on the other hand, didn't mind one bit. So much for keeping her personal life personal.

Taking Kara's hand in her own, Sierra proudly led her back to the table she had been sharing with Blake, Ronni, and Nicole, where they were met with applause for their hot performance. The raucous behavior left Kara wishing she could crawl into a hole and hide, but at the same time, the memory of the kiss made her skin flush and she wished they could relive the moment again and again.

Nicole sidled up and draped an arm around Kara's waist. "If I know you, right now you're wishing you were invisible. But I must say that was one of the most romantic things I have ever seen. You know Sierra is over the moon for you, right?"

With the sting of tears in her eyes, Kara quickly glanced at Sierra, then back to Nicole and nodded her head. Still overcome from the emotional whirlwind, she took a deep breath as she struggled to speak. Feelings were not her forté, but she was learning. "I know and I can tell you the feeling is definitely mutual."

Kara smiled at her old friend, giving her arm a squeeze before meeting Sierra's adoring gaze once again. There was something else in the way they looked at one another now. Kara could feel it sparking in every nerve ending in her body. That kiss was more than a notice to Harley. Sierra had given herself fully to her and she had returned the sentiment. The deeper meaning of Sierra's actions had not been lost on either of them as they so publicly claimed ownership of one another. Kara could clearly see spending the rest of her life with the amazing woman staring back at her and for the first time in her life, she wasn't opposed to the idea.

***

Enjoying a romantic Italian dinner, the couple finished off their main course and awaited their Tiramisu. The pace had been hectic over the last few weeks and Sierra missed their quiet nights together. Their schedules were about to get even crazier as Nicole had gotten her a gig as a stunt rider in a movie filming in Portland that would keep her occupied for several days and she would soon be leaving for the World Cup circuit overseas. Nicole moved fast and it was overwhelming, so she would milk this down time for all it was worth.

Sierra placed her napkin on the table and rubbed her full belly in satisfaction. "That was delicious. I don't know where dessert is going to go, but I know there is always room for it." Her laugh brought a smile to Kara's face. "Come to Whistler with me."

"Maybe," Kara said, her eyes darting down to the table. She shifted in her chair before glancing back up. "I can't leave with you Thursday, but maybe I could fly up after work on Friday."

"That would be great. I always do better when you're there."

The hint of a smile touched Kara's lips. "I'm always with you. You'll do great. You've been amazing these first four races."

Sierra couldn't quite put a finger on it, but even though they were relaxed and having fun, there seemed to be something off with her girlfriend. She hoped there were no more lingering doubts in Kara's mind, because Sierra was all in and ready to take this relationship further. She had been trying not to push too much, knowing that Kara was more reserved and calculated, especially after her break up with Jamie. However, patience had never been one of Sierra's stronger attributes, so she hoped they'd make progress soon. She didn't know what else she could do to prove to Kara that she was completely committed to their relationship.

Kara placed her napkin on the table and sighed. Sierra was not a fan of that look and held her breath, bracing for the impact of whatever was about to occur.

"So, I've finished most of my research projects at the lab and I've decided to go back into practice."

Panic swept through Sierra, clamping a cold hand around her heart. What did that mean for them? She didn't think she could do a long-distance relationship, even if it was just a couple of hours. "What does that mean? Are you leaving?"

"No, nothing like that." Kara soothed her with a gentle touch of her hand and Sierra released her breath. "Um...actually, I'm going to open another clinic here. I'm going to move out of the apartment and I um...well, I wanted to know if you would like to get a place together?"

Sierra fell silent. Her brows knitted in deep thought as she analyzed the words. Slowly, the cold that had taken hold of her dissipated and everything clicked. This was what she had been waiting for and she couldn't be happier.

Apparently, her reply had taken too long, as Kara had shifted into damage control rambling. "I mean, you don't have to, but I'd like to see you more and we could pick out a house or something together...if you want...no pressure...I don't want to stress you out, Sierra. Your body's stress response is perfect in the short-term, but damaging if it goes on for weeks or years. Raised levels of cortisol for prolonged periods can dampen your immune system and decrease the number of brain cells, impairing your memory. It can also-"

Sierra's eyes sparkled with delight and a giddy response of, "Hell yes," broke Kara's long-winded explanation. Leaning over the table to kiss Kara, she stopped halfway and said, "I love you, Doctor Kara Davies, and I would love it if you were at my starting gate and finish line every day."

The relieved smile on Kara's lips made Sierra grin knowingly. "You were afraid I would say no." It was a statement more than a question, and when Kara sheepishly nodded in affirmation, Sierra laughed in disbelief. "Kara, I am crazy about you and I want to spend every second of every day with you. I know you know that." She waited for her girlfriend to agree. "Good. So just remember, Doctor Davies, that I will go anywhere, do anything with you. Quite literally." Sierra waggled her brows, loving when her innuendos garnered a heated reaction. "So yes. Let's plan some time to go pick out a house or something."

With a comforting squeeze of her girlfriend's hand, they shared an intense gaze across the small table. Sierra now craved something off the menu and the sexy "you're in for it later" smile Kara had just flashed had her hot and bothered. The waitress arrived with their dessert and set it on the table between them. The tiramisu looked amazing, but Sierra's mouth now watered for something even more delicious.

Her brow quirked and Kara nodded. That was all she needed before flagging down the waitress. "Check please."

CHAPTER THIRTY-THREE

Overlooking the Pacific Coast Mountain Range, Sierra enjoyed an unusual feeling of peace. She breathed easier these days. Everything felt like it was falling into place. She was committed to her training and she had found the woman of her dreams. For the first time ever, she felt as if she was exactly where she was supposed to be.

Next week, she and Kara would look for a place to live together and she couldn't wait to embark on their new journey. It would be the first time she had lived with anyone besides family or Ronni. She thought it would be scary, but it felt so right. They had only been together nine months, yet it seemed like years. Everything flowed so easily between them that it frightened her sometimes, but Kara was worth facing her fears.

Speaking of Kara, Sierra wished she were here already. She never thought she'd fall into the corny, romantic notion of missing someone, but that was exactly what happened every time she was away from Kara. Forget about being apart for a couple of days, what would she do when they were apart for several weeks? As exciting as trying her hand against the big names in the World Cup was, she was dreading the idea of the European trip right now. Perhaps, it was the proverbial honeymoon phase. It wasn't that she wanted it to end, but as much as Kara empowered her, her neediness made her feel weak.

Determined to regain control and focus on her purpose for being there, she strapped on her helmet and began her descent. Shredding some of the most exquisite singletrack Whistler had to offer, the flow of the trail helped center her thoughts and she knew she would be okay.

As she exited the final switchback, it occurred to her how much life was like that hairpin turn. In the mountains, just like life, there was seldom a straight path to the top. There were always twists and turns to navigate. Sometimes they took you higher and sometimes they took you out. But Sierra was determined and never allowed her failures to keep her from staying the course.

She skidded to a stop in front of the rented truck and smiled. Patience may not have been her strength, but she was stubborn as hell and now it was all paying off. It was only a matter of time before all her dreams would come true.

Two hours later, she was back at the mountain house Nicole had rented for the weekend. Leo took her bike out to the garage for maintenance while Sierra headed to her room. Tired and dirty from her ride, she wanted a recovery shake and a hot shower before heading to the village to check out the scene. If she could squeeze in a nap it would be great, but she doubted she'd be able to fall asleep.

When Sierra opened the door, she was dumbstruck by the sight of a familiar face. There, in her bed, lay Kara comfortably on her side with her head propped up on her hand, wearing only a see through black teddy and biting her lip.

"Hi, Honey. Happy to see me?"

Taking in the sight resembling something from one of her more enjoyable adult dreams, Sierra couldn't move. She couldn't speak. All she could do was focus on the deliciousness lying in her bed right now.

Pleased with the reaction, Kara smirked and ran her free hand slowly over the curve of her thigh. "It's not polite to keep a lady waiting." Her voice was low and silky smooth, eyes glistening with mischief.

Not needing to be told twice, Sierra dropped her hydration pack on the floor and pounced, ignoring the fact that she was a sweaty, smelly mess. Wrapping her arms around her girlfriend, she rolled them over, coming to a stop once she was on top. She cupped Kara's face in her hands and stared at her as if she hadn't seen her in years. "I thought you couldn't come until Friday?"

Kara brushed a few stray hairs from Sierra's face and smiled up at her. "Well...I couldn't wait until Friday to *come*."

"Oh, you are a little vixen, you know that? If everyone knew that the controlled Doctor Davies was such a bad girl..." She didn't finish the thought as Kara narrowed her eyes in jest, but there was a hint of seriousness that was not missed.

Sierra loved that Kara reserved this side of herself strictly for her eyes only. Her smile grew and she tightened her hold on Kara as she pressed their lips together, both of them moaning into the kiss as it deepened. A whimper of protest escaped Kara when the kiss was broken—the sound evoking a primal need deep within Sierra that she was more than happy to explore.

"I missed you. I'm so glad you're here early. Maybe we could do some sight-seeing? You know, after I help you out of your lingerie." Her fingers were already tugging at the lacy strands of Kara's top.

"I missed you too and that would be fun, but there are other sights I've looked forward to seeing." Kara grabbed the bottom of Sierra's jersey and pulled it over her head. She trailed a finger down between two perfect breasts before teasing the hardening nipples through the thin barrier of her spandex sports bra.

Sierra gasped and arched into Kara's touch—her short breaths threatening to match the speedy pace of her heartbeat. It didn't take much for Kara to get her going and the roaming of agile fingers had her body ready to soar. "I know for a fact that they missed you," Sierra said, breathless and ready to take things further...but not like this. "I'm a mess. How about we take this to the shower?"

A silent nod was all she needed. In a matter of seconds, a trail of clothes marked their path to the bathroom and soon soft moans of pleasure filled the air.

***

Three hours and two showers later, Sierra hadn't gotten much of a nap, but she wasn't complaining at all about the distraction. With Leo acting as chauffeur for the evening, Sierra and Kara occupied the back seat of his four-door Dodge truck in comfortable silence. While Kara enjoyed the breathtaking sunset, Sierra had found a far more beautiful sight to behold. The orange, blue, and pink sky over the mountain tops was a work of art, but it couldn't hold a candle to her girl.

Sierra reached down and intertwined their fingers, drawing Kara's attention away from the landscape. Her soft smile and adoring eyes always made Sierra's heart pound a little harder. She recalled her thoughts a few hours earlier as she had sat atop the trail. It truly was astonishing how perfect her life was right now and this moment was proof positive that there was nowhere else she would rather be.

When they reached the village, Leo headed off on his own, planning to meet back at the truck at nine. As much as Sierra would have loved to stay out later, she was here to race and she would not break her routine. At least Kara was supportive, always making sure nothing they did interfered with her usual flow of events. She understood that athletes tended to be creatures of habit and deviating from plan could affect their performance. Sierra chuckled as she remembered Kara explaining how she also relied on a set protocol in the lab and that there was no shame in being superstitious about her process, as it was a form of diligence.

Taking her girlfriend's hand in her own once again, Sierra led them down to a little steakhouse she always liked to visit. After they had ordered, they made small talk and narrowed down their wants and needs for the houses they would look at next week. As they waited for their food to arrive, Sierra filled Kara in on her weekend plan.

"Tomorrow we'll go to the track and walk the entire thing. We'll check the course and pick out lines. Later, we'll ride it and make a plan for the race. Then we pray no weather comes in and messes it all up." She laughed. "On race day, as you know, Ronni and I always have a pancake breakfast together before heading to the track."

Kara nodded in understanding, seemingly analyzing the race routine. "I can make everyone pancakes. I'll just take mine over and have breakfast with Leo and you guys can do your thing. Then, I'll ride up with him and meet you at the race."

"You don't have to do that. You know how much Ronni can eat. It's too much work and I want you to relax. We can go to a restaurant."

The waitress arrived with two medium rare rib eyes, loaded baked potatoes, and asparagus. The pair sat back, their eyes lighting up at the sight of the thick, juicy steaks. Both ladies were starving after their afternoon rendezvous and ready to dig in.

Returning to the conversation at hand, Kara waved her off. "I insist. I enjoy cooking and you know Ronni loves my pancakes."

"That she does." Sierra slowly took the first bite of her steak, taking a moment to savor the oak wood flavor before asking, "I thought you said Leo was an ass?"

Kara forced a thin-lipped grin while chewing her food. She swallowed and chuckled at Sierra throwing her words back at her. "He is, but we actually have some rather stimulating conversations. He's like an idiot savant of the mechanical world."

"You're the best. I don't know how I got so lucky." Sierra reached across the table and placed her hand over Kara's. The warmth of her skin was always comforting, something she never failed to miss once it was gone. "You should come with me tomorrow to walk the course. You'd love it. I'll show you what we look for and you can analyze everything." Sierra knew with certainty that Kara enjoyed making a science project out of everything. The doctor just loved to learn how things worked.

"Ah, appealing to my inner scientist again, huh?" Kara teased with a cheeky grin. "It would be interesting and it'll be a beautiful day...I'm in."

"Excellent."

The rest of the night consisted of sultry glances and lingering touches as they made good use of every minute until their self-imposed curfew. The evening had been perfect. Sierra couldn't have planned a better date if she had tried and took it as another sign that Kara was the one for her. As if she needed one more.

***

The next morning, they awoke to a beautiful sunrise. Sierra found herself cuddled in Kara's arms and rather than jump out of bed, she snuggled in for another ten minute snooze. Today, they didn't have a strict time table, but that would change the rest of the weekend, so she took advantage of a few more minutes of laziness. A smile struck her lips just before she drifted off, thinking of how she would soon be waking up to Kara every day in their new home.

After a quick breakfast, they hopped into the truck with a cooler and headed up to the race course. Sierra was excited to share a behind-the-scenes look at her work with her girlfriend since she had had a chance to experience so much of Kara's jobs—including an adjustment this morning. It did pay to have your own personal chiropractor for those days when your unmentionable extracurricular activities left you a bit sore.

She smiled at the memory of the previous evening as she stared at her lover.

Feeling as though she was being watched, Kara turned to look at her girlfriend and immediately blushed upon reading the look on her face. Kara knew her all too well and Sierra loved it.

The trip to the top of the mountain was over all too soon. As they exited the truck, Ronni was leaning against a Jeep talking to Kourt while a handful of other riders milled about preparing to walk the course. This was one of the few days when the riders would all be together, so it was a good time to exchange ideas and meet new competitors. Sierra would be doing that at some point too, but watching Kara in her tan shorts and blue tank top, studying one particular area of the course map and geeking out over the physics of the banked turns and biomechanics of riding them was a total turn on for reasons she would never understand.

Sierra's mind drifted to other things. Oblivious to the world around her, Sierra didn't even notice Ronni by her side until the clearing of her throat had her jumping in fright.

"You're all googly eyes, so you must be stuck in Kara-land again. You sure it was a good idea to bring her?"

"I can't help it, Ron. When she gets all nerdy like this, it's such a turn on." Sierra smiled wide, then cast a sideways glance at her best friend. "It's fine. I'm focused. Why? Is it a problem for anyone else?"

"Besides giving them plenty of ammunition for jokes, no, doesn't seem like it. She's not the first betty to walk the course."

"Good, because I'm more relaxed with her here and you'd be surprised at her insight into the biomechanics of riding."

"Yeah. I'll have to chat her up about that...like never." Ronni chuckled. "Just don't biff while you're busy staring at her ass. They'll be no saving you from that shame, Wiley." Ronni slapped a laughing Sierra on the back and nodded to Kara. "Now, go get your girl and let's get this party started. This boulder garden is going to be an ass-kicker." Ronni sighed and shook her head.

"I'm on it. Catch ya in a few." Sierra trotted over to Kara, who had moseyed over to the starting gate, and scooped her into her arms. She kissed her hard and then whispered, "You are so irresistible when you use those big words."

"Like centrifugal force?" Kara asked with one brow slightly arched.

"Just like that," Sierra replied with darkening eyes.

"You should be focused on the course, not me." The gleam in Kara's eyes said otherwise and her smile silenced the last vestiges of protest as she loosely draped her arms around Sierra's neck. "But I do like that you find me distracting." Her fingers sifted through Sierra's hair as she pulled her down for a long, slow kiss.

"Oh, gross over there. Can't you two act professional for ten minutes?" Camryn hissed with her usual smugness.

Sierra flipped her the bird and took Kara by the hand, leading her down the course. Kara ate up every piece of strategy Sierra revealed and Sierra loved the little peeks into Kara's life—like when she explained how each activity had its own set of skills and that watching an athlete use every bit of their body's intelligence was like a symphony she could never get her fill of.

Little shared moments like these were the building blocks of something big for them. This had been the most fun and informative course walk ever and Sierra was glad they had both had the chance for greater insight into one another's lives—especially since they would be taking the leap and living together soon. Once again, Sierra was struck with the feeling that she was on the cusp of a monumental year.

***

As promised, Kara was up early on race day to prepare breakfast for the crew. She kissed Sierra on the cheek before rolling out of bed, slipping into her sweats, and heading to the kitchen. Knowing how much Ronni could eat, she was sure to make more than usual. When the last cake was flipped onto the heaping stack, she set aside two plates, one for Leo and one for herself, complete with fruit, syrup, and bacon—because protein provided a more stable energy source than carbs—then covered the rest for the best friend duo to devour.

With plates in hand, she pushed open the front door to leave, but Sierra caught her before she could get away.

"Hey. You didn't think you could slip away without a proper good morning kiss, did you?"

"I hoped not, but I didn't want to wake you," Kara said. Her eyes immediately fell to Sierra's mouth.

Sierra noticed and couldn't help but tease as she slowly licked her lips and smiled. Leaning in, she pressed her hands to the wall on either side of Kara's head, trapping her in between. "Good morning, my love," she breathed soft and low, then captured Kara's lips with a delicate kiss. She desperately wanted to leave her girlfriend weak in the knees, but with her holding a plate in each hand, she reeled in her desire.

"Mmm, good morning to you," Kara mumbled, her eyes still closed.

"Thank you for this, Kara. I'll see you soon." Sierra kissed her again, slowly, thoroughly.

"You're welcome." Kara's eyes fluttered open as a soft smile curled her lips.

That was Sierra's favorite smile, because the green in her eyes would soften and the golden flecks shimmered like the sun.

"You'll most definitely see me soon, Ms. Cody." With one more kiss for luck, Kara headed out, shooing away Ronni's hawk-like advances as she passed.

"Is this heaven? Did I die?" Ronni was practically drooling as she walked through the door.

"Kara is a domestic goddess. She knows how much you love her pancakes too, so she made you all you could eat—or so she hopes. I'm supposed to let her know if she met your quota."

"Me thinks I'm in love. If you aren't going to marry her soon, I may do it," she joked as she helped herself to her first plate.

Sierra took three cakes and covered them with syrup, shaking her head at the pile of food on Ronni's plate. "I've been thinking about that, Ron. I'm finally ready for forever and I want it to be with Kara."

Ronni nearly choked. She hurriedly sipped her orange juice to wash the food down, then cleared her throat. "Shit, Sierra. That's intense. I mean..." She stared blankly at the table as she processed the news. "I think you guys are great together—although a bit gross sometimes with all the touchy-feely—but damn...I've never heard you talk about marriage in all the years I've known you."

"I know. I guess I never thought it would happen to me, but I did have the dream growing up. The one of spending forever with someone you loved more than anything. Wearing a beautiful dress and walking down the aisle."

"When are you going to ask her?" Shoveling another bite into her mouth, Ronni watched with rapt attention as Sierra contemplated her answer.

"I don't know yet, but I know it's her. I hate when we're apart and I can't get enough of her when we're together. I don't want to be with anyone else."

"So whipped." Ronni laughed and punched her in the arm.

A giant, toothy smile graced Sierra's face. She didn't care if she looked every bit the lovesick fool she was, she loved Kara and Kara loved her. That was all that mattered. "Call it what you want, but I'm finally happy, Ron. Really, truly, happy."

"Wiley, my friend, that's all I ever want for you."

CHAPTER THIRTY-FOUR

Several weeks and umpteen houses later, Kara and Sierra had settled on a rustic A-frame with a small yard, two bedrooms, and an office for Kara, twenty minutes outside of Bend. The large front window overlooked the mountains and bike trails were within riding distance. Add in the hardwood floors, an open floor plan, and a fireplace near the window and they instantly agreed that they'd found their new home.

Unfortunately, moving mid-season had been less than ideal. Though they had recruited every one of their friends to help, there was still painting and unpacking to be done. Kara had been more than busy opening her new clinic, but pushed herself to work on the house while Sierra was away.

Every time Sierra returned from a race, she was amazed at how much progress had been made—a truth that saddened her since she couldn't be as involved as she wanted. Sierra honestly had no idea how Kara did it all. Heck, she could hardly manage to get her clothes out of her suitcase between races.

As she walked up the steps and slipped her key into the lock, she tingled with anticipation at seeing how much closer they were to making their house a home. The sensation spread lower, warming her in a way that only Kara could. Her girlfriend was on the other side of the door and of all the things she was excited about, seeing Kara was at the top of her list. Being away had begun to take its toll. She felt disconnected and it was infiltrating her psyche. She knew her fears were irrational, but she had been powerless to silence them. But she was home now and she was sure holding Kara again would solve everything.

"Honey, I'm home," Sierra called out as she walked through the door. She never thought it would feel so great to say those words. Her smile pulled into a frown when she received no answer, but the distant sound of music summoned her to the back bedroom. Along the way, she made note of the deep gray walls with white trim in the living room and the light blue of their bedroom that reminded her of the sky. Everything had been done just as they'd discussed. Kara was nothing if not meticulous.

She smiled at the thought of waking up tomorrow in a completed bedroom with Kara in her arms, unlike the last time, when paint cans and half-empty boxes littered their room. Her smile exploded when she found Kara dancing to a bubbly pop song while unpacking the guest room. Sierra leaned against the doorframe and watched with wonder and amusement. Kara had no idea how adorable she was and would argue whenever Sierra told her such a thing. Resisting the urge to run over and scoop her up was a lesson in self-discipline.

It was nearly a full minute before Kara turned around and nearly tumbled over the box in fright. "Holy shit! You scared me!"

Laughing heartily at her blushing girlfriend, Sierra readily moved in to wrap her up in a tight hug. "Sorry, but it was too good to interrupt."

Kara scrunched her face and dipped her head in embarrassment for a beat and then glanced up through her lashes. A soft smile appeared. "I missed you."

The words "me too" had barely made it from Sierra's mouth before Kara's lips were on hers, humming her happiness as their tongues met in a needy kiss.

Getting her fill of Kara was impossible, but the need for oxygen won out, forcing their lips to part. Sierra looked around the room as she fought to catch her breath. Pulling Kara's body close, she admired the earthy tones of deep brown and blue. In awe of the woman in her arms, Sierra placed a kiss to Kara's hair and said, "Wow! You've been a busy girl."

"You know me. I have a hard time sitting still. Since the office isn't in full swing yet, I found other ways to keep busy."

"I'm sorry I haven't been able to help more."

Kara shrugged at her own poor planning, then looked up and met Sierra's regret-filled eyes. "Well, that's what I get for wanting to do it mid-season. How are you feeling?"

The race hadn't gone as well as she would have liked, but she couldn't complain. Her season was going extremely well. "I'm a bit sore from that spill I took in qualifying, but finishing fourth helped ease my bruised ego."

"Good to know. I can't do too much about your ego, but I can help you with your other aches and pains."

"I think you're my good luck charm."

They were busy people and couldn't be together all the time—she understood that—but the emptiness without Kara sapped the extra energy and enthusiasm she had become accustomed to having. The last two week stretch had been miserable and even Ronni had commented that Sierra needed a little "extra special doctoring" to keep her on track. Maybe, just maybe, she could convince Kara to travel to the next race.

Not wanting to be clingy, but desperate to recover their intimate connection, she asked, "What would it take to get you to come with me next weekend?"

"Oh, Honey," Kara deflated and pressed her hand to Sierra's cheek as if hoping to soften the blow. "I wish I could, but I'm speaking at a Sports Chiropractic Symposium in Vancouver."

Disappointment quickly shifted to agitation and Sierra's body tensed. A cold front had moved in, chasing their warmth away. Removing Kara's arms, Sierra stepped free and stomped to the opposite end of the room, doing her best to not say something stupid. Words were not her forte. She was a reactive person and no matter how hard she tried to tame that part of her, it always found a way to push its way to the front. "Kara, I'm worried."

"About?" Her girlfriend's forehead creased in concern and confusion, obviously still spinning from the sudden change in mood.

"Worried that I'll lose you to your career like Jamie did." Why couldn't she just shut up? The second the words left her mouth, she knew she had been an ass. If she hadn't already figured it out herself, the death glare she received from Kara would have made it abundantly clear. "I don't want to lose you. I can't lose you." That was the truth and she hoped it would help soothe the anger brewing in Kara's eyes.

Rather than getting into a fight, Kara retreated into the solitude of a persona Sierra hadn't seen in months and she berated herself for being the reason behind its resurrection. Gone was the smile and spark that set Sierra's heart aflutter. The happy, easy going woman who had existed mere seconds ago, had reverted to the cold mask of professionalism she had donned early in their relationship.

"I'm sorry you feel that way, Sierra." Her jaw may have been steeled, but Kara revealed her fragility with the tremble in her words.

Kara's tone was flat, emotionless, and it hurt. Boy, did it hurt. Sierra wished like hell that she could take it all back, but it was too late for that.

"I thought I'd done more than enough to prove my love for you. You're right. I have chosen my career over my heart time and again, because no one had ever stolen my heart away. Until you." Kara sighed and ran her hand through her hair, seeming to ponder whether she wanted to walk out or finish speaking her peace.

Avoiding Sierra's eyes, she crossed her arms over her chest and hugged herself as she continued, "You're the only person I have ever left work early for, much less taken time off for. Never before had I had to worry about thoughts of another person consuming me while at work. Until you. Now, I find myself counting the minutes until I can see you again. I hate it and I love it. And I love you,

Sierra. You make me feel things I never imagined—that I never even cared to imagine—I was capable of feeling for another person."

Kara uncrossed her arms and shoved her hands into her pockets. "But as much as I feel for you and as much as I love to be with you, I am not going to give up who I am or what I love to do to spend every minute with you. I love my work. I love helping people live a better quality of life or perform better through my adjustments and research. While I'm sorry our schedules conflict, I will not apologize for it. I refuse to. And if this is going to be a problem, we should probably reconsider our relationship right now." As she finished, she looked Sierra dead in the eyes with unwavering determination, her jaw clenched tight.

There was no room for negotiation. An ultimatum had been issued and Sierra would undoubtedly concede. She had messed up questioning Kara's commitment and needed to make amends fast. Her legs moved with great haste as she strode across the room and stopped a foot from Kara. She wanted to reach out to her, to hold her close. Her arm moved Kara's direction, but pulled back when clear thought prevailed. Now was not the time.

"I'm so sorry. I am. You're right. I know you've stepped out of your comfort zone with me and that so much has changed in you. I can see it, feel it, and I love you more for it. I will never be grateful enough that you chose me. It's just...I have never been so happy in my life and I guess deep down, I am afraid it won't last. My being away and you being so busy...I felt like you were slipping away. I..." Her shimmering golden eyes begged for forgiveness. She was ready to get down on her knees if she had to. "It was stupid. I'm sorry."

"I had that fear for a little while too." Looking to the ceiling, Kara inhaled a deep, labored breath.

The statement caught Sierra by complete surprise, but also set her at ease. She was not alone in her doubts and fears. "Yeah? You don't now?"

"No," she replied definitively and shook her head.

What had occurred that would make the ever-cautious Dr. Davies so sure when it came to their relationship? She had to know. "What changed?"

"You slapped the shit out of Harley." Laughter followed and Kara relaxed her posture. "Believe me, Sierra, we would not have gotten this far if I was going to choose work over you. I would've pissed you off months ago." She smiled lightly, a gesture Sierra mirrored in return.

"My default setting is work. It's as much of a passion as a defense mechanism, but with you..." She sighed hard and reached for Sierra's hand. "With you, I find myself wanting to run *to* you, instead of away. So, I know what we have is real and lasting, even if we have some work to do."

Kara stood before her so open and honest, exposing her raw truth in a way Sierra had never seen before and it struck her in the chest like a lightning bolt. Looking down at their fingers entwined, Sierra allowed the words to envelop her like a warm embrace. The sting of tears defied her will and spilled over. "That is the most romantic thing anyone has ever said to me."

"Give me time and I'll come up with many more," Kara said, her eyes full of mirth and undeniable love.

"All my time is yours, Kara. I'm sorry. So, so, sorry. I..." Sierra didn't know what else to say. She just wanted them to go back to their happy bubble. Was that too much to hope for?

"Shhh, Honey. I know. Look at me, please," Kara requested, her voice soft and comforting.

Tilting her head up, Sierra wiped away her tears and met Kara's loving gaze.

"You love me, right?"

"God, so much. I really do."

"And I love you, so much." Kara smiled and tugged her closer. "You are forgiven."

The tension that had held her body hostage for the last many minutes was banished by the pardon. A deep, honest, smile rose from the ashes. "Thank you." She would never be able to say that enough.

"I think we have a better understanding of one another now, how about you?"

"I believe so."

"Good. Anything else you would like to discuss?"

Sierra searched her memory. She hadn't really had any complaints. Today had been the result of her own insecurities. The last thing she wanted was to upset the peace they had just reached, but it seemed like this was the time for communicating, so she thought long and hard before coming up empty. She shook her head. "I don't think so, no."

Accepting her answer, Kara nodded. She stepped forward as she pulled Sierra in, bringing them breast to breast. Her free hand found its way into Sierra's dark hair, her fingers weaving their way through the long locks. With heavy-lidded eyes, Kara leaned in and ghosted her lips across Sierra's, but fell just short of a full kiss. Their breaths, shallow from the anticipation of releasing their pent-up desire, intermingled.

"Good. Then no more talking."

***

Four weeks of domestic bliss had flown by. Their talk had done wonders for their relationship and Kara felt they were stronger than ever. But the last few days had become more and more tense. For the first time in her adult life, she was experiencing what it was like to be so passionate about a person that she couldn't stand to be away from them. It was a new experience, yes, but she was embracing the warmth and feeling of wholeness that came with being in a committed relationship—especially a relationship with a woman she literally could devour every time she laid eyes on her. The problem was, they had been apart so often lately that her heart and her libido were giving her fits. She had no fear of losing Sierra, but she missed the hell out of her.

She laid on the bed with the newest issue of *The Journal of Chiropractic Medicine* hoping to read up on the newest research studies, but she couldn't focus—not with Sierra moping around the bedroom tossing things into her suitcase.

"What's the matter, Hon?" Kara asked, knowing good and well what the problem was.

The block of European races Nicole had scheduled were upon them and neither were looking forward to three solid weeks apart. Kara had made a decision though—a tough one given how dedicated she was to her work—but she hoped it was the right one for their relationship. Too much time together could be as bad as too much apart. She might still have been learning to navigate the whole relationship thing, but Kara felt good about their path so far—even if she still couldn't believe she had taken the leap.

Sierra shrugged and tried to dismiss her behavior, "It's silly."

Kara set her magazine down and scooted to the edge of the bed. She took Sierra's hand and pulled her brooding girlfriend to stand between her legs, her hands finding purchase on Sierra's hips as she gazed up lovingly. "You can tell me anything. What is it?"

Her eyes took a trip around the room before settling on Kara's and then Sierra replied, "I just hate being away from you." She quickly cast her gaze aside, embarrassed at her confession, even though it hadn't been the first time she had uttered those words. It was clear she was worried she would upset Kara.

Kara smiled. Sierra was so adorable when she was vulnerable. That tough exterior she worked so hard to keep always crumbled so easily around her. "That's not silly at all, Sierra. I love you and I would rather be with you than without you too. You know that." She leaned her head against Sierra's stomach and breathed in her orange musk perfume. "You should look at your itinerary. Nicole has gone all out this time. You'll have a great trip."

Sierra shook her head. "Not right now. I want to spend time with you without the reminder."

"I think you should look at it now, so we can spend the rest of the evening together."

"Fine," Sierra relented in a huff and stomped off to her dresser. She tore the envelope open and scanned the itinerary. "Yeah, looks great," she muttered unimpressed and glanced at Kara, who pointed at the page, telling her to continue.

Kara's legs bounced with excitement, as if she were once again a little girl on Christmas morning awaiting her first present. When Sierra flipped to the second page, her eyes slowly grew wider. She looked up with that cute furrowed brow that appeared whenever she was confused. "Kara, why are...?" Words escaped her as realization struck. "Does this mean...? What about work?"

Kara nodded, her eyes shining bright like stars on a clear, dark night. "Yes, I'm coming with you. I figured I could use a vacation before I dive back into work full-time. I hope that's all right."

"Are you kidding? It is so much more than all right. It's perfect."

Sierra wasted no time pulling Kara up and crashing their lips together in a heated exchange. The kisses were hard, but passionate, reassuring Kara that three weeks away from work to support the woman she loved was not a bad idea at all.

CHAPTER THRITY-FIVE

On the cusp of Sierra's first championship, all she needed was a tenth-place finish or better to secure the title. Five long months of travel and competition all came down to this run. Awaiting their respective turns, Ronni and Sierra idly chatted while another rider sped down the track.

"I'm proud of you, Wiley. I mean, I'm going to try like hell to beat you today, but I'm so proud of the work you've put in this season and I will be right there to celebrate when you pull this off."

"Shhh! I don't want to jinx it, you know. I'm trying to stay loose, but it's so close. I'm afraid I'm going to choke," Sierra confessed in an unusual moment of vulnerability.

"Stop talking nonsense. You attack that course like you always do. Don't hold nothing back, cause that's when things go wrong. You do that and you'll ride off into the sunset today with a title and a hot doctor." Ronni laughed and threw her hands up. "Who says you can't have it all?"

Sierra scooted her bike alongside to give her best friend a hug. "Have I ever told you how much I love you?"

"Yes, but I'd prefer you show me with bikes or food."

Sierra chuckled and freed Ronni from her embrace. It was nearly go time. "Of course you would. You know what? After I win, I'm going to propose."

The idea of making that forever commitment to Kara made her giddy with excitement. Combined with the nerves of the race, it was a miracle she could even string together a thought. The final ride of the season would be a tough one in her current state of mind. She needed to calm down.

First things first—win the title.

"For real?" Ronni perked up, her eyes popping wide at the news. "Awesome! We are going to give you the best wedding and bachelorette party ever! I'm the maid of honor, right?"

"You know it."

The guy at the starting gate called for Sierra. One last ride for all the marbles. That thought alone sent her nerves into high gear. Her legs weakened and her head spun. She swore she'd pass out before getting her bike in the gate.

"You're up. Go kick some ass, Wiley." Ronni slapped her on the back in a vote of confidence.

Sierra did make it into the gate and surprised herself with a relaxed focus as she settled into her pre-run routine. Deep breaths lowered her heart rate and strengthened her legs. Visualization dialed her in to every obstacle she was about to conquer.

At the buzzer, she was off, speeding down the mountain with quiet confidence and the rush of adrenaline she looked forward to every ride. There was no longer a fear of failure. Everything in her life had come together and it carried through into her run, finishing with a second-place time.

Letting out an exhilarating yell as she skidded to a stop, Kara, Nicole, Leo, and her team of sponsors swarmed her in congratulations. Searching and finding her girlfriend's hand in the crowd, she pulled Kara in and hugged her so tight she could hardly catch a breath.

"I did it. Oh my god, I did it! I love you, Kara," Sierra cried, overcome with the emotion of her victory and the relief of all of her fears and anxieties falling away.

She wasn't the only one crying. Kara brushed away tears of her own as she said, "I am so proud of you. I love you too," and offered Sierra a prize of her own in the form of an enthusiastic kiss.

Once again Sierra thought she might pass out as Kara's tongue teased her own.

It was over all too soon as Ronni came roaring across the finish line. She dropped her bike and hopped on Sierra's back as she hooted and hollered in celebration. "I told you! Did I not?"

"You did." Sierra laughed, releasing Kara to protect her from Ronni's exuberance. "I couldn't have done any of this without you guys—all of you." She made eye contact with each and every person in their circle before ending on Kara.

Camryn had won the race, but Sierra paid her zero attention on the podium. She had claimed her first championship and gotten the girl—Camryn could suck it.

Once the race winner photos were finished, they swapped places for the year-end standings, where Sierra climbed into the top spot. Her breath caught as the reality of the moment settled in and a tear rolled free to trail down her cheek. Ronni gave her a high five and a knowing wink from second place.

No sooner had the podium cleared than Sierra called Kara up for a photo. She shook her head no, but Sierra insisted and Nicole shoved her up the stairs. Taking her place beside Sierra, they indulged in several photos, then Kara tried to escape. Her retreat was thwarted, however, by Sierra on bended knee with a black velvet box in hand. The crowd fell silent as all eyes settled on them.

Sierra had no doubt what the answer would be, yet asking the question was proving far more difficult than imagined. Her stomach twisting with nerves and her heart trying to break through her chest weren't helping any.

Kara stood in shock, glancing quickly to their duo of smiling best friends, before her hands moved involuntarily to cover her mouth. "Sierra?" she choked out the question.

Clearing her throat and mustering the courage to finally speak, Sierra reached for and claimed Kara's hand in her own as she fought back the tears that threatened to deny her words. "Doctor Kara Davies," she began, her voice trembling. "I am so completely in love with you. I thank the powers that be every day for making me hit that tree. That was the single best day of my life, because that was the day I met you. Since then, my life has been more fulfilling than I ever could have imagined, and it's all because of you. I dread every second we're apart and I want nothing more than to have you by my side until that final finish line is crossed. Will you do me the honor of being my wife?"

Peeling back the top of the velvet box with a shaky hand, Sierra revealed a shimmering diamond encrusted band. Kara had been stunned silent, but the love in her eyes confirmed everything Sierra had believed to be true. Still, she needed to hear the words. Until they were spoken, nothing was a sure bet and she would never jump to a conclusion in a moment of such consequence. Her heart teetered on the edge, unknowing if it would soar or shatter, as the milliseconds ticked by at a brutal pace.

Finally, Kara's head nodded and that billion-watt smile lit her face from ear to ear. Her heart had answered the question before her brain could even form words, rescuing Sierra from the misery of an uncertain future and thrusting her into a world of unimaginable joy.

"Yes, Sierra. Yes to crossing the finish line with you."

Sierra swiftly slid the ring onto her fiancé's hand and jumped to her feet. Her arms wrapped Kara into their own private cocoon, drowning out the applause surrounding them until the only sound was their two hearts beating as one.

Gazing into the eyes she loved to lose herself in, Sierra framed Kara's face in her palms and placed a chaste kiss upon her lips. It was rare that she was truly in the moment, but this was one time where she wanted to remember every little detail. The light coconut scent of Kara's skin cream. The softness of her lips on her own. The peppermint lip gloss that tingled long after their lips had parted. The erratic thud in her chest that left no mistaking her feelings for the woman in her arms.

Kara brushed Sierra's bangs from her eyes, then cupped her cheek and said, "This has been quite the day.

Guess it's all downhill from here, huh?" With an amused laugh, she let her arms fall loosely over Sierra's shoulders.

"Maybe, but with you by my side, it will be one epic ride."

The End

Thank you for reading. Reviews are appreciated and mean so much to the authors. Please stop by Amazon and/or Goodreads and share your experience with others.

ABOUT THE AUTHOR

This is the fourth novel by S.W. Andersen. Having been raised by her mother, a strong female character in her own right, she has always been attracted to stories that depict independent, capable, determined women. While life tends to surround us with negativity, she prefers to fill it with happily ever after's.

S.W. has spent a large part of her life around horses and rodeos and has always had an affinity for the cowgirl lifestyle. Her love of the mountains and westerns were the driving forces behind her Sarah Sawyer western series. When she isn't working, she enjoys outdoors activities and traveling with her wife, Dianna. They share their ten acres in rural Florida with a rambunctious crew of two dogs, four cats and two horses.

.

www.ingramcontent.com/pod-product-compliance
Lightning Source LLC
Chambersburg PA
CBHW051519250626
47156CB00001B/155